All Our Tomorrows

"What's a smart, sensitive, yearning young woman to do? Forget about Instagram, avoid influencers, and pick up a novel. Specifically, *All Our Tomorrows.* DeBellis sharply renders the glimmering surfaces that should send us all searching for more intimate and authentic ways of living. Grab this book as your lifeline and start today!"

— POLLY ROSENWAIKE, AUTHOR OF
LOOK HOW HAPPY I'M MAKING YOU: STORIES

"A triad of flawed, vulnerable, and disillusioned characters cast their existential hopes and doubts into a future marked by ecological and economic disaster. They trust in one another despite looming collapse. Amy DeBellis's fascinating novel enacts the fine weaving of identity construction: the intentional and accidental web of knots and loops, pain and victory, that make up a person and their persona under late capitalism in New York City. Their stories resonate in my hands."

— SARAH GERARD, AUTHOR OF
CARRIE CAROLYN COCO

For Lily

All Our Tomorrows

AMY DEBELLIS

A perfect day to turn back to one's self: these cold clarities which the sun projects like a judgment shorn of pity, over all creatures—enter through my eyes; I am illuminated within by a diminishing light.

— JEAN-PAUL SARTRE, *NAUSEA*

CHAPTER 1

Janet

The latest batch of grievance letters arrived in Janet Ha's inbox in a distressed bunch, flying on ragged wings. Some of them were long-winded and repetitive, some only a few terse sentences. They all came in from people whose identities were unknowable to her, reduced to a string of letters and numbers, with details like their names, ages, and genders buried in the jumble. This was so she would address their concerns without any bias on her part.

Janet usually received around a hundred of these letters a day, and as it was a Monday, a veritable surge had come in over the weekend. She found that people seemed to have the most grievances on Sundays—the day of rest was often also the day of regrets. And Sunday's letters tended to have a frantic feeling about them, as though their writers were scrabbling at the last chance they had to expose their grievances before Monday came, at which point they would have to put on their normal-person, socially-acceptable armor again.

Janet had never really gotten over the term "grievance letter" —the term was so old-fashioned that it seemed almost tongue-in-cheek, but at the same time the seriousness of the name lent a certain credibility to each letter. They weren't crummy little complaint notes. They weren't annoying, bitchy emails. They were *grievance letters,* valid and profound and bursting with reason.

One letter, from the user TY6482920, went:

I'm worried about how often I have to go to the bathroom, to be honest. Not number two, number one. I pee all the time now, like pretty much all the time. Should I dehydrate myself? Is this the answer?? Please, OLT, help me. I'm peeing as we speak.

OLT—online therapist—was Janet's official title, and TY6482920 typing it out was a departure from the norm. Most of the letter-writers didn't even think of her enough to address her directly. They simply flung their grievances out into space, the way one would fling a fledgling from the nest and expect a fully grown bird to come swooping back a few days or weeks later. Whatever happened in between was no business of theirs. But it was Janet's, and her replies needed to take not days or weeks but only minutes from the time she read the complaints. Her specialty was pinpointing the main problems in the writer's life—in some letters they were quite difficult to parse out—and gathering a list of specialists, sometimes just one or two, sometimes a whole battalion, and sending it back to the writer.

The writer would probably achieve a more accurate result if they sought out professional help on their own, going through the necessary steps to wrangle the most suitable psychiatrist or psychologist or couples' therapist or plastic surgeon. But most people didn't have *time* for that. Most people barely had time to go to the bathroom these days. God knew how TY6482920 was finding the time for all that urination.

Janet set the peeing writer up with a urologist, and a therapist for good measure, just in case of any hypochondria. It would be useful if they could track who sent which letters, to see if any of them came from the same person, but this would apparently be a violation of the writers' privacy. Although it wasn't clear how much these people could care about their privacy if they were spilling their guts to her—but then, she didn't count. She was separated from them by so many layers of anonymity it was as though she were attempting to glimpse them through a thick, murky pane of glass. All she would ever see was a shadow.

She stretched and looked out the window, which was her bedroom window, because she didn't have an office. Like many of her peers, she was permitted to work from home. Many companies had adopted this policy after the pandemic that had happened several years ago. It was a blessing in some ways—no bedraggled commute back and forth, no forced small talk with her coworkers—but just as often could make her feel trapped. Her roommate was never home, preferring to spend much of her time in California or with her boyfriend across the city, and while Janet knew most people would envy her situation, she felt lonely much of the time. The apartment was too hollow, with too many empty spaces, too much darkness collecting between the shapes of chairs and cabinets and in the mouths of doorways.

The peeing letter was silly, but it was a relief from some of the other stuff that came in. With the complaints like the constant peeing, or someone bitching about their annoying coworker or friend or boyfriend, or how they hated having to shave their legs every single day, the solution was usually simple. Janet even felt that she'd helped them somewhat by sending them in the direction of a professional who was suited to address their specific complaint. It gave her a fleeting sense of usefulness and purpose.

But then there were the confessions about wanting to die. The letters bristling with anxiety, with the particular depression and emptiness that seemed unique to the last couple of generations. There were so many more of these letters than Janet had anticipated when she'd taken the job. Some days it seemed that every other letter-writer was haunted by the sense of having no future. Not in a performative 1970s-punk way, a costume you could throw on whenever you wanted to bask in nihilism and then discard when it was time to get back to the real world. But in a grimmer, claustrophobic way. A covering you couldn't shrug off, the sense of no-future rolling like an oily wave over your skin and seeping under your fingernails.

There were the letters like this, lacking grammar and punctuation but which flowed out of the screen like a dark river of consciousness:

i know my leg will heal but everything will just be like this for the rest of my life. I am sick and fed up with myself and i cringe everytime i look into a mirror because of the hideous of my right side of my face. i cant even talk to someone normally. i cant even carry on a conversation. i am fucked up. im kidding myself if i think i can draw because i thought i could and some ppl told me and so that's what ive been doing all my life, drawing, and now i just can't do anything good enough.

It raised questions in Janet's mind even as she looked for the appropriate professionals to send XI3529423's way. What had happened to this person's leg? Were they truly good at drawing, or was it only a way of coping? That was the unseen mass, the Schrödinger's puzzle that lurked behind every letter Janet received—XI3529423 might be an acclaimed artist whose paintings were hanging in galleries, or they might be a college dropout who scribbled a few lines on the back of a napkin every once in a while. And TY6482920 might indeed be peeing every fifteen minutes and in the grips of a gruesome urinary infection, or they might be suffering from a bad case of hypochondria and losing touch with what was normal and what was not. Janet had no way of knowing, and no source of reference other than their letters. She was groping in the dark, hands brushing across strange protuberances, not sure whether what she touched was actually a face or just something that felt like it.

CHAPTER 2

Anna

Sunset in the city: orange light mixing with liquid ash and seeping across the skyline. Grit clouded the air, a light dust that settled on Anna Sidorova's tongue whenever she opened her mouth. She blinked to keep it out of her eyes as she walked to the subway, rubbed her chapped lips together—lipstick already cracking and drying on the papery skin there—and adjusted her scarf so that it wasn't tickling her throat quite as much. She hated the feeling of constriction on her neck, and anyway, she dealt with enough of that with Warren.

As she descended into the earth, the subway exhaled its hot breath at her, its corroded tracks and screeching metal and slow inexorable stench. She couldn't remember the last time she had taken an Uber that she'd been the one to pay for. Her day job consisted of folding what seemed like progressively hideous clothing and adjusting the arms of mannequins, many of which had begun to resemble her—or maybe it was the other way around. After spending forty hours a week trudging back and forth in the store, she could afford rent and food, but just barely. And she had realized a long time ago that this would not be enough.

Anna was glad to leave her apartment behind. The streets and buildings downtown seemed increasingly shrunken and unimpressive compared to the glitter of midtown, those statuesque buildings near the river. And to think that there were so many people from other parts of the country who revered this, who watched too many indie coming-of-age movies and wanted nothing more than to live a cramped, aching life in a shoebutton apartment.

She suddenly remembered that it was shoebox, not shoebutton, and then just as quickly dismissed the thought from her head. It didn't matter. She had left her shoebox/shoe-button apartment and was going to meet up with Warren and he was going to touch her on every possible part of her body with every possible part of his body. Last time he had given her drugs before they had sex and she hoped he wasn't going to this time; it had dissociated her from the experience, but in a bad way. In a way that was like peeling herself off the backdrop of reality and watching her body's filmy, flimsy outline shaking in the breeze from a distance. She didn't like feeling so far apart from herself. Without her feeling of *Anna*, there was very little to hold onto. Just Warren, and with that drug he was unreal too, several layers more removed than even herself. And if they were nothing but two transparent images on a film roll, there seemed to be little point in enduring all of this in the first place.

Warren's apartment was located at the top of one of the towers overlooking the Hudson River, high and remote like the room of a princess in a fairy tale. He was twenty-two years older than Anna, which made him exactly double her age. They liked to joke about it sometimes, about whether that made him twice the pervert she was, or whether she was twice as innocent as him. They had first met ten months ago on a sugaring website. After a few meetings, he'd confessed that the relationship between their ages was part of what drew him to her—the fact that she took up exactly half of his life, a precise fraction: nearly a quarter-century younger and with only the faintest stench of the twentieth century clinging to her.

Their perfect fraction would be gone as soon as she turned twenty-three, of course, but Anna liked to think about practically anything other than getting older. Whenever Warren mentioned a birthday, she laughed in a monotone way and attempted to shift her thoughts to something else. The only benefit of spending her birthday with him was that she could anticipate an extravagant celebration, a showering of gifts, and a temporary boost to her allowance.

The doorman knew Anna's face by now, her dirty-blonde hair and pale skin and towering six feet of height, and he let her up like always, his expression impassive. Despite his cool politeness, she was sure he knew what was going on. She couldn't determine whether this made her feel ashamed, or proud, or sly. The emotions blurred together and coalesced to form a silvery, metallic taste in her mouth.

In the elevator, she tried to remember what Warren had told her last time. His daughter had recently gotten into art school, or maybe it was film school. Or perhaps she was studying film at art school. Anna could never remember these things. She should really start a notebook. She clicked her nails together, listening to the sound, the only thing she could hear in the silent elevator. It sounded like the mandibles of tiny insects, chittering behind the shining chrome walls.

Warren must have heard the ping of the elevator arriving, because he had already opened his door before she had even walked all the way down the hall; he was leaning out, smiling, not even bothering to try to hide his anticipation. He had small brown eyes in a wide, round face, and a receding hairline that had crept nearly all the way around to the back of his neck. He also had a net worth of 42.3 million and a fetish for stockings. Anna had a pair on right now, brushing gently against the inside of her dress as she walked.

"How are you doing, doll?" he asked her, holding the door open so she could glide inside. At first she had cringed at this nickname, but it had slowly grown on her, until, to her horror, she'd found she actually liked it. It made her feel strangely treasured. The glass of wine he handed her made her feel that way, too; from the bottle on the countertop, she saw that he had remembered the type of wine she'd mentioned craving last time, a Zinfandel.

The apartment was pale and modern, with long stretches of white wall on which Warren hung a rotation of steadily more abstract art. There was a long navy couch on one side of the living room, a sleek bar in the kitchen, an enormous fridge that could probably crush three people at once if it fell on them. There was nothing frivolous here, nothing extraneous. Everything had a purpose.

It also made the best of its glorious view of the river, with the entire west-facing wall made up of nothing but windows. The first few times she had come here she'd hardly been able to tear her gaze away from the sight, and Warren, annoyed, had moved the two of them to the bedroom. Now he was more secure in their arrangement, and he didn't seem like he would mind so much if she were to go over and stand at the window, gazing down at the great expanse of steel-colored water. But she'd tired of looking at it; it never changed. It looked like the sound you made when you banged metal against metal: hollow, brittle, cold.

Warren had put on some music, a muted classic rock that she'd never heard anyone else listen to by choice. Despite his wealth, she had trouble getting used to some of his tastes, which were steeped in his bland Midwestern youth: woefully over-cooked pasta and meat, reality TV and stand-up comics, Dan Brown novels. Thankfully, when it came time to take Anna out, these holdovers from his earlier life disappeared and he gravitated instead toward places like NoMad, L'Artusi, or Eleven Madison Park. She had a sneaking suspicion that he had found some of these places on the sugaring website restaurant list. They had plenty of lists. These lists—places you might want to take your sugar baby, brands of shoes and bags that were considered "of the moment" among women—varied wildly. Some of the items were classy, some were unbelievably tacky, and Warren never knew enough to be able to discriminate between the two. He would buy her a sweeping, minimalistic, modern gown, and then turn around and present her with a hot pink bandage dress.

(The latter item was one of her favorites, although she would never admit it to anyone besides Warren; she knew the style wasn't "cool," but the bright color made her skin look like marble, and the tight bandage structure gave her a shockingly tiny waist.) One evening he would take her to an up-and-coming restaurant, and then the next weekend he'd bring her to a place that had gone out of fashion years ago. She didn't mind; his naiveté, the clumsiness that he could never quite get rid of, was slightly endearing.

When she'd first started sugaring two years ago, it was restaurants, before bags or shoes or even sex, that had been her first impression of many of the men she went on dates with. These places invariably dazzled her with their looming ceilings and artistic dishes and inscrutable, attentive waiters. But they were all the same, and after a while they blended together in her memory. And although the food was always delicious, its pleasure remained remote and robotic, trapped in her body rather than filling her mind. The buttery-smooth ricotta, the half-sweet Wagyu beef, the king trumpet mushrooms cooked in luxurious layers of seaweed and sprinkled with pine nuts: all of these things were indeed delectable. She lifted her fork to her mouth and felt the textures and flavors of the food on her tongue, tasted the sweet and salt and umami and knew that it was some of the best food that money could buy. But the pleasure of it failed to give her any true satisfaction. It was the experience of eating your favorite food when you were very full; it still tasted the same, but there was no delight in it anymore. Or eating it when you were exhausted or heartbroken or sick. It was the experience, rare though it was, of Warren bringing her body to shuddering orgasm while her conscious mind floated emotionless just outside the window, coolly observing the spasms of her muscles and the nerve cells firing in the pleasure center of her brain.

But Warren had taken her to Mari Vanna as well, and the Russian Tea Room, and those weren't on any sugaring lists that she knew of. Even now, she couldn't decide whether she had loved or hated it. Taking her there had been a kind gesture, suggesting a level of intimacy that went beyond their arrangement, but the taste of the pelmenis and caviar and blinchik—all overwhelmingly fancy, convoluted, nearly unrecognizable versions of what she had grown up with—had triggered a hideous longing inside her. The pleasure of this food *had* gone beyond her tongue and taste buds, had tunneled out a hole straight down through the center of her, pressing back and back and back into her memory. She'd had to go to the bathroom and dig her nails into her palms to hold back the tears.

Now, Warren watched her drink the Zinfandel, barely glancing at his own glass. His gaze made her feel uncomfortably observed at first, but then, as she continued to drink, it made her feel cherished too. Even though the cherished feeling was fake and Maraschino-cherry-flavored, she could convince herself of it. If she let her focus drift enough, let herself unpeel slightly off of reality—the drugs they'd taken last time seemed to have had a lingering effect—she could almost pretend that they were passionately in love, that she had a real fetish for men with heavy guts and hairy arms and more money than they knew what to do with.

"So, what have you been up to this week?" she asked him. "Did you commission any more 'art'?" She emphasized *art* to let him know she didn't actually consider it worthy of the title. He liked this, this lighthearted teasing with the slightest hint of an edge. Last time she'd been here, he'd shown her photographs of the paintings he had commissioned from an obscure painter who lived in Brooklyn: street art that covered entire sides of abandoned buildings, people and animals with heavily exaggerated eyes and drooping lashes and smiles that curved with a loose pliability. Since Warren's company owned the buildings, it wasn't exactly defacement, but Anna cringed inwardly every time she saw another mural splashed across a previously blank facade. Did the world really need more noise, more color, more *stuff*? Hadn't people crammed enough into it already?

"Indeed I did," he said, his voice hearty. He gave her a long, comical wink. "I'd ask you if you want to see, but I know you're chomping at the bit already."

"Yeah, you didn't even have to bother with the Zinfandel,"

she said, with a gritty undertone of sarcasm. "Or this week's allowance. You got me weak in the knees as soon as you brought up the paintings." Sarcasm didn't come easily to her; for some people it slid off their tongues, oily and innate, but for her it was a practiced trait. She had practiced it because men seemed to like it, especially rich men who were used to everyone kneeling at their feet. She'd found that, for all their posturing, these men actually despised girls who were innocent and naïve, holding them in barely concealed contempt. Anna had seen this with her own eyes. Before she'd started seeing Warren exclusively, several of the men she'd met through the sugaring site had been married, and they told her in no uncertain terms how nice it was to meet a girl like her. A girl who knew how things *really* worked. With Anna, they wouldn't have to lie to her and pretend to be all romantic and loving, the way they did with their wives.

This was another reason she'd chosen Warren. Warren did not have a wife, and the things these other men had told her about their wives—sometimes throwing the comments out casually over drinks, sometimes confiding them in quiet voices in the deep intimate space after sex—had shocked her. The cruelty of it was all the worse for being so unthinking, for seeming to come so naturally. Their words slipped out with the smoothness of glass. She had barely been able to conceal her disgust at some points: this is the woman you swore to love forever, the woman you pledged to have and to hold, and you're telling me how loose her pussy is after she carried your children? *Really?*

Warren turned on the massive screen on his wall and showed her a slideshow of the paintings. In one, a collection of vampiric bunnies scampered across the side of a crumbling warehouse. He did many things with his free time, but she had the feeling that this was one of his favorites—imposing his vision on a city, even if the vision wasn't really his, even if it was funneled through the aesthetics of an artist. Men like Warren loved to impose things. Imposing was what they did best.

"How is your daughter?" she asked, at the same time he said, "So, Anna, how is your family back East?" It was an inside reference they had—she'd once looked out the window across the Hudson and joked that she could practically see her family's farm from here.

"They're good," she replied automatically.

"Really?"

"Well, one of the cows died. But she was old anyway, so it wasn't too sad of a passing."

"I'm sure she had a good life."

Anna laughed. "I like to think so too. I think she lived her bovine life to the fullest." She noted the admiration that flashed across Warren's face; most foreign girls didn't use words like *bovine.* It was another way in which she'd differentiated herself. "And my brother finally got a job as a security officer, so that's good, although my mom is worried sick about him. For some reason she thinks that standing in front of a building for a few hours overnight will put him directly in the line of bullets, which is honestly ridiculous."

She had to stop herself before she launched into any information about her family's money troubles, and how they were doing better now that she'd sent the last two weeks' allowances to them. This had been enough for them to buy essential new machinery that allowed them to keep their farm. Not that Warren would care, and he might even offer sympathy, but—silly as it might seem sometimes, even to herself—she didn't want him to know that half the reason she had started being a sugar baby in the first place was to take care of her family. This would place her squarely in the weak, warmhearted category, and would lower his attraction to her. It was much more alluring to hide behind a facade of self-centeredness, of materialism; this would have the effects of him both treating her like a queen and never assuming that she would extend this caring side of herself in his direction.

"She worries a lot, doesn't she? Your mother."

"Yes. That's her main activity. She worried about me most when I came over to America. No wonder she never wanted to have more kids after me. She told me that modeling was a trap, that I would be taken advantage of."

Her mother still thought she was modeling, of course. Red-cheeked, barely five feet tall, and traditional as borscht, Ksenia Sidorova would probably fall over in a dead faint if she knew what her daughter was really doing to earn a good portion of her money. Whenever she asked Anna, "Where are these modeling photos? No campaigns?" she would tell her mother that she was doing something anonymous, like showroom or fit modeling. "Well, I'm glad you don't have to be as skinny as you used to," her mom had replied once. "I like that I don't see all your bones anymore."

Anna had just nodded and smiled, feeling a flash of guilt that was immediately softened by the knowledge that her mother was no longer worrying about money.

Warren laughed. "She didn't count on *you* being the one to end up taking advantage, in the end!"

Anna joined his laughter, but she wondered, was this really how he thought of their arrangement? If so, he was viewing it from a wildly different perspective. If she thought of it the same way he did, she'd be delusional. But perhaps he was simply speaking about her turning the tables and grabbing control of the situation in whatever way she could, even if it was only a slippery handhold on ice, at risk of being shaken off at any moment.

"You know, it would almost have been more interesting if I was taken advantage of in some way," she said, "given how little modeling I actually did. Sometimes I'm convinced they kept me around only to make the other girls look better."

"Oh, hush. You got plenty of jobs, no?"

"A few, after I starved myself down to a hip measurement of thirty-four inches," she said sourly. "I couldn't even video call my mother; she'd have lost her mind at the sight of me. I had to pretend something was wrong with my camera for nearly two months, remember?" She'd told him all this before, many times, but since talking about the future was so precipitous, they often went over the same ground over and over again.

"I remember, doll, I remember," he said, leaning against the sofa and putting an arm around her. She allowed her shoulders to relax but didn't lean into him in the eager way she would have if she were still the Anna she'd been just a couple of years ago.

"You remember a lot, don't you?" She smirked. "You're like an elephant. Elephants never forget."

"Where is that line from? Aesop?" He frowned, gazing out the window. From this angle she could see bristles deep in his nostrils, stiff and dark like thorns. He returned his gaze to her only a moment later; he never seemed to get enough of looking into her face. "A lot of our sayings come from Aesop. Sour grapes, slow and steady, don't count your chickens..."

"Or the Bible, or Shakespeare," she said. "A lot of sayings come from those too. Maybe it's from one of those."

"Silly doll, elephants don't appear in the Bible." He chortled at the thought, the nose-bristles making another appearance. "And did Shakespeare ever meet an elephant?"

"I wouldn't know," she said, gazing into her empty glass. Thinking of Hannibal crossing the Alps, Hannibal who predated Shakespeare by at least fifteen centuries. "I'm only a poor Russian farm girl." She said it lightly, as though it were a joke, but she heard the bitterness behind her words, dark and vinegary as the dregs of her wine, and he must have heard it too because he said: "More wine, more wine." He rose and snapped his fingers, but they didn't make a snapping sound, only a muted click. He had the look of a scientist who had just seized on some unexpected yet promising solution. "That's what you need."

When he slopped some more wine into her glass, it splashed onto her hand, spots of red like blood-flecks on her wrist. Warren took this as a cue to raise her hand to his mouth and lick up the wine, and she had to fight not to giggle at his earnest, passionate expression: this obscenely wealthy, balding, mid-forties man who didn't even reach her barefoot height with his shoes on, leaning down and lapping at her wrist like a dog. His tongue felt rough and shaggy. But she knew what came next, so they went into the bedroom. He expressed pleasure at her stockings, running his heavy hands up and down her thighs. They felt like the slabs of refrigerated meat she saw at the grocery store, thawed to room temperature and full of a red, insistent energy.

When he started fucking her she was surprised at his vigor. Maybe it was the wine, but—"You must've been lonely this week," she remarked, laughing as she rolled on top of him. He groaned and told her to move slower, slower, he wanted to last. Finally they were done and she lay trying to catch her breath and wondering if he'd want to go for another round. He hadn't even choked her today. He had seemed so eager that even vanilla sex was enough for him. He's paying me too much, she thought. This isn't even so bad.

Then she remembered how dangerous this type of thinking was.

They took a shower together. After she'd washed the remnants of makeup off her face, he offered to get her an Uber back to her apartment. He sometimes asked her to sleep over, but tonight was not one of those nights—he snored, and she couldn't sleep with the sound, and he liked to spread as much of his five-foot-eight frame across the bed as possible. Sometimes, especially with the snoring, it reminded her of an old married couple's routine.

"I'm okay taking the subway."

"You sure, doll? It can get dangerous late at night."

"It's not late at night," she said, and it was true; it was barely eleven. She had spent only a few hours with him. The more lax she acted and the more she pulled away, the more he stepped towards her, the less time he was willing to accept with her while still keeping up her allowance. A doll was supposed to remain distant, after all—pliable on the surface, with movable limbs, but untouchable beneath its porcelain coating.

When she was eighteen, not long after moving to New York City, Anna had gotten a bird tattooed on her wrist. An empty silhouette, flying nowhere. She'd kept the size tiny, easy enough to cover with foundation, so as not to risk losing any jobs; she had just signed with her agency and the entirety of her modeling career stretched out before her, opaque and shivering with promise. As the tattoo artist was bandaging the finished piece, she caught a glimpse of the tattoo on his arm. He was covered with ink, but this piece stood out to her. The script that flowed over his forearm said "If I could, I would. Baby, I swear I would." She looked the words up later, thinking they were song lyrics, but found nothing that matched. Maybe the tattoo artist had meant to do lyrics but had gotten it wrong. Or maybe she was misremembering, or maybe they were pathless, lyrics to nothing.

But some memories were crystallized. Like Florida, a four-day vacation to Fort Lauderdale, two years ago, with her boyfriend at the time. A boyfriend with laughing green eyes and an easy, crooked smile. This was just weeks before she quit modeling, broke up with the boyfriend, and decided on other methods of obtaining money. Both she and the boyfriend were broke and were staying with a friend who owned a house there. It was only a six-month relationship, and not serious in the least, but she never hid any parts of her personality from him, not even the embarrassing or weak or awkward facets of herself. This vulnerability caused her to fall frighteningly, precipitously in love in a way she had not been before or since.

Anna's sandals broke the second day they were in Fort Lauderdale, and as she kept forgetting to buy a new pair until they were already on the sand, she ended up wearing her sneakers to the beach for the remainder of the trip. She was still finding grains of sand in them for weeks after she got back.

In Florida they ate gas station cakes and crisp apples and endless bowls of instant banana bread oatmeal. Anna would tear open packages of cake rolls and eat them so fast that she would get frosting on her nose, and when her boyfriend called it to her attention, she dabbed a bit on his nose as well, like sunscreen, so they would be even. (He hadn't minded.) One evening they reclined on beach towels in the backyard and ate hot dogs for dinner; the mustard was the cheapest brand and the buns were nothing more than gummy slices of Wonder Bread, but they tasted like sweet, juicy heaven after a day of swimming and sweating in the sun. They drank so much coconut water that their skin began to smell like it, bright and clean and verdant. They did so much walking and exploring that the calories they consumed simply peeled away like a trick of math, adding up to less than the sum of their parts.

On the next-to-last day in Florida, they decided to take a nap before going out later. They curled up in bed and the boyfriend dropped off with predictable quickness, snoring cute little snores, but Anna couldn't sleep. She lay awake listening to the music that floated from the other room, her arms limp around her boyfriend's sleeping body, thinking how they were in the present but knowing full well that the spirit of this moment would slip inevitably away. And once past, it would decay still further.

She hugged him and watched the blue half-light fade into a deeper darkness. Felt a great emptiness welling within her. Why was her thoughtless tattoo permanent, but these precious days were not? They thinned out, stiffened, shattered like frozen paper. Leaving nothing but a handful of lyrics and sand in her shoes.

Anna took the subway home. As she got on the train, she stepped around a mother pushing a baby carriage ahead of her; she looked in instinctively, hoping to catch a glimpse of an angelic infant face, but there was no baby, only a bundle of bags in the carriage. The non-mother leaned on the handles, looking exhausted. Anna took a seat. A man in a tilted baseball cap and a stained jersey kept trying to catch her eye and she wondered if she smelled of sex. If the men on the train could catch the scent like animals. He kept staring, his gaze piercing a hole in her peripheral vision, but she found it easy to ignore him as long as she kept her mind on other things. A woman in an ostentatious geometrical-patterned dress stood in front of her, so that if Anna stared straight ahead she had an abundance of shapes to focus on, and her eyes darted back and forth from square to triangle to stripe.

She would probably get home before midnight. She just hoped she would remember to text Warren that she'd gotten home safe. There was the question of whether or not it would be pertinent to add an emoji to the end, or to simply leave it as a statement, factual and cold. Probably better to add an emoji. Surely that wouldn't ruin the distance she'd created between them, its careful gravitational pull. The train car rattled on, the woman in front of her moved to sit down, and Anna caught sight of her reflection in the opposite window: hair frizzing and astray, eyes like holes, mouth a blurry dark.

CHAPTER 3

Gemma

"Can I help you?"

Gemma Taylor jumped and nearly dropped the paperweight she was holding. Good thing she hadn't; she'd seen the price tag, and it was $150. "No thanks," she told the woman who had an ABC CARPET tag pinned to her shirt. "I'm just looking."

The woman nodded and backed away, although with a new tinge of suspicion, probably because Gemma had reacted like a startled burglar. Gemma replaced the paperweight on the shelf with sweaty fingers. Even after fifteen minutes here, it was difficult for her to get her bearings: the whole store glittered like the inside of a geode. Everywhere she looked, she was hit with a new surge of aesthetic brilliance. Chandeliers descended enormous and sparkling from the ceiling, gleaming mirrors loomed ten feet tall, and slim candles stood alongside rows of cups and chairs carved from what looked like driftwood. There was an entire section with statues of the Buddha and heavy, ornate Indian jewelry and incense that filled the air with a spicy intensity. Gemma had walked three full circles around the floor before she could actually commit herself to purposeful browsing.

The problem was, she needed everything in her room to be cohesive. No one wanted to watch a video background that was simply a mishmash of various items that had caught her eye, because this would impart not what she desired—a sense of cool, tranquil success—but rather a frantic and desperate grasping. Appearances were everything, particularly when your entire career was based on visual (80%) and auditory (20%). Even people who mostly kept influencer videos on as background noise relied more than they thought on the visual aspects of the videos.

Gemma came face-to-face with a collection of filament candle bulbs that hung like stalactites from the ceiling. They would add an old-fashioned ambiance and form the perfect background; she could already picture them behind her, framing her face as she spoke to the camera.

Then she saw that they cost $980. Well. She did the mental math and converted them to quid, which gave her a slightly smaller number, but still a lot. She considered texting Derek and asking his advice, but then decided not to. She knew what he would say.

The problem was, while Gemma wasn't exactly skint, as her mother had left her enough money to pay rent in Manhattan, she still didn't have the kind of money that would allow her to drop close to a thousand dollars on a bunch of lightbulbs. This was usually easy enough to ignore, but often the knowledge flitted into Gemma's head at the most inconvenient of times. It was impossible for her to do what she was here to do, which was enjoy herself and collect items for her new apartment, when she was continually thinking about her restrictions.

If she found herself focusing on what she did not have, well —that was a path that led to more dangerous places. And the sort of person she needed to become did not do this. The sort of person she needed to become was always grateful for what they did have. If she wanted to be an influencer, she needed to focus on the good elements in her life, and not think about anything that she lacked. No one wanted to watch the videos of someone who was constantly complaining or unhappy with their situation. It was like reading the news all day long; it left you with a sour, sticky feeling, negativity oozing out of the screen.

Gemma did something then, a habit she had never been

totally able to shake. She closed her eyes and pictured each of the objects, the things she had really liked, the things that had seized her gaze and not let it go. She set up a mental scene where all these objects were gathered in her room. The imposing mahogany chest of drawers, the shabby-chic vase that would hold endless arrangements of flowers, the soft gray napkins. She pictured them all in the bedroom she and Derek shared, the living room, the kitchen. And as the rooms filled with these objects, they grew larger and brighter, the apartment transforming from a cramped studio in Chelsea to a sprawling townhouse with tree branches brushing the windows. This was the power of visualization, of focusing on welcoming positive things into your life. Sure, she could picture stacks of money pouring in or her bank balance ticking up as quickly as the seconds on a stopwatch, but that was too direct. Sometimes a more roundabout, aesthetic visualization was better.

Once she felt sufficiently filled with positive projections, she exhaled and opened her eyes. Her body instantly filled with ice: the saleslady from before was standing in front of her, frowning and concerned.

"Are you all right?"

"Yeah," Gemma stammered. "I'm fine—sorry. Just felt a bit faint, that's all, low blood sugar—"

"Low blood sugar?" The woman's eyebrows snapped up. She had slight buckteeth and hair cut so precisely that it lay in a perfectly straight line. The sight gave Gemma anxiety: what would she do if she got a split end? "You need some sugar."

"Right, I know, I'll run out and get something—" Gemma had already begun to back away.

"Where are you going? I have something for you right here." The lady gestured for Gemma to follow, and led her a few steps to one of the circular registers in the center of the floor. She leaned down and fetched a bar of chocolate from behind the counter. "We keep one or two of these around in case of emergencies," she said, her voice low and conspiratorial. "It'll bring your blood sugar straight back up."

"Really? It's okay, you don't have to..."

But the saleslady was already peeling back the paper. "Oh, go on. Are you British, by the way?" she added as Gemma broke off a square of chocolate and took a reluctant bite.

"Yeah."

"I knew I couldn't mistake that accent! You're not from London, are you?"

Gemma nodded, chewing. The chocolate tasted exactly like dirt packed into a square. She swallowed with some difficulty.

"I've never been there," the lady said, looking wistful. "But I always dreamed of visiting. The whole country's beautiful, though... honestly, you're lucky to have seen so much of the world. I'm Nellie, by the way."

"I'm Gemma. Thanks for the chocolate." She tried to figure out how much chocolate one usually needed to eat to stave off low blood sugar. Was one square enough, or was Nellie expecting her to devour half the bar? Goddammit, Gemma could just as easily have told her she liked to meditate at random times. They were right by the incense section. It would have made at least a tiny bit of sense.

"This is a new chocolate we've just gotten in stock. From Brazil."

"Oh?" She turned the bar over and saw that it was 88% dark, organic and fair trade, from some brand she had never heard of before.

"It's a bargain, only $12 a bar."

Good Lord, Gemma thought. She was scared to ask what the more expensive chocolate bars went for around here. It wasn't even large; it was very light and barely longer than the palm of her hand. She realized she had probably overestimated how much sugar an 88% bar of chocolate contained. If she really had low blood sugar, it might not even help. Maybe it was all a trick. Maybe Nellie was expecting her to drop at any moment. She began to sweat.

"Thanks," she said again, but this seemed inadequate. Obviously she was supposed to buy the bloody chocolate.

"You like it, right?" Nellie's friendly expression had begun to harden and glaze over like one of the varnished wood cabinets on the other side of the room.

"Yeah, it's great," she said. "Um, it's only $12, right?"

Nellie's face softened, as though the hardness had never been there at all. "That's right! Shall I ring you up right, ah... well, right over here?" She laughed at the coincidental closeness of the register and Gemma laughed too. She handed over her credit card, moving as though in a dream, and felt the $12 leave her account and sail away forever. Twelve dollars was nothing, but the fact that she wasn't even getting anything worthwhile for it, just *giving* it away, made it seem like so much more. The chocolate bar felt even lighter when Nellie handed it to her in a paper bag.

Feeling foreign and stupid and gullible, Gemma left ABC Carpet & Home with her dirt-chocolate. A candle was burning near the store entrance, protected in a silver case, and the scent of it wafted her way, making her think of homemade oatmeal cookies, maple syrup from deep in the northern woods. There was something horribly nostalgic about it, like seeing the background of your childhood home that now belonged to someone else.

As soon as she stepped into the sunlight, she sneezed, predictably. She always sneezed when she went outside into the sun. She considered giving the chocolate bar to Derek, but he had even more of a sweet tooth than she did. He would wonder what on earth had possessed her to purchase such a dark and bitter bar. And the price tag was stuck directly on the wrapper. Gemma tried to scrape it off, but she'd been biting her nails again and she couldn't even get half of it off. She laughed to herself and finally walked a few blocks away—who knew if Nellie was watching through the window—and placed the bar on a dusty window ledge. Maybe some homeless person would come along and rejoice at their luck, needing the calories more than she did.

Of course, it was equally likely that a dog would come along, a big dog capable of reaching as high as the window ledge, and scarf it down and die. She hesitated, frozen in indecision with her hand half-extended towards the bar. Finally she snatched it back off the ledge and chucked it in a nearby bin.

Obviously, she could never go back there again. Unless she dressed completely differently, put on an American accent, and came in at different hours.

The late September sun cast a weak light over the street. The sky was a hazy, milky white instead of blue; it was something to do with the weather, something about fires on the West Coast, but Gemma had forgotten exactly what.

She turned first in one direction and then the other, wondering where to go. Passersby blended in perfectly with the city, looking as though they'd been here all their lives. Probably some of them had.

Gemma could not pinpoint the exact moment when she'd made the decision to become an influencer. The thought had come about slowly. Around August, the time she left England and came to New York for university, it had begun to glimmer in her mind with an uncanny brilliance. And now, in the last few weeks since her arrival and moving in with Derek and everything else, it had materialized, glinting steady and unwavering like graphite, black with countless prismatic mirrors on its surface. Countless possibilities. Countless other interpretations of her life that she could dive into.

The truth was, she had precious little by which to define herself. She had read in a recent article that your life was determined by two things: the events that happened to you, and your creations. She didn't want to think about the events part, because the biggest event that had happened to her in the last year was a terrible one. The idea of creations, though; that was another component altogether. At first she'd thought that the author was referring to creative projects such as sculptures or paintings, but then she realized there was no reason her own life could not be a creation. On video and the internet, at least, it was malleable. She could assemble it just as she wished.

But in order to succeed at this she would have to improve herself, and quickly. No one wanted to follow a meek, foolish girl as she jumped from one wrong decision to the next, landing unsteadily on them like they were slippery stones in a river.

A few sparrows pecked at the ground by her feet. "Hello," Gemma said to them. They chittered and looked up at her, their dense soft bodies clustering together. She stood watching them for a few moments, tenderness hanging heavy in her chest, and then turned in the direction of her apartment. At least she had Derek waiting at home. At least she had someone to lie to when asked how her day had been. Some people didn't even have that.

CHAPTER 4

Janet

After she finished her work for the day and sent the last letter-writer a package of ophthalmologists, Janet shut off her computer and listened to the new quiet. It had a sort of hum to it, and she spent a few moments wondering if this was what real silence sounded like—a soft purr, the deep breathing of a sleeping animal—before she realized that one of her neighbors was vacuuming. Of course. There was no such thing as real silence at 351 East 104th Street, or anywhere else in New York, for that matter. To get real silence you probably had to either go to a soundproofed room, or just get the hell out of the city—far away, driving out to a spot in the Southwest where the land stretched parched in all directions. Somewhere even animals didn't want to live.

Janet considered visiting her mother and aunt in Queens for the evening, but even that was too far. She was tired, and didn't want to ride on the subway for an hour, breathing in the smells of urine and grease and stale, crunchy French fries. The sun was sinking in the west; the sky would soon be the color of the deep parts of the ocean where animals floated in bioluminescent halos. She hadn't bothered to turn any of the lights on throughout the workday, and now the apartment was full of shadows, a chiaroscuro of nightmarish light.

She checked her phone and saw, with a little shudder of

dopamine, that someone from a dating app had sent her a text. She'd been chatting with this guy Liam for the past few days, and since yesterday she'd been sensing that he was gearing up to ask her out. Right on schedule, he'd just done so, suggesting a bar on the Upper East Side. At least he hadn't asked her to come straight over to his rooftop or his apartment. She always declined these invitations. She had grown fond of her kidneys over the years and wanted to remain attached to them.

Janet almost wore heels, but then changed her mind at the last minute, slipping on a pair of flat boots before rushing out the door. This turned out to have been a wise decision; when Liam showed up he was the same height as her. Clearly the 6'0" on his profile had been an exaggeration, or at the very least the product of a faulty measuring tape. Janet wondered how many inaccurate measuring tapes were floating around, sowing confusion and inadvertently subjecting men to embarrassment.

Despite the height embellishment, Liam seemed friendly enough. He greeted Janet with an awkward head-nod, and actually pulled out her chair for her to sit down. "Apparently chivalry isn't quite dead after all," she said. As soon as she heard herself, she realized that she sounded like her mother. That overly light tone, a manufactured breeziness barely concealing the tangled nest of her *real* thoughts.

"Despite feminism's best efforts," he said, winking at her. She hadn't known they were at the winking stage. And she hated when guys talked about feminism, regardless of whether they disliked it, as Liam seemed to, or embraced it, in the case of the many men who refused to even buy their girlfriend a coffee. "Sorry. That was a bad joke."

"I've never been here before," she said. "Have you?"

"Only a few times."

She wondered if he brought all his Tinder dates here. It was nice, though; the bar was soft-lit and had stacks of ancient-looking books lining the walls. Their spines were worn and flaking at the corners and looked as soft as velvet. She fought the urge to reach up and touch one.

"So I guess you know what's good?" she asked.

"Um..." He scanned the menu. "Yeah, the apple martini is pretty bomb. Although if you're in the mood for something stronger, they have a scotch—it's a Cardhu, Game of Thrones edition."

"Oh, really?" He sounded so happy about it, too. She vaguely remembered Game of Thrones as a show that had been popular at one point, a number of years ago, before eventually becoming passé. She'd never even watched one episode, but guessed that now wasn't the time to tell him this. So she just shrugged and tried to look interested.

He read off the menu: "This Single Malt Scotch honors the legendary women from the House Targaryen, and their unwavering resilience, with a taste that's rich with notes of sweet fruit, dark chocolate, spice, and toffee." His voice was too loud. Janet felt herself sinking down in her chair. "Isn't that dope? I fucking love the Targaryens. What's your favorite house?"

"From Game of Thrones?" she asked, as though he might possibly mean the houses of Hogwarts. "Oh, Targaryen, too."

"They're just so badass, aren't they?" When the waiter came around, a man with a skinny mustache that would have looked more in place in 2010s Brooklyn, Liam ordered the Game of Thrones scotch. Janet got a lemongrass martini.

"Intriguing choice." Liam folded his hands together and stared directly into her eyes across the table. Unsettled by the sudden observation, she took a sip of her water. They went through the whole first-date dance: where are you from, what are your hobbies, do you have any brothers or sisters, et cetera. The stuff you should be able to scribble down on an online form before meeting. When she told him her family was from Queens, he pressed, "No, where are you really from? Ancestrally."

"Well, Korea," she said. She'd been asked this countless times before; the question didn't even surprise her anymore. "But my parents weren't even born there. So I don't have many ties to the region, myself."

"You mean you've never been?"

"No. I don't really feel the need to go. I mean, I guess I'd like to visit someday, when I have the money..." She stumbled over her words momentarily. Money problems weren't the best topic of conversation for a first date. "But it's a far-off idea, like visiting London or Paris. My older sister lives in Florida with her family and that seems to be fine for her. I don't think she's ever even expressed an interest in going to Korea."

"That's sad," Liam said. He was gazing at her with a new sympathy. "To not have ties to your ancestral homeland. Nothing personal, I mean. It's not like it's your fault. It just seems like kind of a shame."

"Mmm. Maybe. What's *your* ancestral homeland?" She knew that Liam, along with most of the other white guys who had asked her similar questions, probably never asked white girls where they were "really" from.

"Oh, I'm a mutt," Liam said, grinning. "I'm from all over. I guess I'd have about five or ten different ancestral homelands? Let's see, I'm Irish, Danish, Greek, Italian..." He frowned and seemed to lose count. "Did I say German already?"

"So just all of Europe basically. Did you ever visit any of those places?"

"Nah. Can't afford it either. Although when I was sixteen, I did manage to take part in a language immersion trip to Paris at one point. I didn't win too many friends there—I kept stealing more than my share of Brie and Camembert from the charcuterie boards."

"Teenage boys' appetites are no joke." The tension was dissolving a little now that she had gotten him to talk about himself. He kept talking about himself until their drinks came, at which point he insisted she try some of his Scotch. "It's got the essence of the Targaryen house," he said, watching her as she took a minuscule sip. She nodded and agreed that it was extremely fiery.

Then he asked the dreaded question: "What do you do for work?"

"Well, it's a little hard to explain," she said, stirring her drink and losing herself for a moment in the tiny whirlpool. "I'm kind of an online therapist."

"Oh boy." Liam's oversized ears perked up, and he sat

forward. "So you have access to all the dark confessions and secrets of the population?"

"Well, some of them. I'm not really allowed to go into detail, though."

"It's okay, you don't have to tell me. Do you do video sessions with clients or something?"

"No, I'm not as fancy as that. I'm not licensed or anything. All I do is answer their letters. They tell me—anonymously—what's wrong with them, what's troubling them in their lives, and I set them up with a specialist or two whom I think could help them."

"Ah, I see." He looked almost disappointed. "So you're more of a matchmaker."

"A therapist Cupid. Yeah, I guess so." The martini was strong and she could feel the blood rushing to her cheeks and forehead, gathering and pooling there, like her entire face was a giant bruise. "The product of a psychology degree and no med school training. What do you do?"

"I'm a continuous improvement engineer."

"Nice," she said.

"You haven't got a clue what that means, do you?"

"Not really."

"I like your boldness. Most girls would pretend to know, they'd make something up."

"They're probably more polite than I am. I guess I've gotten a little jaded after a year of answering letters that begin with declarations of wanting to commit suicide. It's as though it's stripped all the fancy outer coating off me, left me with nothing but the basic necessities for life." She made a face.

"You've had this job for a year? Wow." He shook his head. "I think it would *destroy* me."

"Who's to say it hasn't destroyed me already?"

"I don't know, you seem pretty okay to me." He smiled at her again. There was something vaguely, drunkenly charming about his big ears, his watery blue eyes.

They ordered another round of drinks and then, at some point, he offered to show her his apartment. He mentioned a piano, drawing on an earlier comment Janet had made about liking to play piano. "Sure, I'd love to see it," she said, baring her neck invitingly as she tipped the last of her drink back. The martini had softened and blurred some of Liam's less agreeable features—his slightly crooked teeth, the sharpness of his elbows that were visible through his jacket—and the music floating from the speakers seemed to be reaching her from a long way off.

In a stunning coincidence, Liam's apartment was only a few blocks away. As they walked in its direction, they talked about nothing in particular; they remarked on a passing car and a passing cloud-like poodle and a famous, now-closed bagel shop. Liam said something about his college days and she laughed along as though she'd had a social life in college, as though she'd had Adventures there too.

Liam's apartment had almost no furnishings or knickknacks or any of the other things that were meant to make a place home. There were only a couple of rooms, so it was easy to take every-thing in at a glance. The bed was a mattress lying bare on the floor. The piano was an electronic keyboard propped upright against the wall and covered in dust.

She should have expected it, really.

They sat down together on the mattress, as though nothing were wrong. And then it felt like the opposite—as though they both knew everything was fake, unbelievably so, and each of them was seeing how far they could take it. Liam put his arm around her and kept talking, picking up on his earlier college anecdotes. Janet knew the motions by heart now, knew the way a boy's face and demeanor changed when he was preparing to kiss her for the first time. His movements slowed, every twitch of a muscle purposeful and calculated, all of these actions pointing towards the ultimate goal of getting her on her back in his bed. They were already sitting on his bed, so it wasn't much of a journey from this point to that one. She wondered how he would react if she said *Let's just get this over with* and lunged at him, whether he would be relieved or insulted or some other emotion she hadn't thought of yet.

The steps passed smoothly, although his mouth was wetter

than she had been expecting. They lay down together, and although they were only on a mattress and not quite in a bed, she could feel her body responding. *It* certainly didn't mind Liam's crooked teeth or sharpish elbows. He was already hard against her stomach, she could feel his heat even through their layers of clothing, and she kissed him back hungrily, enjoying the knowledge that she was causing him to respond this way.

But when the time came, when he tried to push inside her, he softened and shrunk. It was almost comical how fast the transformation happened. One or two attempts at thrusts and Liam was no longer the owner of an intimidating member that a romance novelist would be proud to describe, but something closer to an overcooked piece of rigatoni.

She exhaled in disappointment. Liam shrugged and flopped onto the mattress beside her, as though they had just completed a passionate romp and were about to indulge in some pillow talk.

"I'm sorry, this happens sometimes," he said. But from his expression she could tell that it happened all the time. He didn't even seem that embarrassed. "Maybe I shouldn't have jerked off so much earlier today."

Yeah. Maybe not.

"You ever think you do that too much? How often do you do it?"

He shrugged. "A couple times a day, I guess?"

"A couple times a day? That much?" She didn't try to keep the shock out of her voice.

"Sometimes only once," he said, his tone growing defensive.

Jesus, she thought. "What kind of porn do you watch?" She wasn't sure why she was asking, but she was bold, he had already decided she was bold, and she might as well grab that and run with it.

"Oh, just normal stuff, you know," he said, but from the way his gaze slid to the side she could tell he might not be being entirely honest. "The kind of porn where they show people having sex. Want to watch some together?"

She restrained herself from incredulous laughter. Surely he

wasn't serious. Surely she didn't look like she wanted to lie on a mattress next to a stranger while he attempted to stroke his limp dick into some sort of life. "No thanks. It's getting late, anyway." She glanced out the window as though to confirm this, although the view was just the back of another building, whose windows looked like they'd been shuttered for the last ten years. Grime coated the frames, black and muddy like tar. "I should get home."

"Oh, yeah. For sure. Gotta get a head start on those depression letters." His tone was too hearty, its joviality forced, and the reference a pathetic remainder of what their banter had been back at the bar. How sex ruined everything. Or an attempt at sex. She wished she could ask him what the point had been of him taking her back to his place, if he'd known it had a good chance of failure. She thought this as though she hadn't encouraged it, as though she hadn't been hornier than him. And he had rubbed one (or two) out at some point before their meeting—she couldn't determine whether it was because he'd thought he didn't have a chance at getting laid, or rather that he wasn't thinking about it, because he was capable of thinking only a few minutes in advance.

Or maybe it was her fault, for focusing so much on the actual act of sex instead of conversation and connection with another human being, no matter how fleeting.

Outside, she stood waiting on the corner for her Uber. When she turned and looked back up at Liam's building it looked like it was falling towards her. Maybe it was the movement of the clouds behind it, the sound of the wind rushing by like something underwater. With a shudder she turned away and looked at the street again.

At home in her dark apartment, Janet curled up on her chair. The squares of neighboring windows floated in the night: some warm amber, some brighter yellow, some even glowing in shades of navy or scarlet, and all of them as distant as buoys drifting through the dark.

The screen of her phone was blue-lit, bigger on the inside than it was on the outside, and she fell into it. She scrolled through dozens of news headlines, her eyes flicking from one to the next in a steady rhythm. Some of them were so ridiculous that she had to go back and read them again, just to confirm they were actually real. For example: in the UK, psychologists were attempting to learn more about how the minds of wild animals worked. She scoffed, the sound harsh in the empty room. Their mission made no sense to her—all the wild animals were dying anyway, or three-quarters of them at least. It seemed fruitless, almost mockingly so, to try to get to know the inner workings of a mind belonging to a species that was fated to disappear in a matter of years.

It was like the card that came with the issue of National Geographic she'd mistakenly received in the mail a week ago. It was an advertisement for the kids' offshoot of the magazine, called, predictably, National Geographic Little Kids. The card was adorned with pictures of fuzzy polar bear cubs and baby leopards. Janet had read it in stunned disbelief: *National Geographic Little Kids magazine will ignite the young explorer inside your child! Prepare for captivating facts, amazing discoveries, and stunning photographs that will awaken your child's curiosity about the natural world.*

Awaken kids' curiosity about the natural world, just as that natural world was disappearing forever all around them. Great. Sounded like a ton of fucking fun.

Janet recognized the familiar sense of futility—oh, she recognized it as surely as though she had plunged her head into a basin of cold water. She had read too many of those grievance letters not to.

If she were a bit stupider and more gullible, she might try a guided meditation or something on YouTube, but there was no point in trying to convince herself that reality was not, in fact, reality. And she seemed to have a concentration problem; every time she watched a YouTube video she couldn't tear her eyes away from the comments. She often scrolled through them, completely forgetting about the video in exchange for the half-formed thoughts and opinions of random people who were watching along with her. If she took herself a little more seriously, she would say it was because she lacked a sense of community. But she didn't take herself seriously.

She checked in on her older sister, who lived in Fort Lauderdale. It was late, but Izzy usually stayed up until at least midnight, long after her husband and children went to sleep. At the moment, the region was in the midst of hurricane season. They were hitting the coast more and more frequently, bigger and bigger each year, like the food raining from the sky in Cloudy with a Chance of Meatballs. As a child, that book's illustrations had filled her with a sense of dread so profound that she had shoved the book into the back of her closet and refused to look at it for years, too frightened to even pick it up to throw it away. Now that she'd read stuff like *Haunted* and *The Painted Bird*—some of it for no other reason than to prove to herself that she could—she wondered how her younger self could have been so damn sensitive.

Izzy answered the FaceTime call on the sixth ring. Probably busy with family life. Janet was still growing used to the sight of her older sister, who had once had the longest hair she'd ever seen in real life. Since the birth of her youngest child two years ago, Izzy had started cutting her hair shorter and shorter. She'd most recently snipped it right to her shoulders. Apparently when you had three kids, things like hair just got in the way.

"Hey!" Izzy said. "How's my lil' sis?"

Sometimes Izzy got in one of these moods where she started sarcastically calling Janet the kind of nicknames that older sisters used in movies or sitcoms. Janet wasn't sure whether she liked it or not. Despite all the drama that inevitably happened on those shows, there was a comforting sense of stasis that never wavered. It was cozy, in a way—nothing happened unless it was necessary for the plot. The background remained steadily the same, and, unless some centenarian patriarch needed to advance the show by leaving behind a fortune, nobody aged, and nobody died.

"I'm okay. Hanging in there. How's the family?" Janet asked, and then immediately wished she hadn't. Izzy took this as an invitation to launch into the news of Ruby's potty training progress, Henry's interest in beetles (mostly dead ones, and if they weren't dead, he would make them so) and Terry's latest habit of running around the house with his underpants over his head. The question of why her sister and her docile, bespectacled husband had decided to produce not one, not two, but *three* children never ceased to puzzle Janet. The first two had been twins, yes, but she couldn't understand why they had the third one afterwards. Both parents worked and had good jobs in marketing, so money wasn't a huge issue, but there was still the timesuck problem. Izzy often worked a full day, picked her kids up from school and daycare, and then played with them, cooked, did homework help, watched movies with them, and finally worked on her own personal "self-care" projects such as sewing, redecorating the bathrooms, and gardening. All of this took place in one day. The mere idea made Janet dizzy.

"Do you guys have a plan in case of hurricanes?" Janet asked, remembering a news piece she'd read earlier that day. "There's still a big risk of another one landing on the coast before the season ends."

"Yeah... I guess so."

"I don't like the sound of that. If there's a category four or five predicted, you'll leave, right?"

"Um, and go where?"

"You could always come here."

Izzy looked away from the screen for a moment and swatted gently at something outside the frame. "No, Henry, I do *not* want to see that!" She returned to look at Janet, making an exasperated face. "Just abandon my work and impose on you? With my whole family? As you can see, we can hardly contain them here. And our house is a lot bigger than yours."

"Um, on me? You wouldn't be imposing on me. Obviously Mom and Auntie would let you guys stay with them."

"You think so? I wouldn't be too sure about that."

Janet fought not to roll her eyes, irritated by how her sister always downplayed their mother's affection for her. Izzy was lucky enough to have it; she might as well embrace it. "Their place is bigger than mine, for one thing. And I'm sure Mom especially would be happy to have you. I try to go see her a lot, but she gets lonely."

There was an awkward silence. Izzy gnawed at her lip. Since their father had died several years before, their mother had been living with her sister in Queens, who was also widowed. It was as though their family had been cursed. Her mother and aunt even referenced this curse sometimes, and Janet was never sure whether they were serious or not.

"I don't know. I'd be busy with the kids a lot, and that's *if* I'm allowed to work from home," Izzy said hesitantly. "It's not like I'd have a ton of time to hang out with her and Auntie, drinking supermarket wine and gossiping."

"Or maybe you just don't want to get too close to the Ha curse."

Izzy snorted through her nose, and her tone grew stern and disapproving. "You know that's bullshit."

"Well. If you think about it—"

"But I still understand your reluctance to find a partner."

Janet was speechless for a moment. Maybe Izzy was being bitchy, or maybe it was possible that she thought Janet was single by choice. That she believed Janet thought there truly *was* a curse, in some small and paranoid part of her mind, and that's why she had so far avoided anything serious.

Maybe it was partially her own fault. Maybe she shouldn't have regaled her older sister with so many stories about awkward hookups and failed Tinder dates. But then, she didn't know what other stories she could tell her. The grievance letters were off-limits, and too depressing for Izzy, anyway. She was a mother. She had to be protected from those kinds of things. There was a part of Janet that hated this idea, the unfairness that her sister should be the one who was spared and got to live in blissful ignorance, but another part of her stuck firmly to it. If they both fell victim to the depression of the hideous present, there would be no hope for anyone in the future.

Izzy was only seven years older than Janet, less than a decade, but because of the era they were born in, the age difference had created a substantial gap between the two of them. Janet had been born shortly after the millennium and couldn't remember a time before smartphones and Netflix. Izzy, on the other hand, had been born in the nineties and grown up with flip phones and lagging computer games. She had only really dived into the world of social media in high school, whereas Janet had always been completely steeped in it. Izzy also possessed a sliver of the previous generation's distrust of the online universe, a Luddite holdover from the "lawless age" of the internet. To Izzy, the World Wide Web was still a forbidding landscape bristling with sites like Encyclopedia Dramatica and 4chan and dark, wannabe edgy humor. To Janet, though, it was a haven full of memes, videos of teenagers dancing, and people just like her.

"Well, look on the bright side—me not having a partner just means I have more room for you, in case both yours and Mom's houses blow down and I need to shelter *everyone*," Janet eventually said. "Think about it, okay? It really wouldn't be a problem. I want to save you from a hurricane. It would make me feel useful."

"You worry too much, Janet. There's no evidence we'll even see any more hurricanes this season. Maybe your job is stressing you out too much?"

"We can't all have, like, normal 9-to-5s like you. Some stress comes with the territory."

"Want to talk about it?" Izzy had put on her maternal, you-can-confide-in-me voice, and Janet hated it. Probably because it made her feel like one of Izzy's children.

"I really shouldn't. It's confidential. Also, I don't want to."

"You never want to talk about it. You think of that job like it's some... some mythical mission you've been entrusted with. You know these aren't state secrets? These are a bunch of anony-mous emails from hundreds of people who are looking for the fastest, easiest, and cheapest solutions to their various problems."

"That doesn't make them any less important."

Before bed, Janet took a shower. She'd been looking forward to it all day, but as she stepped into the stream, she realized that she wasn't really enjoying it, and was looking forward to lying down in bed afterward. This was a pattern she'd picked up on lately: during each section of the day, she was only looking forward to the next. After work, Janet would look forward to dinner with the single-mindedness of an animal, and only when she ate dinner would she realize, *Oh yeah, this again. Nothing special.* Then, afterwards, she would sit on the floor for long unraveling minutes and crave a shower, imagining the warmth of the water. But then when she was in the shower, soaping herself and leaning into the spray of water and everything else that had earlier seemed so luxurious but now felt like a chore, she would look languidly ahead to the bed, the soft sheets. And then as she lay in bed she would look forward to the next day.

It seemed that it never stopped. That she was constantly doomed to always look to the future, her mind always skipping one step ahead, until it and she reached the inevitable end.

Just enjoy the moment, she thought. Chill. Stop being such a paranoid fucking loser. But the moment slipped out of her grasp like a wet shard of soap and she found herself looking towards what was ahead, unsure if her anticipation was that of excitement or that of a cornered animal sniffing for its hunter. Her skin felt too slick and slippery with the shower gel, like there was something wrong with it, or with her.

She considered writing this down in a grievance letter and sending it to herself, just as a joke, and it was actually a pretty cool idea. Giving herself a new perspective on her problems and all that. Maybe she could even recommend herself a nice set of therapists. But by the time she woke up the next morning the thought was gone, vanished along with her dreams.

CHAPTER 5

Anna

T he September days were quickly growing shorter and cooler. It had only been a few weeks since 80-degree weather and brilliant sunshine and trips to the beach, but already those days seemed so far in the rearview mirror that they were almost out of sight.

That evening, Warren was taking her out to a rooftop bar. Anna wore one of the outfits he liked best on her—a tight red dress and a pair of stiletto heels as black and glittery as the Siberian night sky. She would be about six inches taller than him in this outfit, but he didn't mind. It was one of the things that she liked about him; he didn't have the sensitivity about his height that so many other men did. Darting around men's various insecurities tended to be a bigger task in this kind of relationship than it was in normal ones, because the men were already intensely aware that they were paying for sex and company. But Warren had never seemed to care that she was taller than him.

He picked her up outside her apartment, in a private car big enough for eight people. When he saw her he grinned: a vulpine flash of white in the darkness. "My beautiful dolly," he said. "I love the way you look tonight."

"It's Dolly now, is it?" She climbed in to sit across from him

—not next to him, not yet, as she knew he wanted to admire her outfit. "That's another level beyond 'doll.'"

"In a good way? Well? Tell me what you really think."

"I'm not sure. I'll tolerate it, I suppose. As long as you don't compare me to Dolly Parton."

"Ah, damn it!" He slapped his thigh in mock frustration. "That's exactly who I wanted to fantasize about when I call you that!"

"See? I know you too well." She regretted the words the second they were out. They hovered heavy and clumsy in the thick, close, perfume-and-cologne-drenched air. And they might even be true. Knowing one another well wasn't a good thing, not with them; a sense of mystery, of the unattainable, was important in a sugaring relationship. And ten months was already on the long side; many men like Warren switched up their sugar babies every few months. Desperate to change the subject, she said, "Remind me again where we're going tonight?"

He didn't seem to have picked up on the tension. "I told you earlier this evening. I do hope you're not developing extremely-early-onset Alzheimer's, my darling Anna-doodle. There, is that better?"

She almost choked on her laughter. "No. And I don't think you should be joking about Alzheimer's, if you get my drift."

"Right, that's probably true. The people at Lasetti will think you're my keeper, not my girlfriend."

"So that's where we're going!" She sat up straighter, victorious.

He sighed. "It's so easy to pull the wool over my eyes, isn't it."

Lasetti's rooftop was heated via the floor and boasted a white, faux-rustic trellis. There were a few sleek black tables, each with a bottle of champagne on it, most of them attended by skinny models and businessmen in suits. Even with the heated function of the rooftop, the models looked cold. Anna wasn't surprised. She remembered her own days as a model, starving herself down to ten percent body fat, lacking the warmth afforded by that essential soft layer. She remembered shivering in her room with the heat turned on full blast, piling on layers and layers of sweaters to no avail, because her body seemed to be producing its own inner chill. She had only ever felt warm when submerged in a hot bath. And it hadn't even been worth it; she could count the money jobs she'd gotten on one hand.

The place was bountifully decorated for fall: the railings and trellis were wreathed in electroplated leaves in shades of copper and silver. The lacework pattern of the veins, skinny and fragile as capillaries, made her think of winter frost, the way it settled on the fences on the farm. Back in Russia where winter was actually winter, not a pitiful dusting of flakes (although it hadn't snowed at all in New York for the last two winters), but a white blanket that engulfed the country and didn't let up until spring. She remembered tramping outside in felt boots and a fur hat and a coat so heavy it felt like an embrace. Back there, she'd never had to worry about what she looked like or how others thought of her. There were more important things to occupy her mind: the bare necessity of survival, the slow scraping-out of an existence from the fertile but ultimately untamable earth. When she'd been part of this struggle against predators and the elements, she had felt secure in her anonymity, anchored by the enormity of the past, in this continuation of her ancestors' lives. Her own existence a perfect recursion.

Sometimes she felt that her move to New York was not the glorious renaissance she liked to think of it as, but instead part of a greater aberration, a blip in history. Like the drawing that was meant to represent all the eras that had passed on Earth: an intricately rendered, three-dimensional spiral rising up from a dot four and a half billion years ago, spiraling out of the distant Precambrian and Devonian past, through the Cretaceous and Jurassic periods, growing larger and more defined as it went, and all of it green, green, green. Only the very newest end of the spiral was a different color—the Anthropocene, a slice so tiny you could easily miss it, a fingernail sliver of rust-covered gray. If you zoomed in enough you could see minuscule buildings, cars, an airplane, all hovering precariously just at the edge. To Anna it looked as though anyone standing on that edge was about to fall off into nothing, into the timeless black that surrounded the spiral.

But back in Russia, people were moving from villages to cities at hemorrhagic rates. They too felt the lure of infrastructure, of the rust-covered gray: hospitals, shops, trains, schools. Exposure to other cultures, to new and interesting people, to employment opportunities that went beyond the simple tasks of survival and blossomed into creativity, into art and higher education. And better access to healthcare. Nobody wanted to give birth on their kitchen floor with only a grizzled midwife on hand, too far from a hospital to get real medical help if the baby turned midway or the umbilical cord prolapsed. Nobody wanted to sit around drinking all afternoon because there was nothing else to do, staring at the mute and unchanging sky. Nobody wanted what Anna had left behind.

People were holding low, soft conversations across the roof and at the bar, discussing the fires raging on the West Coast, the hundreds of thousands of acres that were going up in torrents of flame. Anna half-listened with a numbed, distant feeling. No one seemed especially concerned. The attitude among the speakers was one of mild bemusement rather than anxiety.

Warren got them both drinks, insisting she try a pumpkin concoction that was one of the bar's specialties for fall.

"I'm hesitant, but I'm feeling adventurous," she said. "And slightly intrigued, despite myself."

"That's my girl. I'm intrigued too, but I'm not as brave as you. I'll get a screwdriver."

The pumpkin drink came in a martini glass and had a layer of white foam on top of a rich orange base. At first it tasted like the spices that collected at the bottom of a container of Pumpkin Spice Topping, but underneath was an intense, bitter flavor, like pure vanilla extract. "It's not bad," she lied. "Reminds me of pumpkin pie, but airier. Lighter. I'm pretty sure there's no pumpkin in it, but that makes it more authentic somehow."

"Like the original pumpkin spice latte?" Warren suggested. "Before they changed it to include actual pumpkin?"

"Something like that." She stirred her drink.

"Fascinating. I'll never get used to the way people's minds work." He smacked his lips a little as he drank, thinking. "How does a Russian farm girl know all of these things?"

"That's just the beginning. I know how to milk a cow and slaughter a chicken. And—"

He held up a hand, shuddering. "No more, no more. I'm a sheltered city man." He was in an awfully good mood tonight.

Anna looked down and stirred her drink again, even though she'd done the same thing about five seconds ago. She wasn't going to push it, but she had wanted to talk about the farm, even if it was only to shock him. She liked how stunned he was whenever she told him she could do things like kill a goat or skin a deer. It made her feel like she was a stranger from another world —a luminous, savage storybook world that Warren would never be able to grasp.

At that moment, they both caught sight of a man on the other side of the roof, who was gesturing in their direction. He had silver hair and wore crisp, fresh-looking clothes, as spotless as though he'd just slid them off the hanger and stepped into them. Warren raised a hand in greeting. Whenever they visited a fancy enough place, they inevitably ran into a friend of his: sometimes one or two, sometimes a whole group of them. The more exclusive the place, the more friends they ran into. Sometimes Anna joined in the conversations, but usually she knew her place as arm candy and stood mildly by while they joked and traded stories.

"Can't say no to him," Warren said in an undertone. "He's one of my main investors. I'll just be a moment. Wait here, doll, okay?"

"Sure," she said. "I'll have ordered another by the time you get back, so be ready."

For a few moments she stood and watched the two of them conversing, but glanced quickly away when the other man turned his head in her direction. She gazed instead at the trellis, at the plated leaves glinting in the lights, cold and vacant as frozen stars. Her mind was empty. The conversation of the women at the bar next to her slowly sank into her consciousness.

"Are you sure it really happened like that?"

"That's what her sister said. And I don't think she would lie, do you? There just doesn't seem to be a *point* to lying in this situation. I mean, he's got no enemies... although if one *did* want to tarnish his reputation—"

The other woman's voice was hard and matter-of-fact. "Stop playing devil's advocate, Jade, you're not very good at it. What reputation? He's a grocery store clerk, for god's sake. Nobody knows who the hell he is. Her, on the other hand. You'd think she would have seen the signs."

Anna glanced over at them sideways, not moving her head so they wouldn't know she was looking at them. The firm-voiced woman was tall and gaunt, in her fifties or so, with a black updo and a long blue coat that nearly reached the floor. The other woman, Jade, who had a softer, younger-sounding, more uncertain voice, had her back to Anna. Now she said, "No one can really know the signs in these situations. We never thought he would end up smacking her around, did we? *We* always thought he was a *perfectly* nice guy."

"I'm not blaming her. I'm simply saying that she's far too intelligent a woman to have ended up at the hands of such a man. You'd think there would be some kind of built-in guard against this type of thing happening."

"There is," Jade said drily. She didn't sound so young anymore. "*Class.*"

Class, Anna thought. She wondered what they would say if they knew why she was here, that she hadn't been born into a rich family, or even created her own wealth, but just happened to be sleeping with the owner of that wealth.

She pictured Warren hitting her and felt nothing, just a sense of fear that was almost performative, even inside her own head.

Then she pictured her ex-boyfriend hitting her, the one she had gone to Florida with. The idea of the pain exploded in the darkness of her mind, blooming like paint thrown onto a black background.

The funny thing was, of the two men, Warren was the one more likely to turn violent. He liked to choke Anna in bed and slap her face—he never ended up actually hurting her, but there was a sadistic streak buried beneath the mild-mannered business-man. Many men harbored this streak, and although it could vary from a thin sliver to a bold stripe as thick as a road, it was present in most of them. The ex-boyfriend, on the other hand, had always been so gentle with her. Touching her like she was a spun-glass statue that might crumble away at any moment. She remembered the sun-flash of his eyes and felt a sense of panic, a need to get away, to get away from the memory.

She tipped her glass back; the rest of the vaguely pumpkin-y drink slid down her throat. It settled bitter and clumpy in her stomach and she fought a sudden wave of nausea.

Drinking so fast was a mistake. The alcohol chipped away at her resolve, thinned the barrier she'd put up in her mind.

Midway through Anna's twentieth year, she had ended up— somewhat unexpectedly—celebrating her half-birthday with her boyfriend. "I wasn't around for your real birthday," he said later, after she had gotten over her surprise, "and who knows if I'll be around for the next, but I believe that half-birthdays are worth double the celebration." It was the last time in her life she could remember feeling happy around a birthday (or half-birthday), rather than full of dread, and despite their lack of money, he'd made it a celebration for her. While she was running back and forth to castings all day, unaware of what awaited her at his place, he'd been cooking his own homemade versions of blinis, vareniki, and cherry compote. After her last casting, he texted her, telling her to come see him. When she entered his apart-ment, using the extra key he'd had made for her, she was over-come by the scents: fresh dough, ripe cherry. Smell was the oldest sense, and the strongest, and for a moment she felt like she was back in Russia. With her mother, her family. *Home.*

The memory within scent: it was the same reason she had kept her oldest perfume, the one she'd worn during those six months she'd been with him. It smelled the way a crystal might, if it had a scent: white and sparkling, with sunny slices of rose and ambrette and pear. She never wore it anymore to go out, let alone to see Warren, but one spritz on her wrist and she was lost in those months again, the memory of him and the memory of who she had once been. These memories lost their potency with each application, slowly shrinking, inevitably, in the face of her current thoughts and feelings associated with the perfume: the present devouring the past. So she used it sparingly.

She remembered the yellow light in the kitchen that day, the warm, floury air, the cautious pride in her boyfriend's face. The wonder she had felt, the delighted astonishment. *He spent hours,* she'd thought. *I can't believe it.* There were bags and bags emptied of ingredients, kitchen utensils cluttering the table, printed recipes turned translucent in places by blotches of oil. *That someone could love me this much.* It was so far from this icy, glamorous rooftop. So far, and farther each minute. Like the Anna in her memories, it continued to recede into the past.

Inside her memory, she thought: I won't ever feel like that again. And inside that she thought: But he will.

Warren came back over. "What do you think of these?" For a couple of moments, she didn't even realize he was showing her his phone. She focused on the screen with some difficulty; the pumpkin drink had been stronger than she'd first thought. His phone was open to a page of designer bags. Their colors were garish and glaring.

"I was thinking I'd buy you one of these instead of next week's allowance, hmm?" He said it like he was offering her some glorious prize.

"Really?" She tried to sound pleased, but she was wondering what on earth had possessed him to suggest this. Surely he didn't think that she lacked bags. She rarely used them, and she had little need for them anyway. He'd already gotten her several, and she'd kept a couple to bring along on their dates, just so he didn't get suspicious, but the others she had resold. But there were problems with reselling: things didn't go for all that much when bought secondhand, and somehow, the more expensive the designer, the larger the gap between the amount it retailed for and the price it resold for. Besides, she hated the idea of leaving a trail for Warren to find. It was unlikely that he'd be trawling resale sites looking for her, of course, but the thought of him stumbling upon a collection of pieces he had bought for her made her feel sick. And a tiny bit guilty.

"What do you think?" Warren flipped through a few photos. The bags all looked less like bags than dead, skinned animals smeared with cosmetics. "Glamorous, no?"

"Aw, you're sweet," she said. "Thinking I need to be even more glamorous! I'm not already glam enough for you?" She made a mock-pouting face.

"Maybe it was all the farm girl comments you made," he said, pocketing his phone. There was a new, unsettling blankness to his expression, and she felt a sliver of ice in her stomach. "Well, you let me know and get back to me. Do some research on your own time—I know you young girls are computer whizzes, and frankly, old guys like me just can't keep up."

She gave him a smile, but there was a tense, brittle quality to it, and her eyes felt stiff above her mouth. A sudden gust of wind made them water.

The problem was, Anna wasn't in this lifestyle for the bags or the shoes or the dresses. Or the dinners, or the drinks, or the so-called glamour. She was in it for the money. Practically every sugar baby was—other than those silly girls who focused more on their outward appearances than putting anything away for the future. Sure, Anna focused plenty on her outward appearance, but it was necessary for her work. Sugar babies had to look good. But if she had all the money she needed, she would probably never pick up an eyebrow pencil again. She'd let them grow in thick and bushy, her eyes blazing out from underneath like bright berries peeping out from beneath a thicket of leaves.

Anna was sure that she thought more about the future than any of her counterparts did. They were saving with the goal of owning a home or gaining financial independence, but Anna was saving for the disasters of the future. There would probably be many of them, with the current fires on the West Coast being merely the beginning, but she didn't think about this too often. She simply saved and invested. There were "known knowns" and "known unknowns" in this future, effects of climate change that scientists had predicted and drawn out timelines for, but there were also the "unknown unknowns." Things nobody could predict or accurately plan for. It was these she was preparing for most of all.

She could not determine the reason Warren wanted to substitute bags for her allowance. He'd never had a problem with paying it before. Throughout the rest of their night, she was distracted by the thought that maybe he simply thought she enjoyed bags, that they were more unique and memorable than a weekly bank deposit. Maybe she had seemed *too* materialistic, played the *ooh*ing and *aah*ing over fashion a little too much, and now she had to dial it back.

Even if she chose the most expensive of the bags on that page, it was very unlikely that, once she'd sold it, she would get as much as her allowance was worth. Maybe he would buy her two bags. Or perhaps he would look down on her for suggesting this; she had never quite been able to identify the line between greed and the snooty materialism that men like him so admired.

It was getting chilly. Anna stood motionless on the rooftop, smiling a rictus mannequin smile and laughing at Warren's jokes, and although she'd eaten plenty that day and wasn't underweight anymore, once again she felt that the cold was coming from inside her.

Later that night, when she let him fuck her, she realized she had never thought of it this way before. Up until now, they had been fucking each other. Now she was letting him fuck her. Her power was draining away.

Take me away from here, she thought, looking up at the ceiling as her body was jerked violently on the bedsheets. This is my choice but I don't like it, I don't want it. But I need to. My future. My parents. My brother. O god. Her thoughts melted into Russian and then into a hazy reddish liquid.

Standing in her shower later, alone, she tried to wash herself clean. The soap felt woolly on her skin, smelling of pine and fir and fistfuls of snow. She pictured herself incorporeal, rushing like a wind through the Siberian forest, free of the gaze of anyone who walked on two legs: ruthless as Juno, wild as Diana. Nothing more than a collection of heartbeats under the scattered ice of the stars.

CHAPTER 6

Gemma

Gemma and Derek's apartment was smaller than she had anticipated upon moving here. Somehow the photos he'd taken of the interior, the ones he'd sent to her in England, had boasted far more space: empty rooms flooded with sunlight, pale wood stretching from one wall to the other. When she actually moved in, the rooms had diminished considerably in both size and lighting, and the sun never shone as brightly as it had in the pictures.

Moving in with a boyfriend at the age of nineteen was somewhat uncommon these days, and for the first few months it had given her a sense of airy superiority, a separation from the rest of the world and the un-partnered masses. But somehow—and it felt disloyal to Derek to think this—moving to New York had been even more of an adventure than meeting him there.

It was on her tour of NYU the previous fall that she'd bumped into him for the first time. She noticed a tall, slender man getting coffee at a nearby shop (the tour had ended early, thanks to the tour guide crashing backwards into a bramble bush in Washington Square Park, but this only endeared her further to the school), and the two of them started talking. He thought Gemma's accent was cute, and she thought his accent was, well, different. He was also impressed by the fact that she'd taken an overseas flight to tour the school; not many people did that. In fact, practically no one did. But Gemma had the means, so why not.

When she showed him the pictures of her house he was even more impressed. She didn't understand why she had shown him —all he had done was ask what it was like in England, for God's sake, she could've simply shown him a picture of the landscape, instead of bragging so shamelessly—and it reminded her of a child talking loudly about their new Christmas presents. She was suffused by a sense of shame and put her phone away after flicking through a few photos. But Derek was in awe. "I've got to say, that's a lot better than my parents' place," he said with a laugh, his nut-brown eyes wide. "We didn't even have two stories, let alone three."

Then, just as she thought he was going to leave the coffee shop and relegate her to a mere footnote of his day, he asked her if she'd like to have dinner with him at an Italian restaurant. Only a few hours later, they were eating the trattoria's house-made pasta and tiramisu, dishes with flavors that melted together like liquid butter. After dinner he led her on an impromptu tour of the area, and Gemma, hardly believing her luck, trotted along beside him on her new heels. He took her around the area of Manhattan he knew best—Chelsea, on the far West Side, where the brownstones sat regally back from the sidewalk and observed them as they walked by. He was well-spoken and calm, and always seemed to chew on his words a bit before he spoke, as though he wanted to put things as clearly and concisely as he possibly could. He was the exact type of man she *wasn't* familiar with. Her father, for example, with his mercurial moods and gauche demeanor, was worlds apart.

During Gemma's two-day tour in America, she tried very hard not to think about her father. For one thing, thinking about him meant thinking about her mother, who had recently been diagnosed with cancer. The prognosis wasn't good. In fact, the prognosis was terrible: it was stage four ovarian cancer. Just before she left England, Gemma had trouble looking her father in the eye. Her mother was fully supportive of her short trip to America—she had enthused about NYU as much as she could and practically ordered Gemma to enjoy herself—but her father was grim and silent. The day she left, she knew he was thinking the same thing she was, had guessed that part of the reason she wanted to go to university in America was in order to escape the reminders of her mother that would remain in England after she was gone. The truth of this made her body bristle with guilt.

Derek and Gemma rounded a corner. Before them, the entire side of a building featured a mural of the famous V-J Day kiss. The brightness of it astonished her, nearly made her stumble; the saturation of everything else in the area, every other color, seemed to fly towards it as though it were a magnet. A rainbow clustered in tight squares inside the couple's clothes and arced outwards into a dizzying wheel, the spokes of color widening as they pushed outwards, like ripples in a lake. It was a burst of love, lust, passion: a brilliant explosion beneath the low sky.

The two of them kept talking even after she went back to England. Even as she spent the last of her mother's remaining months, from November until April, taking care of her. This surprised Gemma at first, the consistency with which Derek called and FaceTimed her. She hadn't expected a man in his early twenties to want to talk so frequently to a girl halfway around the world—God knew there were enough girls in New York for him—but Derek was there for Gemma all through that year. He was there during late-night hysterical video calls, after the doctors finally said that they were sorry, and that all her mother needed now was to be kept comfortable. He was there to tell her that she wasn't alone.

Now she was in university in New York, and her mother was dead, but Gemma still had a tiny piece of her in Derek. He overlapped both parts of Gemma's life: the part in which her mother was still alive, and the part in which she was not. And he'd been the only other person to know how Gemma felt that whole time, how afraid she was, and how she believed her fear was selfish—because her fear wasn't just for her mother, but for herself, left alone in the world with a distant, perpetually working father. At one point she had been unable to sleep and had lain staring at the ceiling with tears turning sticky on her face, imagining dorm rooms full of shrieking hooligans and pot smoke and other people's used condoms on the floor. But then Derek had suggested she live with him in Chelsea, and something new had opened in her mind, a gasp of possibility. She wouldn't be alone. And it wasn't like she couldn't afford the rent.

It was probably unhealthy, but sometimes, when they were sitting or talking together, she did this: she pretended that one or both of them were going to die the next day, and this was their last night together. It was her way of avoiding the bland and soporific complacency that always seemed to descend on long-term relationships, the feeling of *Is this all there is?* Their relationship was new, and throughout the months she'd been with Derek, that feeling hadn't settled on her yet, but she was always on guard, watching out for it. She had seen it overtake her peers as they languished in relationships where it should have been clear for months that they weren't right for each other. The stretching towards death, the slow decay.

"Success?" Derek asked her as she entered the apartment. It was a Sunday, so he was home. Right now he was sitting on the sofa, his legs propped up on the coffee table, a habit that annoyed her if she paid too much attention to it. She stumbled slightly as she entered, forgetting, as usual, that their shoe rack blocked the door from opening fully. Well. It was her shoe rack, actually, or at least, it had been her idea to buy it. It wasn't fair for her to be fussed about it.

"Kind of," she said. She didn't want to go into detail, so she headed for the bedroom, as though to deposit a haul of stuff. But he had already glanced her way and seen that she had no bags with her. Yet another excursion, this time to Pottery Barn, had ended in failure. She'd gotten overwhelmed by choice and been unable to make a decision, like the fabled donkey who starved to death standing between two bales of hay.

"You didn't actually get anything?" Outside, Derek's pale skin practically glowed in the late afternoon sun, but inside the light turned his face dim and murky. It was the same in the bedroom. Gemma had to figure this situation out before she started filming. Although it could be cozy with the right lighting, maybe. Candles and lights hung up on the walls, aesthetic floor lamps. It was all about the way you framed it. Just like everything else.

"You don't have to decorate your entire room in order to start filming, you know," he said. He finally glanced up from the video he was watching; it looked like a sports game. "You can do it whenever. There's no rules."

"Right. I'm gonna start this week." She meant it. She really did. He had turned his gaze back to his phone before she'd finished speaking.

She figured she would try the last-day visualization later, when they were curled up on the sofa together, watching TV. Something about the warmth of their bodies as they relaxed there, close together and slowed down after a long day of running around, made her believe that they were in sync. It was in those moments that she found it easiest to connect with him, her head resting on his chest, listening to the murky underwater sound of his heart.

Right after moving in, Gemma had hung a picture on the bedroom wall. It was a departure from everything else she had installed in the room: the delicate, lace-like flower studies, the prickly wicker baskets that held her makeup. It was the last photograph she had of her mother. Taken last April, on a cold day.

It showed the two of them arm in arm in front of Big Ben; they'd never been much for typical London sights because, after all, they were *locals,* not tourists, but her mother was dying and they wanted to have an undeniably British trip around the city. They'd made a day of it, taking pictures in front of Buckingham Palace, the Tower of London, and Parliament, but the one in front of the giant clock was her favorite. It was because of their postures, their expressions. She had just hugged her mother right around the middle of her puffy winter coat, the way she used to when she was a kid, and told her she loved her. Her mother's face had filled with surprise, as well as a new life and light that, at that point, Gemma hadn't seen for months. And at that precise moment, the woman holding their camera had snapped the picture. Gemma remembered her clearly: an Asian woman, pretty but quite harried-looking, saddled with two kids and no husband in sight.

Gemma wondered if her mother had envied the woman's future, the children that she would doubtlessly live to watch grow up. Gemma was grown up by that point, eighteen and just accepted into a New York City college, but there were still so many things her mother would never see: her daughter's graduation, her first job, her own potential grandchildren. She had ceased to exist in the present, and with each passing month she would only fall further back into the past, her once-familiar features slurring and softening in the unreliable rooms of memory, her face growing hazy and amorphous and unreal.

Gemma swallowed against the sudden tightness in her throat. She shifted her focus back and forth—one moment looking at the small figures in the photo, the next gazing at her round-faced reflection in the shining glass over the picture. She often did the same thing in cars, and on trains: flicking back and forth, a switch toggling first one way and then the other.

The sight of her face in the glass did not bring her any great joy. Her nose was big and beaklike. Her cheeks were round and soft, as though injected with puffs of air, and she had hooded eyes; if she were skinnier, her eyelids would probably actually show. She couldn't imagine what kind of audience would want to watch a chubby influencer. All the articles she'd read about body positivity seemed meaningless right now. Political correctness meant nothing next to the natural human disgust at an unhealthy body.

Then she pictured her mother's reaction if she knew what Gemma was thinking about, and the idea filled her with a leaden gray sorrow. When Gemma was twelve years old, she'd hit puberty and gone through a phase of what some people might call overindulgence and what some people might call a sugar addiction. She would buy sweets on the way home from school and sit in her bedroom with the door locked, eating cakes and rolls and doughnuts mechanically, growing fuller and fuller until the nausea saturated not just her stomach but her fingers, her legs, her head, every part of her body. After a few weeks her parents both noticed her weight gain, but they reacted in very different ways. One day at dinner her father told her, glancing at her sideways over the table, "I think you've eaten enough for today." It was not what he said so much as how he said it—his eyes flat with disgust, a mocking curl in his voice. Another time he pointed out how thick her arms had gotten, how they were twice as large as most girls'. Although she was chubby, Gemma was fairly certain her arms were not *twice* as thick as other girls', but her father's words remained in her mind for a long time afterward.

Her mother, though, gently encouraged Gemma to sign up for sports and restocked the near-empty fridge with fresh fruits and vegetables. Gemma insisted tearfully that she just needed to stop eating entirely, because clearly her dad seemed to think so, but her mother said, in her amused, affectionate manner, "Oh, Gemma. Calm down and eat some watermelon." The fruit tasted watery at first, but she ended up liking it just as much as the sweets, not least because it never made her ill. "See?" her mother said at this point. "It doesn't make you feel sick because it's not poisonous garbage. Here, have a kiwi."

Gemma gradually lost the excess weight she had gained and stopped feeling sick all the time. Somehow, throughout this entire process, her mother never made her feel ashamed. Never used Gemma's body as a way to illustrate her failings.

Another thing: her mother did not stop speaking in that amused, affectionate manner until the very end of her life. There was a wry practicality to her, a way she had of shrugging things off and not letting them bother her. Gemma remembered them all going on a hiking trip once, when she was about fifteen; her mother had turned her ankle on a stone and had to limp the whole rest of the way on her other leg, leaning on a stick. Gemma knew her father would've thrown a fit had it been him —he was already grousing about not having anything other than water to drink—but all she said about it was "Oh well." That was her mum. She never complained. She always took things on the chin, was always grateful for the good things in her life. Thinking about it, she would have been a great influencer.

Gemma glanced once more at the photograph of the two of them before turning her computer on. It filled her with joy and sorrow at once: their faces, frozen in the thin sliver of existence that made up the space between birth and death. That enormous clock above them, hands like giant black swords, slicing away the time.

CHAPTER 7

Janet

When Janet woke the next morning, she had an immediate feeling of displacement. It wasn't subtle: it was a stark, frightening confusion. Where the hell am I? she thought. What is this place?

A few moments later: Of course. This is my apartment. But it still felt unfamiliar. She gazed around her room, at the exposed brick wall, the many-paned window, the nubbly white ceiling. It was the same room she had been waking up in for years—she rarely slept over at a guy's house, even if she really liked him—but it had been momentarily unfamiliar to her. She had the unnerving feeling that she had been expecting to wake up somewhere else. But when she thought about it, she couldn't determine where. Not in her childhood room, not in her old college dorm room. None of the choices in her memory felt right to her.

Even as she threw off the covers and oriented herself, the feeling was slipping away. Please not Liam's house, she thought. Please let me not have been expecting to wake up *there*. If she caught feelings for someone like that, she would never forgive herself.

As an experiment, she pictured his face. To her relief this did not bring on any flutterings or warmth or any of the other sensations she associated with emotional attachment.

By the time she had brushed her teeth and made herself

coffee, the feeling itself was entirely gone, and only the memory of it remained. It had been a momentary lapse in her consciousness, she decided. After all, the mind went elsewhere during sleep, and who knew what felt like *home* to her in her dreams. She did things in dreams that she would never do in real life: she'd had dreams where she was inexplicably violent, where she attacked people she knew and loved, or engaged in passionate romps with people she'd never look at twice in waking life, and then would wake thinking *What the fuck?* Her dreaming mind was a completely different person, a stranger to her.

Janet reminded herself to turn off the water as she brushed her teeth. Even though this was New York and not California, the whole world was connected, and it was probably only a matter of time before the droughts would be felt here too. She pictured the planet shrinking and drying, a tattered, crumbling leaf.

She started work earlier than usual that day. Usually she took a while to eat breakfast and linger over her phone, but that was quickly losing its appeal. She was sick of doomscrolling through Twitter, rolling her eyes at Reddit, and meekly absorbing the perfect squares on Instagram that cast her own shitty life into humiliating clarity; after all this, her brain felt like a garbage disposal within minutes of waking up. And then there were the dating app texts.

Hey, how are you?

Hey Jane! Sorry, I meant Janet, lol, autocorrect.

Sup.

Hi.

They were all the same version of the sentiment *Greetings, harlot*, just stamped out over and over again, the lines getting blurrier and messier and uglier with each iteration.

The first few grievance letters she read were about the typical, less serious matters—worries about work, spouses cheating, the signs of aging. She was able to set their writers up with specialists fairly quickly.

But she read the next letter twice before even making any preliminary notes.

Dear OLT,

I'm finding myself in a bit of trouble lately. More than a bit, I suppose. I've been feeling more and more like an alien in the world, but not the enviable, science-fiction kind of alien who's figured out all of his (its?) problems and goes whirling across the galaxies to teach less developed life-forms how to behave. More like the kind of pointless life form that scientists would scratch their heads and go "hmm" at. The appendix of the animal world, if you will. Although probably even the appendix is more useful than me. I believe I'm suffering from one of the core problems of my generation: the loss of hope. But that alone isn't what makes me feel like an alien.

No, that part comes from the realization that nobody else seems to think this. I can go on the internet and find them, sure, the world wide web is open to me, and so are you, but when it comes to the people in my daily life, so-called "real life", I find myself completely at odds with them. My ex-girlfriend once said that we're the happiest generation, that we have things our ancestors never dreamed of. We have the highest standard of living ever recorded in history.

But if that's true, OLT, why are so many of my peers killing themselves? Why did three people leap from the roof of my college before they installed a railing? Apparently, there's a tribe in Africa that had never heard of suicide before researchers explained it to them. They didn't even know such a thing existed. Sometimes I think I'm really meant to be in that tribe, and my time here is some lost interlude, that I'm being held in stasis. I don't really know where I'm meant to be, actually, but all I know is, it's not here.

I don't really have much else to say about this, and although this is a grievance letter, I don't want it to be too depressing—I'm sure you get enough of that already—so I suppose I'll end it here.

The letter's conversational tone surprised her. Most people vomited out their problems without a thought as to how she might feel reading it. But this person—UR5739251—had gone to the trouble to explain his metaphors, to actually attempt to create some kind of a dialogue.

And the sensation he was describing was similar to the displaced feeling she had had this morning. The feeling of un-belonging, of existing in the present space only incidentally—that was what had overcome her as she had woken up, and he described that perfectly. The way he wrote was pretty old-fash-ioned, with none of the casual swearing that made up so many of the other letters. This would indicate that he was older, except that he used "our" to reference his and Janet's generation, lumping them into the same age range.

He was also making a lot of assumptions about Janet, wasn't he. Although maybe this wasn't it at all. Maybe he was simply smarter than she'd given him credit for. He could guess what kind of a person had a job as an online grievance letter specialist, the dumping ground for the city's emotional problems—and it wasn't someone in their forties or fifties with a string of degrees.

Even the combination of letters and numbers that made up his persona intrigued her. It began with *Ur.* Ur had been one of the world's first cities, located in ancient Mesopotamia, which was itself the birthplace of the written word. It was a coinci-dence, of course—users couldn't choose their own anonymized names—but it made her think, all the same.

And it made her write something at the end of her own reply to him, something which she wasn't supposed to include under the typical specialist recommendations. She wrote, *I have that feeling too sometimes. Of not belonging. I think it's a symptom of our times.*

She wasn't sure what had possessed her to write this. She wasn't ever supposed to reply to the letters' authors outside of sending them their specialists. But then, no one checked the outgoing messages. She'd learned this early in the job, at precisely the time she should have been under the most scrutiny. She had mixed two letters up—that particular afternoon had been fueled by too many cups of coffee, which made her hands judder, and multitasking was not her strong suit—and sent one a list of fertility specialists and the other a list of psychiatrists. Only a few moments after pressing Send had she noticed her mistake, and she'd had to quickly send follow-up emails addressing the mix-up. This was the type of mistake that would, according to her training, earn her a serious warning. However, none of her superiors had ever addressed it, and she'd realized that the grievance letter quality controls were based more on illusion than reality.

Now, having pressed Send on the letter response, she felt a shiver of nerves. If they did decide to check the responses today, she'd be screwed. But no ominous message appeared in her inbox. No hand came down from above to clasp her shoulder.

Her decision was cemented by the conversation she had later that afternoon, when she was on her "lunch break," with some guy named Reggie on a dating app. Guys with the name Reggie were already suspect, but his attitude towards her job made her prickle with anger. *Your one of those online counselors?* he wrote, after she answered his question about what her work was. *Omg lollll. Wanna tell me some crazy stories from crazy people? Bet you got a lot of em, lol.*

She sure did have a lot of em, lol. She went back to his profile to double-check his age, just to confirm that she hadn't accidentally swiped on a 12-year-old. Nope, 35 all the way. Maybe even older with that hairline.

She closed the app in disgust, wondering what it was that possessed people to laugh at others' misfortunes. Reggie seemed oddly sure that he himself wouldn't be in need of a little grievance-airing when he lost his job, or was evicted from his apartment. Scratch that, he probably didn't even have a job. He probably couch-surfed. She was aware of how vitriolic her judgments were, but she couldn't hold them back.

There was another shift she had noticed: the guys on these apps were all rapidly blurring into the same person. It was like those compilations of the average face across the world: exactly the person you'd see if you closed your eyes and thought of the word Average. The background character in all your dreams. Except somehow uglier and more annoying. Every time she swiped, these words passed through her consciousness: *I hate you, I hate you.* The words came not from her brain but from her heart and her guts, not thought but a reflexive spasm. She hated what these men represented, hated that her personal life, or at least her romantic life, was reduced to gazing at tiny photographs and using the scant information there to decide if she wanted to allow that person into her space, into her body, into her mind.

Janet's friend Miranda was free that evening. *Friend* was a word Janet indulged herself in, although they were more like casual acquaintances than friends. In fact, Janet had the sneaking suspicion that Miranda only texted her to hang out whenever her real circle of friends was unavailable. Her invites always had a tinge of apathy to them, and whenever they hung out, Miranda's hair was usually unwashed and her gaze drifted away when Janet's sentences got too long. They rarely went out, and Miranda was often doing some kind of task as they talked—cleaning her kitchen, shopping for makeup. But she was company, and she was pleasant enough, and she wasn't trying to get into Janet's pants.

When Janet arrived, Miranda was in the midst of re-arranging her closet, or cleaning it up, or something. Janet sat precariously on a tiny footstool as her friend shoved all her purses towards the back of a cabinet and tossed a few expired makeup items in the trash, talking loudly all the while.

Janet tuned out; Miranda spoke extremely loudly and extremely fast. She was from a Middle Eastern family, and was a tall, skinny girl with a cloud of wiry black hair and eyelashes that skimmed her eyebrows. Every part of her face—her nose, her lips, even her eyes—seemed a bit too large by itself, but when you put all the features together they somehow worked. She was an expert at makeup, and when she applied it she was stunning: highlights glittering around her eyes, cheekbones sharp and cruel, lips bold and red and striking.

"I think I can get a place in Philly for half the price, honestly. It's a good thing I've been saving for so long. So. What do you think?" She turned to Janet with her hands on her hips and an expectant smile, like someone who'd been saving up a piece of good news for as long as they could stand it.

It took a few moments for Janet to process what she was saying.

"Wait, what?" Janet asked, sitting up. "You're really considering... going?" She searched backwards in her memory, frantically trying to remember what Miranda had said over the last few minutes.

"Well, sure." Miranda looked over at Janet in confusion, and then examined a tiny mirror. Frowning, she blew on it: puffs of dust spiraled into the air, and she coughed and waved a hand in front of her face. "Not just considering—weren't you listening? I mean. It's getting crazy here, have you noticed? The rents are going up, and anyone who isn't living in a rent-stabilized place is screwed. I almost got stabbed the other day when two homeless guys started fighting on the subway."

"Shit, really? Why didn't you tell me about it?"

"I got a little distracted when I stepped on someone lying in front of the exit. I'm not sure if it was a dead body or just someone passed out."

"That's horrible. But..." She considered. "These things happen all over. Like, not just in New York. Do you really think things are better elsewhere?"

"No," Miranda said, her speech slowing down a bit, "but things are less expensive elsewhere. If I can't get a place where I can achieve self-actualization, I may as well shoot for one that gives me the best chance of being able to feed and clothe myself in the years to come. Especially since they told me I can work from home now. So, literally, there is no point in staying here."

"I mean... I live here."

Miranda's face fell. "Oh, honey. We can FaceTime."

Janet attempted to process this unexpected turn of events. *Unexpected* didn't cover it. Miranda had been living in New York since she'd been born, and she was the only other person Janet knew who had grown up here. Even people who seemed to know the city well turned out to have just moved from L.A. or Europe last year. To them New York was nothing more than a glossy pit stop on the way to a future home, but natives had roots here. It was harder for them to leave.

Miranda was being pretty casual about the whole thing, though. She didn't even seem that sad to be leaving Janet behind. Although she probably thought Janet had her own circle of closer, more intimate acquaintances. Wouldn't she be surprised if she found out that she was the closest thing to a friend Janet had.

"How long have you been thinking about this? It's not some snap decision, is it? You know what they tell you about those decisions. I read it in a Psychology Briefing. You've got to think it over in a hot bath, a cold shower, and... what was the other one? Outside!" She pointed at Miranda in triumph. "On a windy day."

Miranda's eyes narrowed. "Were you even listening? I knew there was something overly dreamy about your gaze. I told you. I've been looking at places for a few weeks now. I just didn't want to tell anyone until I was sure."

"So that means you are sure."

Miranda looked around her room, hands on her hips. "I'd say so. I can move in next week."

"Things aren't great elsewhere, though," Janet said again. She felt like she was attempting to stop a thousand-pound boulder from rolling down a hill. "Even the sky is like this everywhere. The sun looks crazier and crazier the closer you get to the West coast. Have you seen the news lately?"

Even as she spoke, she knew it was pointless. Miranda had never taken Janet's warnings about climate change seriously, except in one area. This area was that of brain-eating amoebas, and how they had recently proliferated due to the rising temperatures across the country. Miranda now never took showers, only baths. This was despite the fact that Janet had told her repeatedly that *naegleria fowleri* wasn't really a danger in a climate as cold as New York, especially in tap water, but Miranda persisted. Janet trying to lift her friend's focus from whatever was directly in front of her nose (in the case of the amoebas, literally—or at least Miranda thought so) was a losing battle.

"Of course," Miranda said. "You can't escape it here! Especially with politics. This city is so political, you can't avoid it no matter where you go. And all it is nowadays is old white men saying horrible things about each other. Back in the old days..." Miranda was fond of talking about the old days, which she had never lived through or she probably wouldn't be speaking about them with such reverence. "They were actually respectful to one another. They didn't stoop to calling each other idiots and losers on national television. It's like watching a bunch of reality TV contestants taking cheap shots at one another."

"Who says politics *isn't* reality TV?" Janet said.

Miranda snorted. "You might be right about that."

She continued to throw things away on top of a pile that was becoming larger and larger. She soon ran out of room in her bedroom trashcan and substituted a garbage bag for it. Janet watched with a feeling of growing unease. She longed for something, but she didn't know what. A feeling of safety, maybe. A sense of security she probably hadn't felt since she was in the womb.

"I must admit, I'm a little glad to be leaving the *witch* behind." Miranda's current roommate was into Wicca, and was fond of burning dozens of candles at once while she looked up spells, filling the apartment with a smoky haze. Her room always smelled sharp and pungent: a mixture of incense, teas, and oils. Janet thought the whole thing was charming—an archaic atmosphere of runes and candle scents, things that could not be scientifically measured but only trusted and believed in—but Miranda hated it. For all her talk about the good old days, she could be extremely intolerant of anything that might have appeared in them.

"I feel really fucking stupid saying it," Janet finally said, "but I'll miss you a lot." It took some effort to say, because it was so true.

Miranda shrugged, careless. The words bounced off her like a compliment from a stranger on the street. "Why do you feel stupid saying it?"

"I always feel like you're never supposed to say what you

mean. And god forbid you ever be earnest or vulnerable about anything. Seriously, I see it everywhere—everyone in TV shows, everyone I talk to on Tinder, even just people posting about random shit online—they're all hiding beneath a hundred layers of irony. Everything you say has to sidestep any sincerity, has to be something sarcastic that dances around what you're actually getting at. If you're too genuine, people get uncomfortable." Even as she said this, she wondered if she herself was being genuine. She was trying to be, but she was also examining each word immediately after it came out of her mouth, turning the sentences around in the air to try to see what Miranda might think of them. This did not seem like authenticity to her. It seemed like a person trying to sound smart to impress someone else, someone who was barely listening and would soon be gone.

In Janet's dream that night, her sister was sitting on the floor in her flooded house, her family huddled around her. They were all underwater, their skin blue and luminous in the light. Despite the water rushing through the doorways, swaying chairs and toppling lamps, Izzy was smiling.

"I'm fine!" she burbled. She held Ruby in her arms; the baby's head lolled loosely on its neck. Her husband Ted's eyes were half-closed and a string of bubbles was escaping from his mouth. "Really, don't worry!"

The next morning, Janet worked her way through six grievance letters before she found the one she was looking for. Before she saw it, she hadn't even known she was looking for it, but the moment she did, the recognition clicked into place. It was like the opposite of the feeling she'd had the previous morning. The opposite of displacement, the opposite of floating adrift.

Hello again OLT. I didn't know you'd write back to me directly. I've got to say I'm surprised, but it's a pleasant surprise. Thanks for the specialists, but I don't know if they can help me. I'm guessing from your message that you're a bit skeptical as well, even if you aren't allowed to directly say it. I mean, how many of these letters do you get a day? Probably hundreds. I spoke to another person who works for a similar company in California—they're called grievance specialists out there, which in my opinion is overdoing it just a bit—and she says she gets over a thousand a week. I worry about her. I've got to wonder how you feel about it. Does it impact you to answer all these messages?

From where I'm standing, or rather sitting (rather pathetically, on the floor), things don't look so good right now. The news confuses me. I keep hearing conflicting things... we're running dangerously low on resources, but we're entering another period of economic growth based on these very things. Does that make any sense to you? I can never parse out what the truth is. I never know what to think anymore. How can one have infinite growth within a closed-loop system of finite resources? Yet everyone is acting like it's fine. Like it makes sense.

I can't even be honest about my opinions in my work, which is somehow the worst part of it. I have access to a lot of impressionable minds (university, hoping futilely to someday get tenure; it is not as glamorous as it sounds) and I want nothing more than to find some way to warn them of what's coming. But I am fully aware that if I do, I will face the wrath of my supervisors. The entire university industry is run on the idea that there is some hope for the future, you see. That the common man (or woman) can make a change. If I strip the students of this hope, the entire point of the institution may be lost.

I'd love to hear your thoughts, if you're open to sharing them. It can honestly get a bit tiring feeling like I'm talking to a wall, or to a screen, as the case may be.

Also—apologies if this sounded completely crackpot. If you don't reply, don't worry, I understand.

- Ur

Ur. So he had paid attention to the identity he'd been assigned in his first letter, and was sticking to it. This was his signature—she could trace his messages through this.

She scrolled through the letter again. Ur wasn't the only one who sat on the floor; she often did that herself. Somehow it felt more grounding than a couch or a chair. She typed up her response, agreeing with what he said about the finite resources and all of that. He'd put it so much better than she could, and she found herself scrolling to the exact phrasing he'd used so that she could repeat it, tweaking it a little so it wouldn't sound like she was copying him. Pathetic, yes, but necessary.

Where are you located? she asked. *You must be in New York City to be able to access this service and for it to be relevant to you, but what kind of people are you surrounded by? You said they were at odds with you. Do you feel like you're the only one who realizes what's going on? Even among your colleagues (who must be pretty smart)? I feel like that, sometimes. Also, what do you teach?*

Towards the end, taking note of his second-to-last paragraph, she added: *I don't think I'm technically supposed to be answering, but you're right, an impartial list of specialists doesn't seem like the best route to take. If only I had enough time to address each of their concerns individually—well, maybe for some of them it wouldn't be the best idea. But it would probably go a lot deeper towards pinpointing exactly what they're struggling with.*

They do that in therapy, don't they? I've got to ask, why don't you go looking for a therapist on your own time? That's what I always wondered about some people who write here.

Shit, she thought, hesitating. That last part might offend him, might seem like she was suggesting he search for a therapist instead of talking to her. She added, *Or did you just want someone to talk to? I totally get it if you do. I can relate to that feeling myself. Therapy is pretty expensive and time-consuming and I haven't exactly dived into it myself. My one friend is moving away, and she's lived here all her life. No wonder I want someone to talk to as well.*

Janet pressed Send. The message arced out into space and was out of her hands forever.

She looked around her room, remembered the conversation with Miranda. She was reminded of that old saying: *Wherever you go, there you are.* What was a bit more in rent to live here, where she at least had some connections, some roots, scraggly and bitten as they were.

One less connection after next week, though.

Everyone else found traveling so easy. So desirable. People's dating profiles were full of lines declaring their passion for flitting around the globe like mosquitoes. Even Izzy had managed to take a vacation last year with Terry, Henry, and Ted (Ruby had been left in the care of a now-traumatized babysitter). They'd gone to London, of all places. Janet hadn't even been envious. Where was her sense of adventure? Liam and Reggie would surely not approve.

But then she thought of Ur's messages. Despite all the shit that was going on the world, despite the fact that *Things don't look so good right now,* her life didn't seem so horrible in this moment, in her quiet room: the dust motes slowly cartwheeling in the air, the spill of liquid sunshine across the floor.

CHAPTER 8

Anna

At home in her sparse, featureless apartment, Anna took stock of her money. It wasn't a stunning amount, but it was so much more than she had ever dreamed of making as a model, even back when she'd thought her career was about to take off. Her retail job alone provided her with more of a salary than she'd gotten back then. And she'd been sugaring for over two years now, jumping from one quasi-relationship to the next before finding Warren, and from all of this, she had saved up quite a bit. She had enough money to, if she really wanted, leave New York and go back home, distribute some of it among her family and use the rest to settle in a nearby city, wait out the future in a relatively stable place. Breathing on borrowed time.

But if she stayed... if she stayed even a few more years, she could save up so much more. Enough to build a buffer for when the real disasters went down. The supply chain interruptions, the food shortages, the famines. They loomed in the future like a far-off shadow, like the darkness cast by an eclipse.

She didn't like to think about it very much, because the more she did, the more unsure she became that her money would even make a difference in the end. Most of the time she could only regard her plan in the abstract, never looking too hard at it but maintaining a single-minded, stoic belief that it would succeed.

She would never be a billionaire, it was true. Would never be part of the upper-upper class. But she might be able to shelter herself at least a little. Every time she looked at the rising number in her bank account, she felt warmer, as though an infinitesimally thin layer of protection was wrapping itself around her. She had already made a difference with her family—and they, when it came to the impact of climate change, still lived in blissful ignorance. They were insulated by their animals and their day-to-day farm chores. Even the steadily rising heat had been favorable more than anything else. The farm's winter crops were not in as much danger of dying due to low temperatures, and there was a greater yield during the reaping season. There was even talk of farming northern lands that had, up until now, been too cold.

But Anna had seen a little bit of the world. She'd heard the predictions, seen the videos, read the articles. She was witnessing them even now in the heat waves roaring across the Western states, the temperatures reaching the mid-120s, sending heat rippling from the pavement and scorching the skin off of dog paws. Warren wasn't worried, but he was twice as old as she was, and he had his enormous wealth to buffer him.

Even in Siberia, the rising heat would eventually climb to the point where it was no longer favorable for crop yields. There was the question of droughts, starting in the regions to the south and east of her parents' farm and gradually spreading north.

There was also the question of her investments. She'd been investing ever since she had built up a large enough balance, carefully siphoning it into stocks like Apple and Pfizer and other relatively sure bets. It was a long-term operation, and she would reap the biggest rewards if she stayed at least a few more years.

No, leaving now was not an option.

Maybe she should find another Warren. But it had taken her so long to find this one. Warren had a small cruel streak in bed, but he wasn't obsessed with anal or BDSM or other horrible things. Piss, vomit, shit—the grosser the substance was, the more likely it was that you would find a charming, powerful man who was into it. She had quickly learned that.

For example: her last sugar date before she'd found Warren, with a European entrepreneur. He'd wanted to watch Anna get fucked—he'd said *fucked,* but what she'd thought as his lips moved had been *raped*—by ten other guys while he watched. He'd offered her an obscene amount of money, but she had refused. Or another guy, who had wanted her to fuck his dog. The memories swarmed across her brain like a surge of insects, biting and buzzing and blackening the terrain.

She exhaled, trying to push these thoughts out of herself along with the air, and went over to the window. Pressed her hands against the cool, solid glass.

Her living room looked out onto the backyard of an elementary school. It was still warm enough for the kids to have recess outside, and sometimes she would catch a glimpse of them chasing each other around the playground. Soon the sky would turn bone-white and frozen, dead leaves would blow across the ground, and the children would be bundled into the classroom during recess. The teachers didn't want them to risk slipping on ice or getting their tongues stuck to metal poles or whatever it was Americans were concerned about during the winter. One would think it was an enemy assault rather than a season with how cautiously they treated it. At least some people would be happy about global warming. People like this would probably rejoice when winter coats finally stopped being sold.

Anna stood and watched the empty playground for a long time. Sometimes she wished she could go back to childhood, just to experience that absolute freedom one more time. How serious she had been then, in a rush to grow up, to not be thought of as a child. Between the ages of seven and ten, she had pouted or even wept in protest if someone referred to her as a little girl—in Russian, malyshka. She'd desperately wanted to be thought of as adult, capable, mature. If only someone had warned her that these qualities came with their own heavy price.

But someone had warned her. Her mother had once told her: "A woman's young years are few and precious, and no matter what, they will end up slipping through her fingers like seaweed." She remembered the words exactly. Attempting to hold onto these years too tightly, her mother had added, would simply crush whatever was left, the slick strands turning mushy and ruined.

Right now Anna was only twenty-two, still too young to worry about wrinkles or age spots, but she had already seen the changes in her face. There was something more serious about her expressions, her eyes more deep-set than they had been as a teenager, her mouth thinner and more firm.

Warren had made her promise not to get anything too drastic done as long as she was with him. A bit of Botox was okay, but for anything beyond that, she needed his permission. "I've seen girls' faces destroyed from too much lip filler," he'd told her once, early on, puffing his lips up like a fish with an allergic reaction. "Don't do anything like that to yourself, please."

"Why do you think they get that stuff when they don't need it?" she had asked, playing at ignorance.

"Because they think it makes them more attractive. Plump lips, puffed-up cheeks—who on Earth knows why that stuff is considered attractive in the first place, it seems so arbitrary to me, but you certainly don't need it. It's sad when a woman's life is controlled by what she thinks is attractive to men. You'd think we'd be beyond that by this century."

She had barely been able to keep herself from smirking. Who on Earth knew why people thought plump lips and cheeks were attractive. Why, Anna knew. These were markers of fertility, the markers that also became exaggerated during ovulation. She also thought it was silly of Warren to bemoan women's lives being controlled by their efforts to make themselves attractive. He gained as much from this as the plastic surgeons themselves did. If women stopped trying to make themselves look attractive to men, poor Warren wouldn't know what to do with himself.

Later that evening, lying on the sofa, Anna called her friend. She had just finished a mind-numbing shift at the clothing store, and her back and feet were aching more than usual; every time she wiggled her toes, pain shot through her arches. It was bizarre how she had never felt this when she was modeling. Back then, she'd literally run back and forth to castings in four-inch stilettos, and she'd felt fine, she'd felt light and winged and incipient, but after eight hours in comfortable sneakers her body felt like it was ossifying. Maybe it was the torpor of the job itself, the dead end of retail. There was no room for upward mobility, unless you wanted to become a manager—and Anna knew she lacked the brisk and domineering qualities that this would require.

Anna and Daria—or as Anna knew her, Dasha—usually spoke a couple of times a week. They hadn't seen each other in person since Anna had left Russia; Dasha had grown up in the same village, and had only recently moved away to a neighboring town with her new husband. They were FaceTiming, so Anna propped her phone up against a heavy vase Warren had bought her, which she used to house the flowers he gave her. And on the table was a heart-shaped box, which had once held Neuhaus chocolates. She'd long since eaten the chocolates but had kept the box to hold her earrings.

So many of the things in her apartment were from him, she realized, not for the first time. They were his gifts, or remnants of his gifts. The sofa itself was a cast-off, a piece Warren had bought on a whim and then decided he was too busy to return. It was smooth and ultra-modern, made of plush velvet without cushions or sections, like a swipe of soft gray paint. He'd asked her, almost jokingly, if she wanted it, and she'd agreed, trying not to appear too eager. (At the time she had not had anywhere to sit down in her apartment besides the bed, the floor, and one lone chair at the tiny kitchen table.)

Even now, though, the apartment wasn't exactly a beauty. The walls were drenched with paint the color of parchment paper. The furniture stood awkwardly at attention, in muted colors that had looked stately in the catalogs and in Warren's home but sickly in the pallid light that filtered through her windows.

Dasha picked up the phone, revealing her own room: walls painted green, cluttered with framed photographs of her and her husband's cats. As they began to speak, Anna relaxed, and the cloud of the last few days began to lift. Just talking was a relief; her mouth loved Russian. The complexity of her mother tongue, the blurry rise and dip of consonants, was a welcome departure from the bland, sibilant plateaus of English.

They spoke about their families and the weather and the political troubles. There always seemed to be political troubles. "Our president isn't so bad," Anna said, after Dasha had told her about the Russian president's latest scandal. "But he doesn't give a damn about the environment either. He just OK'd the opening of a new pipeline, which is going straight through Native territory, and if there's a spill, thousands of people's drinking water is screwed. But as long as the oil companies can be sure of a few more years of profits, it's worth the risk, right?"

"That's pretty dumb," Dasha said, although she probably had no idea what Anna was talking about, as she didn't read the American news. But you didn't always need to read the news to know what was going on, as so many of the changes were undeniable now, even in Siberia: permafrost melting, chunks of ice sliding into the ocean. An inescapable event horizon creeping ever closer. "Why can't people stop doing that crazy shit?"

"Greed, I suppose," Anna said, eyeing her wardrobe. She wondered if Dasha would think she was greedy if she knew what she did for a living. She had told her friend that she was dating a wealthy man, but had ducked Dasha's more detailed questions, and had only sent her a few blurry shots of them together. Dasha had some idea that Warren made it easier for Anna to get by in New York, but she had no idea the extent of it. Sometimes Anna wished her friend knew everything. At other times she was incredibly grateful that she did not.

"How is everything with Anton?" Anna asked.

"Oh, dear." Dasha closed her eyes. "Don't ask me that."

"What? Why not? Are you okay?"

"Yes. I mean, he doesn't beat me or anything."

"Well, *that's* good," Anna said.

Dasha didn't pick up on the sarcasm. Anna did, though, and was startled at how easily it had emerged. She never used to be sarcastic. Now it seemed that every few days something caustic would escape from her mouth, a sentence dipped in acid. She realized, her thoughts slow with dread, that the persona she was practicing for Warren was becoming more and more real, a harsher version obscuring her old self. The past, as well as the Anna of the past, was moving further and further away from her.

"I know, right?" her friend was saying. "But I'm still unhappy. I do my best to keep him satisfied, you know, rub his feet, make him hot meals, keep everything clean. The house sparkles when I'm done with it, I put all the kitchenware on the countertop." She gestured in the direction of the other room. "The spoons are all lined up in size order like—like little *gnomes*. But I try to talk to him and he just looks at me and grunts. Just grunts. Sometimes I feel like I'm talking to a wall. I expected this, yeah—after ten years of marriage! Not six *months*." She rubbed her forehead. "Shit, do I have lines? I feel like I'm starting to see lines here."

"No," Anna reassured her. But she did see the beginnings of lines on her friend's forehead. Every time they spoke, Dasha looked older, just by a tiny bit—not only lines but a new gravity to her face, a settling-down of flesh. Maybe Anna looked like that, too, when seen from another perspective. "Well. Maybe a little? It might be the stress. Try to relax your muscles."

"Relax? Anton is the only one who gets to relax around here."

"And he ignores you if you try to talk?"

"Not literally all the time. But mostly, yeah. If it isn't something to do with him, he doesn't care anything about it."

Anna had never met Anton, but from what she'd learned of him through Dasha, he was a boorish, selfish man who couldn't be bothered to see beyond the end of his nose. His greatest accomplishment that Anna knew of was catching the biggest fish in the village river six years ago.

"I always dress up for him too," Dasha said in despair. "But he barely notices me anymore. I walked into the room in lingerie the other day and he literally didn't even look up. I finally said,

'Hello dear, do you like my outfit?' and he asked if I was cold."
She rolled her eyes.

"Wow." From what Anna had seen on Dasha's social media,
Anton was the one who was too ugly for his wife: he had sunken
eyes, large pores, which gave his skin a pitted look, and an unap-
pealing slouch to his shoulders. With her asymmetrical features
and crooked nose, Dasha wasn't exactly gorgeous, but she had
glowing skin and large, clear eyes: the kind of simple beauty you
might find in a storybook tale about a dairymaid. Anna had told
Dasha this before, leaving out the part about the dairymaid, but
Dasha had just shrugged. "The more beautiful one is the one
who thinks he's more beautiful," she'd said. "And yes, it's usually
the man."

"Don't try so hard, Dasha," Anna suggested now. "By now
he's gotten used to having a dolled-up maid waiting around for
him, and it's made him complacent. What would he do if you
stopped doing those things? Don't put on the makeup. Slouch
around in sweatshirts and old jeans. Maybe he'll realize he's been
taking you for granted."

Dasha sighed, impatient. "It's not so easy for me. I'm not a
girl in New York City, surrounded by hot, wealthy men on the
lookout. In this case, it's easier for Anton than for me, because
he'd just find someone else. Most girls tolerate more than I do,
actually. His friends cheat on their wives and talk about it
freely. I overheard them discussing it the other day." The
corners of her mouth turned down in disgust, carving trenches
in her skin.

"Does... does Anton?"

"No, I don't think he does."

"Hmm," Anna said.

"But he will if he thinks he can get away with it," Dasha said
sourly.

"Are you in love with him?"

Dasha looked stunned at the question; Anna realized that it
would be the same if Dasha asked her that about Warren. How
ridiculous, she'd think. Love never even entered the picture. She
would be speechless, too, if faced with that question.

"There are more important things than love," Dasha said finally. It was exactly what Anna had expected her to say.

Later, Anna went through everything she had in her closet. It wasn't as full as many sugar babies' were. It housed only the things she hadn't been able to bring herself to throw away, like soft woolen sweaters from Russia, and the things she hadn't been *able* to throw away: the clothes that Warren expected to see her wearing. She knew, almost by instinct now, what she could sell and what she could not. When Warren bought her something with a distracted glance, a wave of his hand and a lazy flick of his credit card, she put it in the "to sell" pile. But when he really *looked* at her in the dress or shoes or coat, when he smiled his sticky smile and told her she looked like a goddess, she knew she had to hang onto that one. There were a number of these last items: short bandage dresses that hugged her waist and lifted her breasts, silk lingerie as delicate as tissue paper.

Maybe it was the conversation with Dasha, maybe just the time that had elapsed since Sunday, but Anna realized that she had panicked that night on the rooftop. It wasn't the end of the world if Warren bought her a few bags in place of her allowance. After all, he hadn't said anything about cutting her allowance off completely, because that would, of course, violate the terms of their agreement. There were some sugar babies who subsisted solely on dinners and presents, but Anna had specified an allowance. It wasn't like he was trying to back out of that completely.

She paged through the dresses in her closet, turning them as though they were the textured pages of an enormous book: some thick and furry, some ruffled, some watery and smooth. It would be a book about someone else, a stranger she had never met. Her favorite piece was an ombré floor-length gown from a Lebanese brand, and when she came to it, she paused for a few moments. The top part was solid black, lightening into what looked like a cluster of branches near the waist, fading into white on the skirt. It was like something a girl in a fairytale would wear as she walked through the woods, the trees parting before her.

Not a lot of fairytales here, she thought, fingering the material. Not a lot of trees, either. She remembered the taiga back in Russia: dense, heavy with mist, spruces and pines huddling under a snow-heavy sky. Rows and rows of dark conifers that bristled with secrets. No other humans for miles. A feather drifting to the ground; the inky shadow of a fox.

Her chest felt numb. She let go of the dress. Maybe she could sell it. She rarely ever wore it, as it brushed the ground and weighed about ten pounds. It was much too fancy to be practical.

But Warren might invite her to another gala, and she couldn't exactly wear one of her slutty Herve Leger numbers there. She pictured herself tugging futilely at the hem of a bandage dress as all the other guests stared at her, scandalized, older men and women who knew very well who and what she was.

She pictured herself through Dasha's eyes then. Poor Dasha. For a moment, she felt exactly like the girl Warren thought she was. Materialistic, unsentimental, sarcastic. She felt a strange, hard disgust at herself, like a pebble in her stomach.

As she looked at her face in the mirror that was set into the wardrobe—Warren had had it installed so she could admire herself at all times—she felt a shudder of awe, an odd thrill. Dasha might be Poor Dasha, but was she Poor Anna? No, she decided. She was not a victim. She didn't know who or what she was, but she wasn't that.

Maybe this is what I'm meant to do, she thought. Maybe this is me after all.

CHAPTER 9

Gemma

The next morning, Gemma sat down cross-legged in front of the camera. All of her classes today were in the afternoon, meaning she now had several long, sunlit hours in which to film. If her advisor knew that she'd set her entire schedule up this way, she might be concerned, but she *didn't* know, and Gemma certainly wasn't going to tell her.

"Hello," she said. She cleared her throat; her voice sounded weaker than normal. "Hi."

Maybe it was that her bedroom was painted all the colors she associated with the trends of today—pastel pink and muted pale blue—maybe that was making her voice sound softer, more vague. She swallowed. Her mouth felt cold from toothpaste.

It was a Tuesday, so Derek wasn't here. He was at work, so at least she didn't have to worry about him overhearing her. Not that he'd judge her. He had a quiet supportiveness that was so much more valuable than other couples' overenthusiastic, often false-sounding cheerleading.

She looked at the lines she'd scribbled down last week and edited several times since then, ran them through her mind one more time, and then looked up. Her cheeks looked rounder than ever, and heavy, too, with the beginnings of jowls.

"Hey, guys," she began, doing her best to imitate the cheery tone she'd heard in every single influencer video. "I decided to move to New York City—all by myself!"

Right. That was crap. She looked down at the lines again. They didn't look all that saccharine on paper, but they definitely came out sounding like it. She tried again. "I decided to move to New York City... all by myself."

Yes, she had been all by herself, hadn't she? Her mother hadn't even been alive to come over on the plane with her.

She swallowed, opened her eyes very wide for a few moments, and when the swell of emotion receded, she looked back at the paper.

"I decided to move to New York City all by myself. I applied to NYU early decision, was accepted, and didn't hesitate to come all the way across the..."

She ran through the lines several times until she felt she'd gotten them right, until she thought her voice contained the right balance of cheer and humility. This was the key: to avoid any sense of longing in her videos. The influencers she watched never had any indication of loss or lack. Some of them had started with nearly nothing, but they had been able to convince their audiences that they were still worth watching, that they were happy with their lives. Even if their lives were simple, they were content with them—just as Gemma's mother had been. They radiated joy and self-satisfaction to their audiences. Some of them were rather humble about it, but some brimmed with an almost disgusting smarminess, which their audiences, loyal as mirrors, radiated back.

But when she watched her video, her stomach dropped. She looked terrified in the footage, as though someone were menacing her just offscreen. Her face was stiff, her voice clogged and muddy, and the words she had chosen, which looked so good on the page, were coming out all wrong.

She stopped watching and simply listened to the video, but when heard rather than seen, her delivery was even worse. She sounded like she didn't believe what she was saying. Like she was being forced to speak about a fresh and beautiful new life that was happening to someone else.

Maybe this was how amateur actors sounded before they got good. An actor had to believe their lines on some level, and this took practice. Or maybe it worked the other way around—maybe they spoke the lines and only then did they start believing them.

Boil it down: *I am happy. I am not alone. I am happy.*

Boil it down and only the bones were left.

She told herself firmly to stop thinking of bones. She opened her eyes very wide again, but this time it didn't work, and the tears came anyway.

Gemma rubbed her hands over her face several times, and when she took them away her palms were moist and felt grimy, as if her skin were covered with a layer of oil. She closed her laptop with a snap and went to class.

As a freshman, Gemma didn't need to come up with a major until next year, so for the time being she had split her schedule among core courses and electives. As it turned out, her creative writing class was one of the few where her presence was actually noticeable; most of her other courses were huge, anonymous lectures. She thought that she might eventually want to focus on political science or film, but these were more like backup plans, vaguer even than the approximation of her influencer success.

She finished her last class by seven and walked home along Greenwich Avenue. She never tired of gazing at the architecture of New York, which was, in most of the city, so much sleeker and newer than the old-world structure of Britain. Down here in the village, though, everything was smaller and lower to the ground, as though in imitation of a much older country.

As she walked north she glanced up at the buildings, whose windows, blanked out by the light of the setting sun, gleamed like blinded eyes. It unnerved her, and she was only cheered when she saw a dog with exceptionally short legs passing by. This was a necessary tool for survival, or at least mental stability—finding small bits of happiness in the midst of all the uncertainty, all the doubt. Her mother had told her this, once. A long time ago.

Derek came home around the same time Gemma did,

shaking the hair out of his face. He needs a haircut, she thought, and felt a twinge of tenderness, as though he were her child and she in charge of setting up his barber appointments. When they hugged, the edge of his cheekbone pressed into the softness of her own face. These sharp features of his—his long, lean figure, the hollows of his cheeks—gave him a studious gravity that was at odds with his casual, mild demeanor. She often joked that he looked like the ultimate idol of a nineteenth-century scholar, especially when he wore his glasses.

They ate dinner. Sitting at the table, Gemma was about to mention her experience filming that morning, but Derek had already placed his phone sideways on the table to watch some sports game. He inserted his earbuds, hunched over to better see the screen, and was lost to her.

Gemma's noodles lost heat, crusted and hardened. She stared at the contours of his shoulders and the slopes of his arms, feeling a frustrated urgency. This could be their last night together, and he was wasting it looking at a screen. Her mother had watched nothing on screens during her final weeks, preferring to spend as much of her time as possible in the real world, with real people.

Gemma felt a kind of rage in these moments, as though she were pounding on the side of a thick glass, unable to reach him. The rage was hard to deal with so she buried it with fear. She imagined again that it was their last night together, and then it was easier, she could just sit there and watch him and be in awe of the perfect sharp structures of his face and the concentration in his eyes and admire it all, laid out before her as perfectly as flowers on a grave.

He looked up. Looked at her. "Are you okay?"

Later that evening, able to stand it no longer, Gemma reached forward and tapped Derek's shoulder. They were both on the couch and no longer eating, but besides that, nothing had changed. He was still hunched over watching his game; she was still staring at him.

He raised an eyebrow at her, not lifting his head but rather turning it slightly on his neck like a jointed mannequin. "What's up?"

She smiled, feeling foolish. "I just thought we could talk."

"About what?" He finally paused the video and removed his earbuds. This had the effect of making her feel a new pressure to perform, and in the sight of an invisible viewfinder, she groped around for something interesting to say.

"Um. I dunno. About anything. The weather. How my classes are going. How your work is going."

"How are your classes going?" he asked dutifully.

"Good," she said, and then added, jiggling her leg, "Well. The classes themselves are. But I don't know how I feel about the other students there."

"Yeah? Like, you don't like them, or what?"

"I feel that I can't relate to them. Everything they talk about is so bizarre to me, it all sounds so stupid and foolish."

"They're just not as smart as you, Gemma."

"No. I don't know about that," she said. "I'm not so clever. It's not like my head is alive with genius thoughts, or ruminations on philosophy or life. Maybe it's partially that I'm living here, so far away from all of them, walking home at the end of my classes whereas they all go back to campus together. They all live in dorms and go to parties and hook up with people whose names they don't even know."

"And?" He sounded as though she were regaling him with the mating habits of South American tree frogs. "What do you think about that?"

"I think it's nasty... and a drag to talk about. But they probably have the same judgments about me. They'd probably call me boring, a prude."

"Actually, I think they'd look up to you."

"Yeah? I doubt it. Who'd look up to *me?* There are students there who are models, writers—I think some senior in my creative writing class has a *book* out, in which case, like, why are you even *taking* the class—students who have actually done something. They're the ones to look up to."

"Gemma, you're only nineteen. And a freshman. Look, think about it this way—" He paused, his mouth curling into a hesitant smile. "—you're probably one of the only people there who lives in their own place. Most of them live in crummy dorms with three or four other people. But you have your own apartment in Manhattan, and how many of your classmates can say that? Not many, right? I'd be surprised if they could afford even half of your rent."

"Right. Except they didn't get the rent money through their parent dying."

Her voice had turned to acid. There were a few moments of silence.

"I shouldn't have said that," she said, at the same time that Derek said, "Shit, Gemma. I'm sorry."

"It's okay."

"What I was trying to say is... well, what I *should* have said, is that you don't need to have accomplished anything to be worthy of admiration. There are plenty of people with achievements and certificates who are probably the most boring people in the world. And, conversely, I'm sure there are a lot of 'normal' people who are really interesting to talk to."

"Yes, but am I one of them?" she asked drily.

"Of course you are."

Then why are you already turning back to your phone? she thought.

"What do I have to say that's interesting, though?"

He glanced back over at her, the tiniest hint of annoyance in his gaze.

"I mean. What stories do I have? What about my life could possibly be interesting to an audience?"

"I don't know if I'm the best person to ask," he said. "I'm biased, aren't I? After all... I live with you."

Sometimes Derek talked slowly. So, when he said, *I live with you*, there was a split second where Gemma heard only *I l*, the infinitesimal gap between the beginning of the word *live* and the end.

For that tiny second she'd thought he was about to say, *After all, I love you.*

Well. Wasn't that stupid.

That night, Gemma lay awake. Her body was tired, melting into the mattress and growing heavier with each moment, but her mind was on edge, fully alert. A siren went by, and then another, and she lay listening to this chorus for what felt like ten minutes. Ambulance wailing after ambulance wailing after ambulance. There seemed to be an innumerable amount of people who were sick, dying, in trouble.

Finally she got up to check, pulling the curtains aside with a prickling of dread, but the street outside was dark and empty. She stood there for long minutes, wondering if the sirens had even been real. Maybe she had been dreaming; maybe she would be able to fall fully asleep if she went back to bed.

But when she lay down again, her mind remained awake. With every moment that passed, she felt her body waking up, too: a restlessness filling her limbs, a desire to kick her legs out as the muscles slowly stiffened.

Finally she could stand it no longer and took her phone from the nightstand. Walking quietly so as not to wake Derek, she crept into the bathroom, put in her earbuds, and sat there on the cold tile, squinting at her phone. She re-watched some of the year's top-rated influencer videos. The lighting and backgrounds were perfect in most of them. But then she scrolled to the very beginnings of their channels, to the videos they had filmed years before that had kicked everything off. Here there was a stark difference: their video systems were much less sophisticated, the backgrounds either cluttered or far too spare, and the lighting was barely decent.

But what *was* there? The content. They had interesting content. Their stories were interesting, their lives fascinating, their personalities engaging. They charmed their audiences, even if they hadn't done much of note. She didn't need to focus so much on the aesthetics of the whole thing, as on the content. The main problems with her first video were mostly in the material, not the execution. She had a decent lighting system and background, and her face was... her face. Nothing to be done about that. All she needed to do was make sure that her intro, the things she would say, were perfect.

And she had the ideal feedback at her disposal in her creative writing class. It would be her turn to submit a story later this week, and in her first few classes, she had seen countless stories about dragons and elves, snippets that looked suspiciously like essays for other classes, and free verse poetry. Surely a video intro wouldn't be too far out of their comfort zones.

CHAPTER 10

Janet

Sometimes Janet had faint thoughts that skimmed across the glassy surface of her dreams: ideas, realizations, designs, fragments of song. But when she woke up they were always beyond her reach, having left only traces of their existence: an idea that would be groundbreaking, if she could only recall what it was. A beautiful melody she couldn't quite remember. They always seemed to take something out of her when they disappeared, as though her entire being were comprised of these insubstantial thoughts. As though one day she would wake up to find countless holes in her center, the vanished fragments threading flight-trails out like spiderwebs.

Janet hadn't spoken to Miranda since the night before last. She was aware something was necessary, some wish of goodwill before she left, but even as Janet picked up her phone, a juvenile urge kept her from typing anything. Their last messages stood in symmetry, stiff and polite, Janet's followed by Miranda's:

Got home safe.

Cool, good night.

Janet put her phone down with a snort. Hopefully the people in Philadelphia were more selfless and mature. Hopefully they could handle their old friends' abrupt departures without any ill will. Miranda would probably love them. She probably already had a circle of them set up there.

Now it was just Janet and the letters. She screamed into her pillow and then got up and turned on her computer. It took a while to boot up, just like her.

Her first letter of the day was from a mother who had lost both children to suicide. *Everyone says their overdoses were deliberate, but I don't believe they would do something like that. They'd know how much it would hurt me.*

Yeah, right. Janet gnawed her lip and recalled Ur's mention of the students who had jumped from the roof of his college. She skimmed all the letters—something she wasn't supposed to do, she was supposed to go through them one by one, like a robot—looking for Ur's response. He hadn't replied yet. With a feeling of defeat, she returned to the grievance letters. It seemed that there were more and more of them each day, descending like a deluge of water. Like a hurricane.

Janet drank her dirt-tasting coffee and stifled an acidic burp. Then she wondered why she had even stifled it. There was no one here to see her.

But on the other hand, if some hacker creep had installed a pervy surveillance camera, she didn't want to gross him out too badly. He had already watched her pick her nose and sneeze all over her bedsheets this morning, and she didn't want to be so disgusting that even a pervy surveillance guy didn't want to watch her. That, somehow, would be the ultimate rock bottom.

She read more and more of the letters. They began blending into each other the way the dating app guys did. She had to walk away from the laptop every few minutes, looking out the window at the cold cloudless sky to clear her mind.

There was something grotesque about the real tragedies that appeared in these accounts. They were so raw, so real, that they felt almost fake. There was a sense of futility about them. She wasn't sure how anyone could anyone expect her to respond to these grievances in a genuine manner when she had already become so numbed to bad news. For god's sake—through her phone alone, she'd been exposed to six traumatizing news stories before the workday started, and then, via the letters, a dozen more afterwards. So someone's brother had died in a car accident. She could top that: another grievance letter featured a girl who'd been sold into a sex trafficking ring and only escaped after ten hideous years.

Fuck, Janet thought. She pressed the heels of her hands into her eyes. Tiny squares exploded across her vision, geometric shapes like endless walls of bricks spiraling across the reddish black.

This wasn't how humans worked. Surely they could automate this shit; surely there was some kind of AI technology that could recognize certain keywords—*trauma, hangnail, divorce*—and point these people in the right direction. But AIs were instead happily churning out art and music and writing, leaving humans to perform the mechanical clerical work, the rote tasks that dimmed creativity and deadened hope. And it was Janet's job to look through people's grievances, rooting around in their letters for clues to all their sadnesses, all their pain, all of the negative spaces inside their souls.

When Ur's letter came after her lunch break, it was a relief.

Hello again OLT.

To answer your questions, I teach a rather opaque subject: anthropology. Humans and their subspecies. You'd think it would be a simple undertaking, because homo sapiens et al are so familiar, but there's actually a huge challenge in teaching humans about other humans, particularly ancient ones. My students just can't develop enough distance from the subject to properly gaze at them with a clinical eye. They're always thinking about how these ancient humans, these Denisovans and Neanderthals, would have coped without iPhones or porn. Modernizing them. Drawing little cartoon speech bubbles with "Sup bitches" next to their textbook pictures of Julius Caesar. It's fairly unsettling.

I'm in a place you've probably never been to in your life (trust me, that's not a bad thing), in an extremely run-down part of Brooklyn. Therapy is rather out of my price range, I must admit, shameful though it is. As to what people I'm surrounded by, I can't honestly answer you. There are so many of them, and they're all wrong about things in completely different ways.

Mostly, I wanted someone to talk to. I find that online you can concentrate more on what the other person is saying—as opposed to the real-life circus of small talk, where you make eye contact, nod, smile, half-absorb what the other person is saying and half-focus on what you're about to say, repeat ad infinitum. Everything is so rushed like that.

Even in films, there's this perfectly balanced exchange in conversations that never really occurs in real life. Think of the way nobody says "Bye" when they hang up their phones onscreen, except blown up to gigantic proportions and spread across every conversation. Everything has a subtext, there are always two or three layers of meaning, and people speak much more precisely than they do in reality. If you tried that kind of thing in real life everyone would think there was something off about you. Funny how that works: they say life imitates art, but if you actually try to imitate art in real life, you'll probably get carted off to a psych ward. Once you see it you can't unsee it.

I hope your day is going well, or as well as can be expected at the moment. Mine isn't so terrific... half my family lives in Detroit, and according to the news, they can't drink their tap water. There's a rush on bottled water at the stores, people getting trampled, it's horrible. People always worry about food, stockpiling it like no tomorrow, breaking into cold sweats about perishability and maximum calorie counts... but it's water that's really going to matter in the future. Can't go three days without it, and everybody is losing their mind over beans and toilet paper. It's insane.

All right, I had better end this letter before I build up a head of steam and rant on for pages and pages. :)

-Ur

People always worry about food? Certainly nobody Janet knew. The only time she'd ever seen Miranda worry about food was when she stressed over the carbs in her bagel. Even her mother and aunt didn't fret too badly. Their concern only went as far as price hikes. They never thought all the way back to the roots of the food, to the supply chain that brought the food to their doors. It was as though everyone thought it just sprang up, fully packaged, from the floors of the food shops, and had only to be fit with a price tag before it was ready to be sold.

Janet didn't reply right away. She wanted to give Ur something more substantial and thought-out than the replies she dashed off to the other writers throughout the day. As the sun went down, she finished up her last few responses and smoked some of the weed she kept stashed in a zebra-print box on her nightstand. Not pure sativa, which made her taut and paranoid, but a hybrid, just potent enough to soothe her mind. To tone down that frantic feeling in her brain, which sometimes reminded her of the insectile buzz that emanated from high-voltage power lines: trapped energy, blank meaningless drone.

When she logged out of the computer and checked Instagram, her sister's post was the first one on her feed. Her stomach contracted at the sight: Izzy and her kids were standing in their backyard in the midst of a downpour. Izzy was laughing and the kids were shrieking with joy, their faces frozen in delight. Everyone's hair was plastered to their faces and their clothes were completely soaked through, turned heavy and transparent. It looked like someone had dumped an enormous bucket of water on them. In the background a palm tree was bent at a painful-looking angle.

Ted must have taken the photo, and Janet felt a jab of resentment for him: the doting, docile husband with his gentle cow-like eyes, doing whatever Izzy asked. Enabling her even in the middle of a storm during fucking hurricane season.

Izzy clearly treated it as a joke. The caption to her post read *Don't think I need a shower today ;)*.

Yeah, very funny. Let her see how many showers she needed when her entire house got blown away.

Janet had been checking the weather forecast for Florida and while there were no signs of any hurricanes immediately approaching the coast, there were several reports of unseasonably rough seas and heavy storms. And this picture fit right into that prediction.

Izzy let the phone ring several times before answering. When she finally picked up, Janet fought not to ask her if she'd done this on purpose.

"Hey, Janet. What's up?"

"Not much. How are you?"

"Oh, ya know. Just relaxing. It's been a long day. Ruby threw up on me."

"Ah. My sympathies." Great, now she sounded like Ur. "How was the storm?"

"The what?"

"The storm? The enormous deluge that cascaded down upon you in your last Instagram post?" Janet made to show Izzy her phone, but then remembered that she was using it to talk to her. "The one where you made the crack about, like, not needing to take a shower ever again?"

"Um, I wouldn't exactly call that a storm. Just a summer rainfall."

"It's not summer anymore."

"Okay, a fall rainfall then." She could hear Izzy shrugging. "What's the problem with that?"

"You don't think these storms are getting worse? I mean, even in the city we had a pretty bad hurricane a couple years ago." Her mouth was dry; she kept forgetting to hydrate after smoking.

"Oh my gosh. Not this again."

"Not what again? Not me caring about you again? Look, Izzy, it's better to be prepared. The next hurricane could be a really bad one, miles and miles of flooding, and your house has a good chance of being directly in its path. This isn't 1995 anymore, you know. It's not even, like, 2012. They barely even *have* category one or two storms anymore."

"Janet, what the hell is up with this doomsday attitude? I think maybe those letters are doing a number on your brain. Listen, have you tried compartmentalizing? I do it when I attend to the kids and the house, and it's really pretty easy. All you've got to do is section things off in your brain—"

"Yeah, of course it's because of my job," Janet snapped. "That doesn't take a genius to figure out. I have access to everyone's worries, everyone's fears, from petty shit like their hair not growing properly to suicide and PTSD and incurable illnesses. But it's also what's made me more aware of everything. I don't have—I don't have a happy little family home life like you to distract me, to pull the shades over my eyes. I can see what's really going on, Izzy, and it's *terrifying*, it's scary as hell."

She kept talking for several more seconds before she realized Izzy had hung up.

Anger surged in her skull. Fucking bitch, she thought. Fine, get swept away in a storm. She couldn't remember what was supposed to make a sister so special, anyway. The blood of the covenant was thicker than the water of the womb—and apparently the water of the hurricane, too.

The phone screen, restored to its default home page, stared back at her. As she watched, a notification came down and proclaimed merrily, *New message from Charles!* As though the message were anything more than a jumble of characters that Charles thought would provide the maximum amount of return for the least amount of effort. Her mouth tasted like ashes. She tossed the phone onto her bed and went to the kitchen to chug a glass of water.

She knew she should go visit her mom—it had been a couple of weeks since she'd last taken the trip out to Queens—but she couldn't stand the thought of being around anyone right now. Especially her family. Her mother's judgmental stares. The dim lights of the apartment, the dusty black-and-white photos on the walls. The pointless, cheap-looking ornaments and the grim, funereal silence. The rise and fall of their chests as they slowly consumed all the oxygen in the room.

After dinner, Janet turned her computer back on and replied to

Ur. The letter came out of her like a gush of air, released in a clatter of keys.

Hi again, Ur. I hope you know the origins of that word. Nobody else really seems to know very much, which is disappointing. Even my own sister doesn't believe me when I tell her how bad everything's getting, and she lives on the coast of Florida, if you can believe that. Not worried about hurricanes at all. I worry about her. Or I did, before she hung up on me in the middle of our conversation today.

You're right about the water. I'm sorry about your family in Detroit. I did see the news about that. New York is supposed to have one of the best water sources in the world, so if things really go to shit it'll likely be a while before we have to start worrying. But then, that's probably just the kind of thinking that was popular among European Jews in 1935. Or the aristocracy of France in the 1780s. Nobody thinks it's going to happen to them, do they, until it's too late. Do I think it's going to happen to me? Everyone's got a false sense of security. Prom and college and interviews and weddings and anniversaries—we've got all that stuff to keep track of, and so the panic has nowhere to go amidst the tidy markings of the calendar.

The thing you said about movies really intrigued me. I was thinking about movies recently too, but for a different reason. Every movie I've ever seen about an athlete, an artist, a hero—anyone, really—follows a course so predictable and so scientific you can plot it on a chart: early achievements, then the struggles, a dark night of the soul, the event that we might think our hero is Not Coming Back From... and finally, inevitably, a triumph. Bugles and trumpets. Confetti flying from the ceiling, a shower of petals, victory, joy.

But then I thought. What about the stories that don't end up that way? The ones that happen so many times in real life? The ones that fail, the people who get back up on the horse—or the balance beam, or the stage—and fall, maybe not every time, but at the time it matters most? Instead of the champion who fails the first two events of the tournament and wins spectacularly in the last one, the one that really counts... what about the reverse? What about the ones who never have a triumphant comeback? The ones who walk out of the stadium with head lowered in defeat, with no one there to celebrate what didn't happen?

You have it absolutely right. Try to imitate art in life and they'll think you're insane.

After pressing Send, she read the message over again, just to try and see it through Ur's eyes. To her horror, she had actually written out what she could have sworn was only a thought: *Do I think it's going to happen to me?*

Her palms grew clammy as she read it. This was one of those things that pushed her ever closer towards the at-risk category of *completely* losing her shit. Fortunately, the rest of the letter didn't have anything else of that nature. She read it over and over again just to make sure.

She realized it was nearly nine p.m. and she hadn't been outside all day. The apartment at night was febrile, tense, noxious with the smell of something she couldn't describe. Peelings under the garbage: a bag tied up tight, oozing wettish stink. She needed fresh air, but in this part of the city, the "fresh air" was anything but fresh. Discarded junk littered the sidewalks, the reek of liquefying garbage hung around every corner, and pigeons looked at you out of their beady eyes like they knew just a little bit too much.

It was less effort to stay inside. Janet slumped onto her bed and began watching a TV show on her computer. But the TV show didn't stand a chance. Within five minutes she had picked up her phone and was scrolling through various apps and articles, her concentration fractured into a million glittering shards, none of them reflecting anything worth notice.

CHAPTER 11

Anna

Wednesday was not a day one might normally hold a dinner party, but Warren liked to buck tradition. *Wear your green dress tonight,* he texted Anna that afternoon, when he told her about the plans. Anna selected the aforementioned dress from her closet, thankful that she hadn't sold it. It was a shade of green that had a hint of silver, a chill to it like the snow-bitten tips of a fir tree, although she couldn't for the life of her figure out how the designers had done it.

That evening, Warren had the same good mood he'd had on Sunday. When he greeted Anna in his apartment his face was alight with energy. "You look amazing," was the first thing he told her, his gaze settling on her lips. She had painted them a dark, blossoming red, the color of the deep inside petals of a rose.

"Thanks. I didn't want to let your guests down." She looked around the room; he'd had several new art pieces delivered and placed at strategic intervals around the apartment. One featured a chunk of dry brown hair taped to a white background; at first she thought it was a photograph but when she walked over to examine it more closely, she saw that it was an actual lock of hair taped to the canvas. It wasn't even protected by a glass barrier. It seemed unhygienic, not to mention difficult to ship. What would happen if the hair got tangled in the process? Would someone have to comb it out? Another piece depicted a glass eye, the iris a brilliant and fervid blue. Wherever Anna walked in the room, the eye followed her.

"Did you decide on a bag yet?" he asked her. For a moment she had no idea what he was talking about. Then she remembered.

"Oh, not yet. I'll decide by the weekend, I think."

"You do like them, right?" His eyes narrowed, as if in concern.

"Of course I do. They're beautiful." Her smile felt like a layer of putty drying on her face. She reminded herself again that one week's allowance meant nothing, so there was no need to take it as the end of the world.

"Good!" He clapped his hands and rubbed them together. "Let's focus on this party tonight, then."

"Will I need to talk to people?" she asked delicately. "As opposed to... other times?"

He got what she was saying. "Dolly, I am not in the *least* ashamed of you," he told her. "Don't you even start thinking that, all right? You don't have to stand off to the side or anything, if that's what you mean. You're the hostess of the party." He smiled proudly. "We've never hosted a party here before, have we?"

"I suppose not." *We?* She was hardly involved. She was as much a bit of decoration as the abstract, pointless art on the wall. And after this long, it was where she was most comfortable.

The guests began arriving shortly after eight. They started in a slow, hesitant trickle, but after eight-thirty they began flowing in full force. Many of them were older than Warren: Upper East Side society ladies, aging investment bankers, alcoholic day traders. They lingered over the food. Warren had had an assortment of it catered, delivered by waiters gliding around the party, blank-faced and professionally unobtrusive.

From across the room Anna caught sight of one of them, a blond with a chiseled, haughty face, taller than anyone else in the room. She felt the air leave her body. He looked so much like that old boyfriend—so much that she had to take another look to assure herself that it wasn't actually him. On second glance the differences became obvious. His jaw was softer, his hair thinner.

She thought, in a flush of anger: Why did everyone she compared to him wind up being so much *lesser*?

Turning to the window, she watched the water below, its glinting metallic black. She drank more and more slowly, feeling the wine turn warm on her tongue. When another waiter passed, Anna snatched a shrimp from a tray and nibbled on it. It tasted like nothing. She remembered reading that shrimp, both farmed and wild-caught, were even more unsustainable than beef. Apparently, small fish like anchovies and herring were a much better choice. She imagined telling Warren that he needed to replace his shrimp appetizers with anchovies, and stifled a laugh as she pictured his face. He would never be capable of caring about anything like this. He was too well insulated from the impacts of climate change—not because of blissful ignorance, like her parents, but because of his wealth and privilege.

She reminded herself that this was what her goal was, to be insulated just like him, probably never on the same level but with a similar buffer between herself and the floundering, drowning world. Perhaps one day, because of this, she would become just as uncaring. Perhaps the only reason anyone cared about what was happening to the world was because it affected them, too; remove that connection and the changes became inconsequential. Right now the idea horrified her—but then again, the idea of fucking Warren would have horrified her when she was seventeen or eighteen years old. It was only at twenty that she had begun to think of things like this, to accept them into her mind and eventually her life. Perhaps she would continue to grow and change and warp and the person she became at thirty would be utterly unrecognizable to her twenty-two-year-old self.

She ate the remainder of the shrimp, sucking the meat from the tail. It felt greasy in her mouth and she swallowed with difficulty.

Another thought shouldered its way into her mind: what her old boyfriend would think of her if he was at this party, working as a waiter, noticing her from across the room through a thicket of people. He would probably think her just as shallow and ignorant as everyone else here was: eating appetizers and gazing out the window at the filthy Hudson, dressed in a gown the color of the vanishing forest.

"You're supposed to put the shrimp tail back on the tray," an older woman said from beside her. She raised an eyebrow at Anna, cocked her head, and smiled. Her skin was so pale as to be almost translucent, and she was one of the few female guests whose faces hadn't been nipped and tucked to inhuman proportions. After seeing them, Anna understood better why Warren had been so cautious about the idea of her getting work done. They looked like balloon animals.

"The tray. Of course." So that's why the waiter had hesitated for a moment before walking away. Apparently she was supposed to eat it in front of him, and then drop it back onto a dish on the tray. How awkward.

"What an adorable accent!" the woman exclaimed. She had a string of pearls around her throat; their smoothness was startling against the wrinkles and sagging skin of her neck. "Are you from Ukraine?"

"No, I'm from Russia."

"Moscow? St. Petersburg?" the woman suggested quickly, as if she were on a quiz show.

"No," Anna said, and named her town, feeling a perverse flicker of satisfaction at the lack of recognition on the woman's face. "It's pretty small."

The woman took a sip from her glass of champagne. Rings bristled on her fingers, the stones glossy and iridescent like scarabs. "I suppose what they say is true, then."

"What do they say?"

"About the most beautiful things coming in the most humble of packages." She winked. "I do wonder how Warren found you? Was it pure luck?"

"Oh... you could say that. There's probably a saying about that, too. About the things fate brings us, and all that." She smirked into her wineglass and immediately wiped the expression from her face, but luckily the woman missed it and thought she was serious.

"That's *adorable*!" she crowed, grasping Anna's arm. Her rings were cold against Anna's skin. "I need to get a photo of you two together."

"Sure," she said. "I'm flattered. Let's find him?" She was still holding onto the shrimp tail.

"You probably have a *sixth sense* when he's around, you adorable girl." The woman beamed, trailing after Anna as she walked across the floor. She was clearly not on her first glass of champagne.

"My sixth sense seems to be failing me now," Anna admitted, after they'd made two laps of the room and failed to retrieve him. She had, however, managed to discard the shrimp tail. "Sorry, but what's your name again? I'm afraid I didn't catch it." As she spoke, she realized with a horrible thrill that her speech had changed just from the few minutes of being around this woman; there was a clipped quality to her accent, an exaggerated politeness.

"Talia Britsburg," she said. Anna recognized her surname from one of the wings of the MOMA. "And you?"

"Anna," she said. "Just Anna."

"Just Anna?" boomed a voice from behind them. When Anna turned she saw that Warren had walked up to them unseen. His face was bloated with drink, his eyes smaller than ever in his face, and his breath smelled like champagne splashed on the ground. "That's no way to introduce yourself. *Just* Anna? Talia, please forgive my rudeness. This is Anna Sidorova, my lovely partner in crime." Talia simpered. "Anna, this is my dear friend Talia." His speech, too, had gotten overlaid with mannerisms, words like *dear* and *lovely* hanging on like little leeches. "She's been a great help in selecting the decor."

"Oh, please," Talia said, waving a skeletal hand, although she looked very satisfied with herself.

"You helped pick out the artwork?" Anna asked.

"Only a few pieces. Did you enjoy the *Fabric of Meaning* one?"

"Which one was that? I must have gotten the names mixed up."

"Why, the one with the lock fastened to the canvas. You couldn't miss it. It was so... *tactile*. Really reminiscent of the very essence of life."

Lost, Anna scanned the room, thinking of keys.

"The one with the hair," Warren offered. "The lock of hair." Glancing at Anna, he added, "Maybe it's time for some dinner? These hors d'oeuvres don't seem to be holding me over very well."

By the time the meal was served, a good portion of the guests had left. This was fortunate, as even Warren's enormous banquet-style table wouldn't have seated them all. Anna wondered if he had planned it this way. He had really gone all out on the food, if nothing else: the light appetizers of before had given way to mushroom soup, roast quail, bruschetta. Anna kept an eye out for the blond waiter she'd seen before, but he appeared to have gone home. Only a few of the staff remained to refill water glasses and carry empty plates back into the kitchen.

Anna tried to sit next to Warren, but he told her she would be better off making friends for a change, winked, and nodded at an empty chair in between a man and an elderly lady. Feeling chastised, she trailed to her "assigned seat" at the other end of the table.

"So you're Warren's girlfriend?" the man on her left asked. He was dark-haired and handsome, but there was something lazily cruel about his attitude, the way he posed the question. There was a tinge of skepticism in his voice, and something close to amusement.

Anna felt herself stiffen. This guy was no drunken society lady; he was alert and sober, or close to it, and he was looking at her a little too intently. Like she was a piece of modern art he was trying to figure out.

She tipped her champagne glass back to give herself time to

think. "Something like that," she said with a one-shouldered shrug and a smile.

He cocked his head. "Wondering how that works. He's been telling us you're precisely half his age. That's interesting, right?"

She tried to conceal her shock. At the other end of the table, Warren was laughing uproariously. He must have had quite a bit to drink, as he wasn't usually in the habit of bragging about her. Somehow she'd thought he had more subtlety than that. But maybe that was foolish to assume of any man who participated in a relationship like the one they had.

"Yes. It's one of those interesting tidbits about us. Every couple has their intriguing detail that they can't help themselves from sharing with the world—some have completely opposing horoscope signs, for example, or were born on the exact same day."

Her hastily invented speech failed to distract him. He didn't even blink. "If you don't mind me asking, how did you two meet?"

She glanced again at Warren without meaning to. Her skin prickled. Now she had to guess what Warren had been saying to this man about them. Not that she was sure it even mattered; probably this man, like the doorman downstairs, had no trouble figuring out their arrangement. Yet he was asking her as though he couldn't puzzle it out himself: feigning ignorance, feigning innocence.

The pause stretched out for the longest time. The conversations of the other guests surrounded them, stories and questions pattering like gentle peripheral rain. She wished she was part of one of these discussions instead, even if it meant talking about stocks and investments and business deals. "Can't remember?" he said, looking like he was trying not to laugh.

"Online," she finally said. She drank some more champagne. It was some of the finest anyone could get, but it tasted sour in her mouth, with a sickly-sweet tinge like fruit gone rotten.

"Yes, that's the way it works nowadays, isn't it? Not like in days gone by, when your parents would simply set you up with a wealthy older man."

"I suppose so."

"What website was it?" He arched a precisely shaped eyebrow. "Plenty of fish? Match.com?"

"I think those are a little outdated," she said. The champagne glass felt brittle in her hand, about to snap. Across the table, Warren was engaged in conversation with a middle-aged woman and a silver-haired man—from the looks of it, they were swapping hilarious jokes. He hadn't had her sit by him, hadn't guessed that this would happen. Instead he had left her to fend for herself. Maybe he thought she would be able to charm everyone like she charmed him. With a lurch in her gut, she recalled how the other day he'd told her, face alight with good humor, that she was the one taking advantage. She kept trying to catch his eye, but he hadn't even glanced in her direction. She felt like she was trying to send SOS signals to a satellite.

"What's your name, by the way?" she added, not eager to stay on the conversation of herself and Warren. "I'm not sure we've been introduced."

"We haven't, or I'd remember." He gave her a false, watery smile. "The name's Yohann Straut. Unfortunately, I'm only one and one-half times your age, not double."

"That's a shame."

"Can you guess what that would make me?"

"Thirty-three," she answered dully, serving herself another slice of fish. It was soft and perfectly cooked, flaking apart at the barest touch of a fork. But she had completely lost her appetite. Just as with the painting of the eye, she could feel his gaze on her even when she didn't look at him.

He cleared his throat. "So. What do you do all day? In this apartment." He looked around at the vast windows, the magnificent glittering chandelier, the ornate sculptures standing at either side of the entrance to the kitchen. His expression was one of barely concealed amusement. "I'm not sure I believe a girl who hails from a Russian farm would really know what to do with herself around here."

The mention of the farm caused her stomach to lurch even more violently. It was the way he said it, too—scornful and disparaging, as though he thought she knew how to do nothing more than pet cows and pick berries. A memory flashed into her head: slicing into the carcass of a rabbit and peeling the skin back, exposing glistening muscles and tiny dots of gelatinous fat, the dark bruised purple of the veins underneath. If only she could do that right now, right here in front of this man, and then smear her bloody hands on his fancy suit, push him backward into a pit of snakes.

She took another swig from her glass and gave Yohann an icy smile. "Why even ask? I'm sure Warren's given you the answer to that too. He seems to have told you an awful lot about me."

"Careful, Anna," he said. "I'm probably the most important guest at this party." He smiled, his mouth moving separately from his eyes. "Care for some more crab cakes?"

Yohann didn't speak any more to Anna through dinner, but she was aware of his presence with every movement she made. She made desperate, doomed attempts to engage the woman on her right in conversation; this was difficult because the woman was about ninety years old and hard of hearing. Anna had to shout her own name three times into her companion's shriveled, whiskery ear before she understood, and from across the table, various people gazed at her with pity.

She excused herself multiple times to go to the bathroom. She wasn't sure to whom she was speaking when she got up, saying *Excuse me*—to Yohann? To Warren, who couldn't hear her anyway? To the dead fish on her plate?

The bathroom was echoey and strange with the noises of the party leaking in from the other room. Fresh flowers were laid out next to the sink, the taps freshly polished. In the mirror: Anna's feathered lipstick, flushed cheeks, mouth tight like a wire. She smiled at herself and saw lines form on either side of her mouth, digging in like fingermarks in clay. Then she pursed her lips until they resembled a strawberry: too red, overripe, beckoning future rot. She watched herself for a few more moments, trying to mentally place her personality, her outline, somewhere on the timeline of existence. Somewhere that would make sense.

She was unsuccessful. Her transparent film-roll self remained unattached to anything. The background was a vertiginous dark.

The party dragged on and on. Finally the last guest departed, and Anna allowed herself to drop the smile that had been clinging to her mouth all evening. Her cheek muscles ached.

"Do you know that guy Yohann?" she said to Warren. "The one who was sitting next to me? Mid-thirties, dark hair?"

"Yes? What about him?" He kept wiping his brow; he sweated a lot after drinking. In a sudden movement, he sat down on the bed, making the springs creak. His body looked like a paper sculpture that was collapsing.

"Well, what's up with him? He kept asking me all these questions, and it made me a little uncomfortable."

Warren laughed. Then he laughed again, looking ecstatic. Anna watched him, unnerved. When he was able to speak again, he said, "Oh, dolly, you really are the sweetest thing."

"I... am I?" She hated feeling sweet around him, hated feeling innocent, silly, pure. She had only gotten to feel that way with the ex-boyfriend. Sometimes she thought of a balloon with two dots drawn on it, labeled with their initials, and pictured the balloon being blown up. The dots moving slowly and inextricably further and further away from each other. They said the same thing was happening to the universe.

"You have no idea why I'm saying this, do you?"

"Not really. Enlighten me."

He shook his head, his mouth twisting in a wry smile. "In the simplest terms, you don't want me to get jealous. You were seated next to him all through dinner and now you're sheltering me from any suspicions that would shatter an old man's heart."

"You were the one who told me to make friends," she said, flustered.

"It's okay, Anna. Come here." His attitude had turned fatherly, which she hated. He patted the bed beside him, and she sat.

"I'm pretty sure he was making fun of me, or trying to." For an instant she wondered if she was being paranoid; but no, the things Yohann had said went beyond good-natured teasing. And of course there was that final comment he had made, the comment that had made her unable to swallow any of her food afterwards. *I'm probably the most important guest at this party.* "Who is he?"

"He's the son of a business partner of mine. Oh, he can be high-spirited sometimes. But that's because of his youth... and you're so much younger." He smiled, his eyes boring into hers. "You can be high-spirited too." He traced the curve of her waist, trailing down to her leg. Only now did he seem to perk up, to really focus on her face as he spoke. "You feeling high-spirited now? The party didn't take too much out of you, did it?" His touch turned heavier, more insistent. Anna remembered what Dasha had said about feeling like she was talking to a wall when she spoke to Anton.

The pale ghost of a bird streaked past the window and she wondered if it was flying south. If it was flying to Florida. Maybe even to Fort Lauderdale, where perhaps it had a nest, and other birds it knew.

Warren pressed her back onto the bed.

She couldn't see it from here, but she knew that the river snaked below: its chill, its rope of glittering dark. It was very unlikely that the bird would end up in the city where she had once been. More likely that it would crash into the river and drown.

CHAPTER 12

Gemma

G emma typed up her video intro that evening. It was a harder task than she'd thought, as every few minutes a noise intruded from outside: a car honking, a child's screeching, the clatter of something falling to the pavement. She closed her eyes and concentrated. She could type pretty well with her eyes closed, actually. It felt like her fingers were hitting the right keys.

She opened her eyes to a jumbled mess of letters, words cut off and ending in the wrong places, and below all of it the bright red scars of the spell checker.

Okay, she could keep her eyes open as she typed. No problem. Everyone had to start somewhere.

Within an hour she had her new, revised intro. It was a fairly basic description of her life, with various details peppered throughout the timeline, but most of it concentrated around the recent past. There were bits about Mum—hopefully she wouldn't choke up at these—her life in New York, even a few asides about her father: his emotional distance at odds with his goofy humor, his complete lack of self-awareness, his famous (failed) attempt to catch a fly between two chopsticks. And through it all ran a current of accomplishment. A self-confidence that would make Derek proud.

She had thought of including a memory of horseback riding

with her mother, but had ended up cutting it because it was too long. She'd gone back and forth on it a few times, though. Around the age of ten, Gemma had had a horse-crazy phase, which most girls seemed to go through at some point between ages nine and twelve but which in Gemma's case had been extremely short and extremely intense. Seeing this, her mother had taken her to a stable that offered pony riding, and they'd gone every weekend for the next year, until Gemma's obsession waned and she found horseback riding made her more sore and bored than happy. But her mother was much more impressive on horseback than Gemma was: she had ridden as a teen, and she hadn't lost all her skill at it. Ten-year-old Gemma was astonished at her mother's balance and coordination as she, in dun jodhpurs and no-nonsense boots, switched her horse seamlessly from a trot to a canter while Gemma (who never advanced very far herself) watched in openmouthed glee. She'd felt the inverse of what parents might feel at their children's sports games: *That's my mum.*

Even after Gemma quit riding, her mother had continued to go to the stables and ride, driving up every weekend. She'd gone for years, coming back home late on Saturday afternoons with helmet hair and a satisfied, hay-scented air around her.

She had only quit when her fatigue had gotten too bad to manage, just around the time she was diagnosed with cancer.

Gemma went shopping for dinner. Derek was still at work, so she went alone, as she usually did. While she did most of the cooking, they always split the grocery bill squarely in half, because Derek was a feminist and supported women's financial independence.

The supermarket was only a few blocks away, and was exactly like every other food market she had seen in this area: refrigerated, vaguely chemical smell, soft but inescapable whine from the freezers, glacial taste to the air. Stark white lights that rendered time meaningless.

Gemma took her time deciding between Atlantic cod and

Chilean sea bass, and eventually chose the sea bass for its exotic flavor. She could even add some cooking material to her channel, in an organic way, through vlogging or a recipe video. Perhaps once she'd lost some more weight.

Then she reminded herself that appearances weren't what mattered; it was the substance that counted. She pictured herself stirring the fish in a pan over a low flame, smiling beguilingly at the camera. Nobody would care if she had a little extra weight on her frame. She could even try to tie it in with a body acceptance theme.

Gemma got distracted searching for the avocados. They had been here last week, although marked up to a hefty price. But they weren't here today, and in their place were a few sad piles of mealy-looking tomatoes. She hunted around the vegetable section some more before finally accepting defeat and heading to the checkout with her meager basket.

This late, less than ten minutes before closing, she was the only shopper at the registers. The lone, dour-faced cashier rang her items up with mechanical smoothness. Gemma grappled with her courage, and finally, as she slid her card into the reader, gathered up the nerve to ask, "So, did you guys get rid of the avocados?"

The cashier looked up as though she were surprised Gemma could speak. "Yeah, I think so," she said after a pause. "The California avocados, right?"

"Yup. They're not there anymore. Are they... are they going to be restocked?"

"Don't think so. Don't expect me to know why, though. The management here doesn't pay me nearly enough to keep track of these things."

"Oh, right, of course," Gemma said hurriedly, prepared to back away as soon as she got her groceries.

The cashier must have sensed her discomfort, because as she handed her the bag, she added, "Probably all the droughts out west."

Gemma caught sight of the cashier's face again—plum-colored circles under her eyes, sallow skin, all the signs of exhaustion—and felt a wave of sympathy come over her. This woman wasn't much older than she was. She probably worked here for minimum wage, struggling to support herself, maybe even caring for a family. Spending hours staring at the unchanging displays of meat and chocolate and fizzy water, her legs growing stiff under the colorless lights.

"It's okay," Gemma said, trying to impart the sudden warmth and goodwill she was feeling. "Things will get better."

She should know. Things always did eventually get better. Those first few days after her mother's death had been full of a sick, slowly dawning realization, like being asleep and realizing your dream had slurred seamlessly into a nightmare. It had been nightmarish, all of it: the funeral, the service, the deluge of relatives who had poured themselves like liquid into her arms, as though they were the ones who needed comforting. The bright spring day, unseasonably warm for England. All those flowers blooming in a perfect mockery. But after a few months Gemma woke up and no longer felt the same sharp pain. It still hurt, but it was blunted like a burn scar, the nerves deadened and dull from so much damage.

The cashier stared back, uncomprehending. For a moment Gemma wondered if she'd even understood her, but finally she managed a wooden "Uh, thanks."

As Gemma left the store, doubt set in. She'd meant to impart a sense of companionship towards the cashier, the message that no matter how tough things got, things would eventually get better. But she hadn't exactly made this clear. For all the cashier knew she could have been talking about the droughts, which Gemma knew almost nothing about. She'd heard some vague warnings, but most people didn't have time to read all that depressing stuff.

Even if the cashier had somehow grasped her meaning, who did Gemma think she was to say something like that? She'd lost a parent, yes, but she had no experience with the kind of suffering the cashier was experiencing. And who was to say if she was suffering at all. Maybe her face just looked like that. Maybe she really enjoyed her job and thought Gemma was a nutcase.

She breathed through her nose and reminded herself to think positive. But this was made more difficult by what she saw when she got home: a dim apartment, meaning Derek was still at work, and a missed call on her phone.

It was from her father.

Well. It was one in the morning in London, which meant he had been working right up until this point. He had been doing this since her mother was diagnosed: waking up at six, working straight through the day until midnight, getting a few hours of shallow sleep, and doing it all over again. Sometimes he would stop for a week or two, probably to avoid being hospitalized, but inevitably the cycle would continue. He was clearly still doing it. Gemma suspected she might have gone the same way if she had stayed in London. She would be suffocating, trapped in close proximity to actual grief, without the distraction of the imagined grief she indulged herself in when she did her last-day visualizations with Derek.

Gemma unloaded the groceries into the fridge, taking her time, and then called her father back.

"Gemma, dear," he said. His tone was jovial. Too jovial for one a.m. He had probably had a drink or two. "How are you?"

"I'm good. How are you?" She was starkly aware of the forced politeness in her own voice. Anxiety writhed in her chest, right above her stomach.

"Well, good, good. What's going on?"

"I'm not sure. You called me."

"Ah, yes, so I did. I was just running through my list of contacts and realized it's been a while since I spoke to my daughter."

She hadn't bothered to turn any of the lights on. Darkness filled the apartment as she listened to him ramble on about the complexities of teaching economics at one of England's most prestigious universities.

It was hard for her to listen to him without hearing a second voice overlapping his current one like a shadow: his pleas not to leave, his furious denouncement of the American educational system. As that dreadful summer had crept towards autumn and her flight date had approached, he began to grow desperate, his tactics vacillating wildly between entreaties and threats.

Now, every time she spoke to him, she felt twin shivers of guilt and anger. He'd always known that studying in New York was her dream. How dare he make her choose between this and the only family she had left. Shortly before leaving, she'd snapped, "You weren't there for me this entire time." It was the closest she'd ever come to yelling at him. "You were working all the time. When Mum wasn't in the hospital, I had to take care of her all by myself. You never helped. And now you want me to stay for *you*?"

"I couldn't bear to see her like that," he'd protested.

"And I could? I could bear to see my mother like that?"

Now she listened to him rambling on. He was in the midst of telling her a humorous story about a colleague, or a story he thought was humorous—it involved a mix-up of cold medicine and sleeping pills, a biology class, and a gerbil who dreamed of escape—but even as she stared into the gloom of her apartment, listening, she saw his face. His eyes, fathomless and desperate, as he pleaded with her not to leave him as his wife had. He had needed to make it so bloody hard, hadn't he. No seamless transition to college for her, no, nothing she could talk breezily about in a video; it had been one of harsh, tearful fights, stumbling over landmines of guilt and obligation.

"You're doing well?"

"Yeah, Dad, I'm good. Thanks."

"Don't need any care packages?"

"Nah," she said. "I'm good." She realized vaguely that she was on her third *I'm good* of the conversation by now. Unless it was her fourth.

"You're eating enough over there? They're not starving you at that cafeteria, are they?" It was almost obscene, this sudden show of goodwill. He was asking all the right questions, but only now that he had no choice in the matter.

"Nope, but I don't eat there much anyway. I just picked up some sea bass at the store."

"Hmm. Perhaps not the most sustainable choice," he said, and she heard the low sound of him chuckling.

"I don't know. Actually, I have to go start dinner. I'm pretty hungry."

"Awfully late over there for dinner, isn't it? Past eight already?"

"I guess that's the way they do things over here. Bye, Dad."

Gemma hung up in between *Good* and *bye*.

As she waited for Derek to come back—it was quite late by now, but he worked late often, and this wasn't outside the usual parameters—she went back to the video intro she had typed up. The screen glowed bright white like the supermarket lights, arctic and empty.

She highlighted the part about her father and pressed Delete. It was funny, but without it, the intro immediately looked so much more genuine. It was obvious she couldn't fake any enthusiasm about him. And she would simply avoid any detail when it came to her actual journey to New York. Leave out the fact that she had had to go to the bathroom on the plane three times, staring at her trembling lip and pink-rimmed eyes in the mirror, before she could compose herself.

Speak only about the good stuff and only that will be true.

Boil it down enough and even the bones will be gone.

She printed out sixteen copies: one for each student in the class, one for her instructor, and an extra copy for herself.

CHAPTER 13

Janet

It was pathetic. Janet wanted to leave her apartment, but she had nowhere to go and no place to be. Finally, alone, she just took the subway downtown and walked around for a bit. It had been days since she'd taken an actual walk outside, other than runs to the drugstore for more toilet paper or ice cream.

She walked past Washington Square Park and the lounging and/or languishing NYU students who were soaking up the warm sunlight like cats. She passed the picturesque row of houses that made up the college's language department. Among them was a punny little sign saying:

Learn German
if you DER.

Janet didn't der. She dered only to wander over to the bodega and purchase a cheap ginger lemonade that made her throat burn. She hung around, thinking of her response to Ur. She had received another letter from him that morning, and hadn't yet composed a reply.

Hello OLT. (Sometimes I think the word "owl" in my brain when I type that up.)

I think you're right to worry about your sister. She's probably one of those people who bury their heads in the sand—forgive me for assuming, but it does seem that way from your description—and focus on the minutiae of their own lives as a distraction. Like pinching yourself when you've got a broken leg. The smaller pain distracts you, if only for a little while.

But the world hasn't just got a broken leg, has it?

I hope you can be there for your sister when it matters most. When, as you so astutely explained in your last letter, the current crisis reaches the end scene—the triumph, confetti, et cetera—only I think it will be rather the opposite, don't you? Not confetti but ash.

I was never fortunate enough to go to college or attend all those fancy classes, so I must admit I didn't know the origins of the word "ur," but Google stepped in and assisted me just now. They're fascinating, aren't they, the little coincidences that make up our lives? Perhaps OLT too has some alternate meaning and neither of us has grasped it quite yet. Although the meanings of Ur are interesting enough. Thinking of all those ancient generations, lost to time, to history, to memory... only around three percent of human history is recorded (that's another Google for you) and even that small percent holds so much. I wonder what mysteries are lost to us forever. How many stories there are that we can never know.

But they say history repeats itself, don't they? Perhaps there was a man in the Stone Age who had all the genius of Newton, but nothing with which to record his ideas. A cave-painting Leonardo da Vinci. An Iron Age Hitler or Mussolini. Perhaps there was even a Paleolithic copy of you or me, scaled down in size and a great deal hairier. Who knows.

Forgive me, I'm rambling on a bit too much now, as I warned you in my last letter.

I do hope your day is good and not disturbed too much by my rather ambitious missive.

- Ur.

There was something in his letter that had confused her, that clashed with the image of him she had, but she couldn't put her finger on what it was. The more she thought, the more it danced away, like a dust mote disappearing in a beam of sunlight.

Janet spent that evening at her mother and aunt's house. She took a book to read on the train, but found herself unable to focus: every loud noise, every movement of a stranger into her personal bubble, broke her concentration. Finally she closed it and simply stared at the graffitied tunnels going by outside the window.

At least her mother would have some homemade food to eat for dinner. Janet had made pasta for lunch, but her strainer had broken and she hadn't had the energy to go out and buy a new one, so she'd drained her pasta of water by holding it upside-down above the sink and pressing a paper towel to it. It was a subpar job, and when she ate it, the pasta was still far too watery, the fake Parmesan cheese sliding around in little wet lumps.

She got off the subway and walked to her mother's house. The streets of Queens were emptied out, piles of garbage stacked along the sidewalks, a conspicuous absence of trash cans. As the days grew shorter, she knew, the streets would become dirtier, rust blooming on fenders and the sparse plant life wilting in the brittle cold.

At the door, Janet's mother gave her daughter her customary nod and small smile and beckoned her inside. Janet wondered if her mother could smell the evidence of the weed she'd smoked just before leaving: the fecund, piney odor that clung relentlessly to her clothing and hair. Probably not. She hadn't tried very hard to rid herself of the smell, not even bothering to wash her hands or apply perfume afterwards, but it was already overshadowed by the rich scents wafting in from the kitchen: Buldak, Abiko curry, spicy Korean food that she could no longer stomach after too many trips to the American deli on her corner.

"Hi, Janet."

"Hi Mom. It's good to see you." The Korean felt strange on her tongue, though she had learned it as an infant, around the same time she had learned English. She remembered Liam asking with such vigor about her ancestral homeland. Wouldn't he be disappointed.

"How's Izzy?" her mother asked, as though she hadn't spoken to her other daughter herself. Janet knew from her sister that she had more conversations with her mother than Janet herself did. But Janet's mother liked to get a story from every angle, like a skeptical reporter. She'd ask Janet and Izzy how they were doing, and then she'd ask Janet about Izzy, and Izzy about Janet, and finally compare notes.

"She's a little oblivious, but she should be okay," Janet said. Then she remembered that her mother was woefully uninformed. As her aunt emerged from the kitchen, Janet told them about the hurricanes that were striking the coast and the danger for the people who lived there—including Izzy.

Even as she spoke, she felt the importance of her words diminishing. The adjectives she chose to illustrate the direness of the situation came out sounding melodramatic and overwrought. It was the same feeling she'd gotten when she told her mother about her sixth-grade science fair project or the fact that cows killed more people than sharks—the feeling that if she was the one who had to tell her family about something, it couldn't be all that important.

Neither of the women looked too concerned; Janet might have been informing them about dust storms on Mars or the conditions on one of Jupiter's moons. She trailed off in disgust, wishing Ur was here to witness this. He'd probably lose his shit.

Then she wondered how it would be if her and Izzy's places were reversed, and it was Izzy who lived in New York and was trying to inform her family of the danger Janet was in. They would probably react the same way in the end. There would be added credibility due to it being Izzy's opinion, of course, but that would be balanced out by the fact that it was only Janet in danger. Not Izzy.

When her mother left the room, Janet finally cracked her knuckles; the urge to do so had been building for long minutes now. They popped like dry firewood. Funny how she never wanted to do this when she was alone, but when she was around her mother, who hated it so much, the urge became almost irresistible.

They ate dinner as the sun began to go down. Janet filled up a glass with milk, pilfered from the back of the fridge and nearly expired, so that she could handle the spice better. Her aunt didn't miss this; she gave her a glance like, *Really?* Janet thought: Yes, really.

Her mother and aunt spoke about several things during the meal, and Janet contributed to the conversation, but after a few minutes found that she couldn't name one thing they'd been talking about. Maybe there was something in the milk. Maybe her mother had finally decided to get rid of her least favorite daughter. Janet started to laugh at the thought and then choked on her rice. Her mother and aunt stared at her in horror as she coughed up a few wet grains. "I'm okay," she managed, and this made her laugh even more. She wiped the rice grains on the edge of her plate, where they lay, moist and plump, like larvae.

After dinner, the three of them went up to the roof—concrete floor, dirty tarp, rickety beach chairs—and drank glasses of cheap Chardonnay. The wine was as dry and ashy-tasting as the burnt sky looked. As Janet sipped it, her mother and aunt traded intense, breathless gossip about two family friends who had run off with each other. Janet attempted to follow, but something about the wine was slowing her thoughts.

She thought that maybe her mother and aunt were drinking a bit too much lately. Every time she visited, the two women had a fresh bottle of wine to open. There were also the endless bottles of liquor stacked all the way to the back of the cabinet, like some alcoholic Narnia. Although it could be worse. They could be doing meth, like XS9284115. Janet stifled a yawn and tuned back into the conversation. Now they were talking about another woman, a distant relative who had died in childbirth, and they kept saying how sad it was, but there was something grimly satisfied about their faces.

Janet closed her eyes.

A memory came back to her: another dinner, this one from nine or ten years ago. The four of them—herself, her sister and her parents—had been eating some hot, delicious meal. Her father was still alive then, sitting at the head of the table, tight-jawed and remote, sullen gray bags under his eyes. Her mother, dark hair sleek and foxlike around her face, had been unaccountably irate that evening. She snapped at Janet three times for eating her food too fast, but when Janet protested that Izzy was devouring her meal even more quickly, her mother rolled her eyes and ignored her. Janet glanced at her father for backup, but he was intensely focused on his own food, chewing slowly as if to reprimand Janet for her greed.

"Izzy ate more than I did," Janet muttered again, and her mother told her to shut the hell up. In Korean, of course.

Izzy smirked at her across the table and mouthed what might have been "fatty."

Janet *was* chubbier than her sister, she knew, her face rounder and puffier. Puberty was not being kind to her. The heavy hand of shame pressed down on her shoulders. She felt like she was filling slowly with hot water. Her cheeks scorched; her forehead bubbled with sweat.

After dinner she went to the bathroom and tried to throw up, jamming her hand clumsily down her throat. It was her first and last attempt at doing this, and ended in miserable failure. Her only result: a few strings of saliva, burning eyes, the phantom taste of acid and a face covered in drool.

"Are you okay?" someone asked.

Janet jolted back to the present. That was bizarre: without her eyes open, she couldn't tell whether it was her mother speaking or her aunt.

Maybe they couldn't tell who she was, either. Maybe they had mistaken her for Izzy and that's why they were so concerned. At least someone was wanted around here. Shame she was all the way in Florida.

Janet smiled, her eyes still closed. "For now, I'm just fine. Please, go on. What happened with Miho?" Wouldn't want to miss a single detail. She could practically see the pleasure settling back onto her relatives' faces as they returned to the conversation.

CHAPTER 14

Anna

Warren's good mood held up throughout the rest of the week. Usually he and Anna saw each other between two and three times per week, but this week it was four. On Thursday night, knowing she couldn't put it off any longer, Anna selected a bag that she thought she could resell fairly easily. Adding a sassy emoji, she sent the link to Warren. Hopefully this would be it for the bags.

She put her head back and sighed; she felt like she'd just sacrificed a week's allowance. Which she basically had. The bags weren't even that expensive. If she didn't know better, she'd think Warren was trying to cheap out on her. Then again, he kept talking about a new business deal, so he should have more money if anything.

Days passed. The clothes at the store where Anna worked grew cheaper and uglier: stretchy neon dresses, polyester sweaters with sarcastic slogans like THANKS FOR NOTHING and PRINCESS BUT ONLY ON THE INTERNET. The cheaper and uglier they got, the more Anna labored over them, folding them with fastidious precision and arranging them at perfect, mathematical angles. Sometimes she would touch a pilling sleeve as she passed by, or brush her fingers over the hem of a pair of acid-wash jeans, as though in reverence. Her manager started to give her odd looks.

The weather grew colder. Warren's mood grew colder as well. He began to seem not to hear her when she spoke, and she would have to repeat herself if she asked him a question. Sometimes she didn't bother to repeat herself—it felt too nagging, too weak—and her words would drop like stones to the floor between them. What's happening? she thought. Her thoughts swarmed and wheeled frantically.

Despite his low mood, Warren did not stop taking Anna out. He brought her to more rooftops, heated this time, handed her drinks that tasted like the color pink: fresh, fruity, sparkling with alcohol. The layer of crushed ice on top reminded her of the frozen coating on a pathway of snow, crackling beneath boots in midwinter, illuminated by faraway lights.

She felt sadness expand inside her, rising in her chest, in her throat. Taking up the space in her lungs, making it hard to breathe. She thought: I miss snow.

On Sunday, the two of them were lying on the couch in Warren's apartment. He had been quiet throughout their meeting and had only come to life when they were fucking. Now, afterwards, he had returned to quietude. So it was a surprise when he said abruptly, "Doll, have you thought of any other presents you want?"

Anna's insides stiffened. The bag had arrived in the mail a few days ago, its seams looking less expertly sewn than she would have liked, and she had put it up online the very next day. So far she hadn't received any offers on it. She had brought it today, in a gesture even she thought might be a little too pointed. The material was rough under her fingertips, like the desiccated skin of an orange.

"You mean... instead of an allowance?" she asked, as lightly as possible.

His face didn't change. "Well. Perhaps. Is that a problem? Honestly, I noticed that you've been lacking in the style department lately." He looked her outfit up and down. "No jewelry? Maybe we need to get on that next."

Anna's eyebrows shot up. He didn't usually criticize her like this. "If you want to buy me jewelry in *addition* to allowances, I wouldn't say no."

"Ah. Now I feel you're just taking advantage of me."

This *taking advantage* again. His words were so unfair that Anna had to struggle not to let her anger show on her face. "Warren," she finally said, as calmly as she could, "we agreed to weekly allowances when we started seeing each other. I didn't expect that to change."

"Anna, do you have to do this?"

"What?"

"Refer to our relationship as some kind of... *arrangement,*" he said sadly.

"It is an arrangement."

In the new silence Anna heard faint, distant music, perhaps coming from the next apartment, percussive and vague like something out of a dream.

Eventually he said, "Is that what you told Yohann?"

"What?"

"I've been introducing you to people as my girlfriend. At the party, you remember. I didn't tell people we had an arrangement. Just—to hear you speak about it like some kind of cold system, I don't know. It's a bit of a shock and to be completely honest, it doesn't feel good."

Anna felt a deep, tidal pull of guilt. She knew it was ridiculous, but she felt it anyway.

"It's okay. If you want to get me jewelry this week instead of an allowance, I'll... well... I'll allow it." She gave him a dazzling smile. His face lightened at her words and he moved closer to her on the couch. "And to answer your question," she continued, "no, I didn't tell Yohann about our arrangement. I sort of danced around the question as much as I could, actually. I said we met online. I was very uncomfortable. I felt like he was interrogating me."

"He was," he said. His face fell and for a moment he looked much more than twice Anna's age. "I'm a little worried he guessed the truth anyway. Not that that would matter, but he's not too fond of me, I guess. Thinks his father's making a mistake by going into business with me. He's a little too spoiled, if you ask me. It's not that there's anything to be ashamed of with us, you know—but he'd use anything he could against me. Maybe he wasn't hugged enough as a child." He chuckled, his old light-hearted demeanor surfacing for a moment. Anna realized that she had actually missed it.

"So why did you have me sit next to him?"

"You're pretty well-spoken, dolly. I'm always impressed by how you can talk to people, and I know they don't all expect girls like you to have been speaking two languages since you were six years old. I thought you might win him over, so to speak." He made a face. "But he's something of a tough customer. I probably shouldn't have put you by him. It's all right, though. Don't think too much about it—I'm pretty sure even the most charming guest would've been overwhelmed by him."

She thought again of her conversation with Dasha. *What does love have to do with it?*

She also realized that she could no longer picture her ex-boyfriend's face. Except in her dreams, but then his face was out of focus, grainy and pixelated like a photo that wouldn't load. Sometimes she tried to picture it manually, loading parts of the photo one by one—there was the bubblegum-pink scar on his chin, the full-lipped smile, the green eyes—but as soon as one part stabilized, the others slid out of focus. Slipping out of sight under a black water.

Warren held another party, this time on his roof. It had a heated deck, and the drinks he had catered were heated, too: spiked hot chocolate, warm buttered rum. Anna wore a dress he had bought her months ago, a silver wraparound that was cozier than it looked.

There were fewer guests at this party, and fewer caterers; Anna didn't see the waiter she had noticed at the last one. This was probably for the best. Yohann wasn't here, either, which surely had not been some oversight.

But Anna knew she wasn't imagining some of the glances people were giving her. A woman passed her and shot her a look of derision as sour as a splash of acid. Maybe Yohann had been talking about her—although he probably had more important things to do than tell everyone that Warren had a sugar baby. Arrangements like theirs weren't even that rare. But she felt observed, and not in a good way. She sipped her buttered rum and made awkward, halting attempts at conversation with a woman who looked to be around her own age but was positively dripping with precious metals. Rings and bracelets and earrings hung from her body and seemed to suck up all the light in the atmosphere, rather than reflecting it. She had a Southern accent and a pampered, well-fed look that was at odds with sleek New York glamour.

"I'm studying ecology," the woman said, and named a prestigious university in a nearby city. There was a spattering of freckles across not just her nose and cheeks but her forehead and chin as well, like someone had flung a handful of sand at her.

"Ecology. That's fascinating."

"It's not that fascinating. But at least I didn't go into environmental sciences. Apparently..." She leaned in close, as though she were about to impart a juicy secret. "Ap*par*ently there's going to be some sort of protest this weekend. Something to do with climate change and saving the rainforests, et cetera."

Anna took a cool, impartial sip of her drink. "Don't you think that's important?"

"Of course! But you know half the people in attendance aren't doing it for the right reasons. They just want a selfie to post on Instagram, or even if they don't take any pictures, they're just doing it to *feel* like they're doing something good for once. Then they can check it off their lists along with petition-signing and recycling and only then can they sleep soundly in their beds." She rolled her eyes. "They don't put their hearts into it."

"That's sad," Anna said. She wondered if this was in fact true, or just something the woman told herself so she could feel better about not doing anything. To clarify, she asked, "Are you going?"

"No. What would be the point?"

Sensing that the conversation was spiraling, Anna said, "What are you going to do with your degree?"

"Do with it?" She looked surprised. "Well, nothing. Do I look like I want to go digging around in parks with dirt up to my thighs?" She gave a throaty laugh. Anna realized this woman was probably one of those people who didn't give a damn what happened to the natural world as long as they could continue living in their apartments, with their screens and entertainment and endless feedback loops.

"It would certainly mess up those gorgeous boots," Anna said, nodding at the woman's white stiletto heels. She couldn't stop herself from adding, "But I'm wondering, why get a degree if you don't want to use it?"

The woman was silent. "I'm pretty sure half the people at this party have at least a master's degree," she said eventually. "Oh, that's damn rude of me, I haven't even asked—what did you study?"

"Nothing," Anna said blithely. "I didn't go to college." She felt a flash of pleasure at the surprise that washed over the woman's face.

As the woman unpeeled herself from the conversation and Warren came over, Anna's sense of victory cooled, and she realized how stupid her comment had been. If Warren had been listening, he wouldn't think she was good at talking to people. No, definitely not.

"How do you like the necklace?" Warren asked, referring to the sautoir he had given her earlier that week. She was, of course, wearing it around her neck right now.

"It's wonderful," she said. It was a lie, at least partially. It wasn't her style and the metal wasn't as heavy as she had expected. She hadn't put it up for sale yet, but hopefully she could get something for it. She had no way to know exactly how much it had cost, but the lightness of the material in particular had given her a sinking feeling in her stomach.

"I'm glad," he said. "It brings out your eyes."

"Thank you. You know, a boy once told me, 'I love your beautiful gray eyes.'" She snorted. "And I responded, 'My eyes are blue.' That was very awkward. I mean, he was looking right at me."

"What idiot was this? Should I take care of him for you?" Warren arched an eyebrow, playing the aging but still dangerous Mafioso. "Some young Russian fool?" Beyond him the city glimmered like a sea of dying fireflies.

"Pretty much. He was fifteen, rough-cheeked with acne. Sometimes I tell myself he was color blind—when I'm in a generous mood—but I don't think so. Maybe his eyes were messed up from playing too many computer games. I suppose there isn't too much else to do over there." The sassy tone of her voice was feeling more natural every time she used it. And she could tell Warren liked it. As she spoke, the life that had seemed to be leaching out of his face returned. Having this effect on someone, even someone she wasn't actually attracted to, warmed her in the same way the hot rum did.

"Your eyes were one of the first things I noticed about you, you know, dolly? Blue like crystal. Or water, real clean water, without pollution in it. Hard to get water like that nowadays. I'm not really sure how he could have mistaken blue for gray, to tell you the truth."

The burble of other peoples' conversations washed around them like waves on a beach. Anna remembered a childhood trip to the ocean: the cries of wheeling gulls, the sea and its slow language.

People spoke about money and fame as though those two things were everything they wanted. They so vehemently made them the frontispiece of their lives. Forget love, they said. *Fuck* love. But if they were to stop and think about it, money and fame were still connected to love—it was just that they represented perceived love, not actual love. They were a pale substitution.

Looking at Warren, she thought: Is this the closest I can come to love? At that moment, she knew that it was, and the knot of anxiety in her stomach loosened. Giving up, after all this time. It felt like an exhale.

The door to the roof banged open. Two cops scanned the roof and then advanced across the floor in Anna's direction. Voices crackled from their walkie-talkies; guns hung heavy on their hips. Someone actually screamed.

Anna's thoughts splintered like glass. Realization loomed in her mind, nightmarish, immense: *They're here to arrest me for prostitution.*

But the cops didn't even glance at her. They descended on Warren like carrion birds, handcuffing him, the metal glinting in the light coming from the nearby heater. One of them said, his voice clipped and unemotional, "Warren Gohrmansen, you're under arrest for fraud."

Anna felt her mouth fall open. She tried to say something, to ask him what was going on, but the words didn't even make it to her lips. The cop continued, his voice rehearsed and robotic and unreal: "You have the right to remain silent and refuse to answer questions. Anything you say may be used against you in a court of law."

"What the hell?" someone said, striding into their circle of light. It was the silver-haired man who had been sitting on Warren's right during the dinner party. His face was alight with indignation as he confronted the cop. "Who do you think you are?"

The cop didn't even look at him. He continued speaking to Warren. "You have the right to consult an attorney before speaking to the police and to have an attorney present during questioning now or in the future."

"Holy *holy* shit," someone said from behind Anna. They sounded gleeful. Someone else was sobbing, caught up in the drama.

"Excuse me?" The silver-haired man's voice climbed an octave, skipping up unsteadily. "Can somebody tell me what's happening?"

"James," someone hissed, and Anna saw a middle-aged woman with black hair and thick, stiff-looking lips—the woman who had been on Warren's other side at the dinner party—pulling him away.

"Warren?" Anna finally said. "What's going on?"

He didn't respond. Didn't even look at her as they took him away. He had turned his face away from her, and in his slumped posture and hunched shoulders, she was reminded of old engravings: a man kneeling in stocks, a prisoner on the way to the executioner.

CHAPTER 15

Gemma

Gemma and Derek hadn't been sleeping in the same bed lately. It wasn't a habit, or anything—it had only been going on for the past few days. It was because Derek felt constricted in the bed, unable to stretch his long legs out as far as he would like. So he had been sleeping on the couch.

It was a big couch, and soft, and Gemma hoped he was comfortable there, but she felt strange lying alone in that bed. Without the shape of him next to her, it felt too large and flat and empty. Like a desert. She'd wake in the middle of the night and see moonlight spilling across the vacated side of his bed. Then she would realize that it wasn't moonlight, just streetlights from outside. But he'd assured her it wasn't anything personal. He simply wanted some more space.

Late on Monday night, as they were in between episodes of Love Island, she asked him, "Is everything okay?"

"Yeah, sure. Why wouldn't it be?" He didn't even turn his head.

But things had felt different lately. She had begun to suspect that picturing it being their last day together, that a fatal accident awaited one of them in the near future—screaming metal of a train, dripping maws of a truck—was actually bringing this fate closer to them and inviting bad luck to their door. She decided to stop. Whether it was their last night together or their three-thousandth-to-last night together, she would try to appreciate it equally. After all, she shouldn't have to pretend that one of them was about to die in order to enjoy their time together.

But it was hard to enjoy time together when they sat so far apart at dinner, when he watched his sports games with his earpods cutting him off from her. At one point that same night, he asked her how her video was coming. She blushed and told him she wouldn't be filming anything until she got her intro back from her creative writing class. He nodded, as though this was precisely what he had expected, and turned back to his game.

She felt twin prickles of anger and shame; how could she be mad at him for not expressing interest in her life when there was nothing for him to express interest in? Next time he asked, she would have an answer to give him. Tomorrow, actually. Tomorrow was Tuesday, and since Gemma had handed in her intro on Thursday, she would be getting it back the next day. The class met twice a week and Thursday was submission day. Tuesday was feedback day.

But the anger stayed present all night, despite her attempts to push it down. It built every time she noticed Derek was still on his phone, still had his earpods in and was clearly unwilling to interact with her. Since she wasn't picturing tonight as their last night together, or next-to-last-night, or anything of that sort, she was forced to face the evening as exactly what it was: one featureless night in a long, long series of similar ones. They had already passed the point where they were excited by one another, Derek in particular. Now their relationship was embarking on its final phase: a gradual winding-down towards complacency and eventually death. This phase would take up the majority of their relationship, the way the majority of a person's life was spent dying, beginning at age twenty-five, when the number of dying cells overtook that of new cells being formed, and ending at eighty or ninety. Or fifty-five.

Some couples tried to keep their relationships alive by going on adventurous trips together, or even inviting other people into their arrangements. In this case, though, it was Gemma, not Derek, who was the one trying to keep their relationship alive. And he didn't seem to care at all.

The next day, she walked downtown to her creative writing class. Her Starbucks was cold by the time she got to the room. She was one of the first people there. Her professor Hélène, a tiny French woman, gave her a smile as she walked in. Gemma's stomach did a little flip. Slowly, slowly, people began to file in. Gemma's toes fidgeted inside her shoes.

Finally, at five after, everyone had arrived. They always started class a bit late, and Hélène, who had begun the semester by saying that she *expec*ted punctu*al*ity, had by now mastered a gently resigned expression. "We'll start with Jessica's piece," she said. "Who wants to go first?"

Gemma knew they did these in alphabetical order, and since she had the last name Taylor, she would be next-to-last of the four people being workshopped today. But she couldn't conceal her excitement as she waited for the class to dissect the pieces by Jessica and Harry. She spoke only once, as it was difficult for her to concentrate on anything beyond what the reception of her piece would be. Whether they would notice the metaphors she had used to describe her life with her mother. Whether they would say that her tone was too basic, or enjoy the pared-down aspect of it.

She only half-listened as Peter, the bookish, bespectacled star of the class, dissected Harry's story. He pointed out the inconsistencies in narrative voice and gratuitous use of adverbs. Then he added how fabulous Harry's characterization was, how the people in his story really jumped off the page. That was Peter's thing; he always found something good to say about your piece. By the end of his comments, Harry's stricken expression had changed to one of cautious pride.

"Shall we do Gemma's story next?" Hélène said. She phrased

it so gently, like it was a suggestion, even though of course it was not.

A rustling of paper filled the room as everyone searched their bags for Gemma's story. Gemma fished her print-out from her bag, where it had been lying ready for half an hour, and put it face-up on her desk. She was intensely aware of the focus of the class turning to her, and each one of her movements—crossing her legs, brushing her hand through her hair—was bloated with self-consciousness, as though she were moving her limbs not through air but through thick mud.

"Peter? Want to go first?" Hélène said, as Peter raised his hand. Gemma's stomach lurched with anticipation: Peter had a calm and open expression, as though he knew exactly what he wanted to say. She had seen this look on his face right before he delivered a piece of particularly astute, pointed praise.

Peter cleared his throat and said, "Well, I didn't really... get it." He gave an apologetic chuckle to the room. "Maybe it was just me? And Gemma can definitely answer this when we give her the floor, to, you know, help clear stuff up, but I'm confused at what this is supposed to be about. I mean, we have a lot of description and a clear chronological structure. But there's something lacking about it. I feel that there isn't enough substance, somehow."

Hélène nodded wisely, and spotted another raised hand. "Go ahead, Annabelle."

"Yeah..." Annabelle chimed in. She had actually put her phone down to contribute, which was rare for her. "I mean, it was kind of clear what happens in the story? But what was the point of it? It was kind of. Pointless? No offense."

Gemma forced herself to keep a neutral expression on her face. Her throat felt like someone was squeezing it.

"Paula?" Hélène prompted.

"Well, okay. I had a lot of questions about this piece," Paula said. She avoided Gemma's gaze as she continued, "Why does the narrator focus so much on what's been happening to her in her life as opposed to how she *feels* about it, and how it's impacted her? She seems to be a little lacking in self-awareness. Do you think she focuses so much on the small events within her life as a way to distract herself from the effects they've had on her?"

"Interesting idea," Hélène mused. She told Eun Jung to go. Eun Jung launched into an interrogation about Gemma's use of articles and adjectives.

"Michael?"

"Sunita?"

"Rachel?"

Everyone seemed to have something negative to say. As the class spoke, Gemma stared at the front page of her piece. Not really knowing what she was doing, she took her pen, as though she were about to begin writing something down. It didn't matter what. She just needed to look like she was writing, like she was doing anything other than sitting there and trying not to cry. She scribbled down a few things Peter had said and then added carefully, in very small, cramped print so that the people next to her couldn't read it: *I am a stupid little poo.*

Hélène wasn't even calling on people anymore. They were just throwing out their opinions left and right. They were so eager, far more eager than they had been to speak about any of the other pieces before hers. Now that they had scented blood, they descended on Gemma, flocking, buzzards around a carcass. None of them would look at her.

"All right," Hélène eventually said. "I think it's time to give the floor to Gemma, what do we think? Unless anyone has anything *extremely* pressing to add?"

Peter looked like he was about to raise his hand, but then lowered it, looking sheepish. He was a little blurry, though, so it was hard for Gemma to tell. She blinked rapidly.

"Gemma?" Hélène prompted. "Anything you want to share with the class? Feel free to respond to any of the questions we've raised and address any confusion that has cropped up. And if you have any questions you want to ask *us* about the piece, anything we haven't touched on that you'd like feedback on, please go ahead."

Gemma was grateful that Hélène spoke as long as she did. It gave her time to swallow and blink a few more times. She crossed and uncrossed her legs, trying to give the impression that she would start speaking any moment now. Her stomach felt black and sour.

"Thanks for your feedback, everyone," she said eventually. "Um... so..." She looked down at the margin of her paper. She'd scribbled down a few notes based on things people had said —*confusing, lacking cohesion, point???*. Seeing those bleak words next to the sentences she had worked so hard on made her throat feel tight.

"Um. To address the confusion," she finally said. "Some people said that it seemed pointless? I guess the narrator is just... just talking about her life. And, well, she's addressing it in a vaguely chronological way. Because, I guess, I didn't want to confuse the narrative with any of that cool time, um, time-mixing stuff. Like Eric did in his piece last week for example. So, that part is pretty simple. And, well, the adjectives—I guess I kind of overdid it, but I like using adjectives because they help describe things, and when I'm writing I kind of like to paint a picture in my head? To, like, describe things to myself, and not just to the reader? I guess I went a bit overboard though, um. And..."

She couldn't stop talking. She went around and around in frantic circles. It was excruciating. The air around her had thickened, grown warm and humid; she was sweating even in her T-shirt. There was a shrill buzzing in her ears. She wasn't even sure if what she was speaking was English anymore.

Finally she ran out of steam and sputtered to a stop, like a mechanical toy winding down. Even though she hadn't looked up from her page once, she could feel the stares of the class. Her face was bloated with blood, boiling, incandescent.

"Well. Do we have any more questions for Gemma?" Hélène asked the class. Mercifully, they did not.

"Thank you for sharing," she said. Gemma nodded, staring at the letter *e* in one of the words on the page. The silence was suffocating, terrible. As soon as Hélène introduced the last piece of the day, Rachel's, Gemma stood up and went to the loo. She started to cry before the classroom door had even closed behind her.

She stayed in the loo for the rest of the period. The floor was sticky and it smelled like pee but at least she was alone. She stood at the sinks, ducking into a stall every time she heard someone approaching, where she continued to stand, not wanting to sit on the toilet. Her plan was to time it so that she would come in at the end of class, just in time to grab her things, and she would be lost in the movement and shuffling of everyone gathering their stuff to leave.

Instead, however, she found herself walking towards the classroom just a minute too late. Or a minute too early—if she had waited another sixty seconds, everyone would have been gone. But she arrived at the precise moment everyone was filing out of the door, so that she had to stand in the hallway, red-faced, to allow the flow of people to exit before she could enter. Everyone passing got a good look at her red-rimmed eyes and splotchy cheeks. Hélène's face was the worst, the awareness and sharp pity in it.

On Gemma's desk were the fourteen copies her classmates had scribbled their feedback on, all of them marked with so many underlines and notes and corrections that she could barely see what she had originally written.

As soon as Gemma got home, she tossed her bag into the corner of her room. She didn't feel up to looking through her classmates' revisions yet. She wasn't sure if she ever would. She felt like her torso had been replaced with a hole, a cavern opening behind her sternum and sucking her lungs into its emptiness. It was a feeling she hadn't had for quite a while.

She should have told them it was a video intro. That was something they'd all gotten wrong. But, bloody hell—she'd thought it was obvious! With everyone else's non-story pieces, it had been immediately clear what they were supposed to be. And after the first few rounds of criticism, the idea of admitting that these weren't just the thoughts of a first-person narrator, but her own thoughts, was excruciating. Her classmates' visible contempt for the narrator—well. How would it have been to tell them that this was actually supposed to be *her*?

One of them, Rachel, had come pretty close to the truth. "You're also British, so it makes sense that your narrator would be too," she'd said. "I do the same thing; I always tend to set my stories in Chicago." She shared a quick, knowing glance with Hélène. "But does it really matter to the reader that she grew up there? Maybe you should shake it up a bit, set it in Texas or Alaska or something. Even another country. Because right now everything that happens is extremely pedestrian."

Pedestrian, pointless, pathetic, Gemma thought. Got it. In the hours before Derek got home, she watched TikToks about cats and puppies. Her eyes were heavy in their sockets. Her mind felt glazed, glassy. Every time an influencer video came up on her screen she clicked the little *X: Do not show me this.*

Derek got home well after eight. He made himself a bowl of leftovers and sat at the table reading something on his phone. The single light shone down from above him, framing him in a neat circle, like a museum spotlight.

Gemma walked into the room, willing him to greet her. To her relief, he did, with a distracted but sweet smile. Of course he wasn't going to totally ignore her. That would be ridiculous.

"Hey. How was your day?" she asked.

"Good, good. Did some pretty cool work for a new client, so that was nice. What about your day? Did you get up to anything interesting in school? Go to a bake sale? Join a cult?" He tapped a finger on the side of his nose and grinned. His expression was toothy, goofy, and she felt a warm familiarity spread through her.

"None of that, unfortunately," she told him. "I finally got feedback on the intro for my first video."

"Right!" He snapped his fingers and pointed at her. "How did that go?"

"Awful." She grimaced and took a seat across the table from him. "Pretty much no one had anything good to say. They were all telling me how pointless and bland it was."

"Oh no."

"And when it was my turn to talk about it and ask questions and respond to people, it was even worse. I totally lost track of what I was saying. I think might've I blacked out at one point." She forced a laugh.

His gaze fell to his phone. The screen had just lit up, and illuminated from below, his face looked thinner and harsher.

"Derek?"

"I'm listening," he said, looking back at her. But something in his expression had changed, and she felt a desperate lurch in her stomach. Please, she thought. All I want is your support. Please give me this.

"Why can't you engage with me a little more?" she asked, trying to keep her tone casual. "You don't really seem like you're listening."

"Ah," he said, grimacing. "Maybe now isn't the best time?"

"Best time for what? You aren't breaking up with me?" She forced another laugh, but it didn't sound like a laugh anymore. "Come on, what's up? Don't act so grim. God knows I've had enough of that today."

His expression was serious. "No, of course not. Why would I break up with you? You're so soft, so sweet." He reached a hand out to her across the table, and then abruptly retracted it, as though there were something inappropriate about the gesture. "No, I was just thinking about some things recently. They were... ah... it's whatever. Not important."

She swallowed. "Can you please tell me?" Her voice was as thin as a spiderweb. She could tell from his hesitation that it was important. Because if it wasn't important he would just spit it out already.

"Okay." But he was silent.

"Please tell me."

"I was thinking about opening up our relationship." He glanced down at his phone again, although the screen remained dark. "I've been thinking about it for a while, actually, but haven't really had the opportunity to bring it up until now."

"What the hell are you talking about?" Gemma managed.

She never swore. "What do you mean, you haven't had the opportunity?"

"I've just—been busy. Things got in the way."

"Why do you think today is such a great opportunity?" She looked around, incredulous. "Because it's been such a hideous day for me, and you wanted to make it even worse?"

Then her gaze, too, landed on his phone, and realization thudded through her. "Wait, what's different about today? Did some girl just text you?"

She could tell from the paleness of his face that she was right.

"Look," he said unsteadily, "I don't believe in couples keeping secrets from each other. So yes, I had to tell you today. Gemma, I'm not a cheater. I'm not a bad guy. I believe in women's right to independence, and sexual liberation, and..."

Gemma interrupted him before he could launch into a spiel about a woman's right to choose. "Did you cheat on me?"

"No!" He looked shocked. "I would never."

Finally she got it. "So what you're saying is... you're not a cheater. But you will cheat if I don't let you, right?"

He didn't say anything, but he looked more uncomfortable than ever. A siren wailed by outside. Gemma felt it as though it were tearing through her body.

"I'm a young guy, Gemma, not that much older than you. We've been together for a while, not long but, you know, a while, and I haven't really had a chance to. How do you put it? To sow my wild oats."

Ironically, she had been thinking of this just the other day—those couples who were trying to breathe life back into their relationship by opening up thirty-year marriages and taking up with other partners. If only Derek were suggesting this for the same reason. But he wasn't. She could tell from the hesitation and discomfort in his voice that the idea of strengthening their relationship, whether it was misguided or not, was the last thing on his mind.

"But... I haven't either," she said. "I was a virgin when I met you, remember?"

"Yeah, well. It's different for guys, Gemma. I'm still young. I don't know if I want to be with only one girl all my life. And we already live together, so it's pretty serious. It was serious from the beginning. I didn't see anyone the whole time I was talking to you over the summer," he added. "Not one girl."

She had never asked him about that. She felt a momentary stutter of happiness at this disclosure, but then, of course, it vanished. "I still don't get it," she said slowly. "How is this going to work? I go out and, what, see lots of guys, and you see girls? So we're just friends now or what? I don't know, Derek, it feels an awful lot like you *are* breaking up with me." Her voice wobbled.

"Actually... I was thinking it would be open for me, mainly."

"What?" Surely she had heard wrong.

"It's different for guys," he repeated defensively. "I'm not sure I can keep living with you if I know you're sleeping with lots of men, you know? It's a male thing. We don't like it when women sleep around. And it's only natural for men to want to be a little wilder than women. If you look at the biology behind it, it makes perfect sense."

"The biology?"

"Yeah. Not to be crude, but... a man can impregnate many women at the same time. Well, not *literally* the same time..." He laughed. It was the most uncomfortable laugh Gemma had ever heard. "But around the same time. On the other hand, a woman can only carry one man's baby at once. It wouldn't make sense for her to sleep with a bunch of guys around the same time. Scientifically speaking, promiscuity makes more sense for men than for women. Not that," he added hastily, realizing that he had gone a bit too far, "not that I'm talking about being promiscuous. Not at all, for sure. I just think it would be healthier for our relationship if I had the option... just the option, you understand... to, well, see other people sometimes. Occasionally."

"That's unfair," she said finally. She knew what he was saying had a gleam of sense to it, but it didn't fit in at all with what he was saying about their relationship. In fact, it seemed completely irrelevant. They were a couple in the twenty-first century, cohabiting and in love. They weren't a bunch of apes tearing through the jungle, having wild sex with everyone. And she was pretty sure that the females of some species did "sleep around" a lot, so that the males of the species didn't murder babies who might be their own—chimpanzees came to mind—but she doubted that Derek would believe her. And he would probably say something about the barbarity of murdering babies, completely missing the point. Or pretending to miss it.

"You don't have to agree," he added, with an expression that made it clear he thought he was being very generous by offering her this option.

So why don't you just break up with me? she thought.

Well. That was obvious, wasn't it.

Gemma went to bed shortly after this conversation. They didn't say another word to each other, and for the first time she was glad he was sleeping on the couch. She was paying half the rent, and she did most of the cooking; she could have the bloody bed to herself.

She lay awake in the darkness for a long time. Derek's words kept running through her mind, fluttering around in her brain with slick oily wings, like a half-drowned moth.

She felt sick. She tried to think about something else, but then her brain settled on the next available thing—the feedback for her intro, that humiliating classroom—and when she pushed her brain away from *that*, it went to her mother. By the time she had distracted herself from thoughts of this, her brain settled on Derek again.

They weren't in love. They never had been. At least Derek wasn't. He was too preoccupied with work and sports and polyamory and impregnation and whoever had been texting him last night.

When you didn't sleep, you got extremely hungry. This was something Gemma was re-discovering for the first time in several months. She went to the kitchen three times that night, creeping softly past Derek, to scoop grated cheese into her mouth. It was expensive Parmigiano Reggiano, aged for 24 months, but it tasted like wood shavings and dust.

Dawn came. She hadn't slept. Light filled the room slowly, weak and cold, pale as a wash of expired milk. She didn't go to class that day. When she finally fell asleep around late morning, her dreams were violent and repetitive: rusty metal scraping against skin, a bird beating its body ceaselessly against a window.

CHAPTER 16

Janet

Over the last few days, Janet and Ur had been writing back and forth regularly. He would send her a new grievance letter every morning, and she would respond to him in the afternoon or evening. Much of her time was taken up by thinking of what she would say in her replies. This waiting period was like having a conversation throughout the day and being able to re-do it over and over again, as many times as she wanted. Even when Janet felt she had no one, she still had Ur in her head, ready to receive the latest iteration of her reply. Only when she put it down on her computer did it become real, but that made the imagined version no less satisfying.

And in real life, she did have practically no one. Miranda left for Philly on Wednesday. Janet had texted her friend, *Have a safe trip!! XO* the day before, but didn't suggest that they meet again before she left. Unsurprisingly, she didn't receive a reply.

Wednesday passed with leaden slowness. There were no messages from Ur when she logged in in the morning, and still none when she logged out at the end of the workday. She frowned at the screen, worrying her lip with her teeth. Had he gotten bored? Luckily, Janet had still received the typical grievance letters featuring yeast infections, colicky babies, and odd-smelling earwax.

Eventually, once the frames on the wall no longer reflected the sunlight but instead glowed silver in the streetlamps, Janet decided to have a drink. Alone in the kitchen, she poured herself a glass of Scotch. She'd been storing it under her kitchen sink for nearly a year, but Scotch kept well (unlike Janet). She took small, measured sips, listening to the crack and hiss of the ice. The alcohol burned her lips and throat and stomach.

With the glass by her side, she lay on her bed and watched a few episodes of an old TV show. Same old shit, same tired lines, she could watch it with both her eyes and ears closed and still follow along perfectly. Eventually she checked her work email. She did so absently, not really expecting to see anything.

There was a new message from Ur. She recognized it from the very first line: *Hi again Owl. I was...*

She sat up, sending her glass flying.

"Shit!" A stain was now spreading rapidly across the bed. She threw the wet cover to the side, stripped the bed, and clicked on the email. She'd clean up the mess later.

Ur's letter was shorter than usual, but he addressed several of the points she'd made in her last message, especially those about her parents. He sympathized with her situation, adding, *Mine don't live in Queens but two boroughs away, in Staten Island.*

Janet frowned at the words, confused. *Two boroughs away?* But Brooklyn, where Ur lived, was right next to Staten Island. Wasn't it? She tried to picture the map of the boroughs inside her head, but the pieces of land kept disconnecting and swirling away from each other.

Then again, maybe he meant two boroughs away from Queens, where her parents lived. It wasn't the most logical answer, but it was the only one that made sense.

Something he'd written near the end of his letter caught her attention immediately. Her stomach twisted in excitement as she read it.

I'm wondering, I hope this isn't too bold of me, but maybe we could meet in person some time. I'd love to be able to discuss my views with a like-minded guy or girl—(forgive me, you weren't clear which it is)—over coffee or some kind of meal. We live in different areas, but I'm sure we can meet somewhere in the middle. Let me know if this isn't too presumptuous and if it sounds like something that would be to your liking.

She read it over and over again, hardly daring to believe what she was looking at. Someone wanted to meet her, someone who wasn't a creep from Tinder trying to get into her pants. Someone who was actually smart. Who wasn't oblivious like Izzy or distant like Miranda.

He had sent it only minutes ago, but she wasn't able to make herself wait any longer as she typed a response, her fingers blurry with anticipation. She added at the end of her letter—it wasn't a long one either—that she would love to meet and talk with him. She almost mentioned that she was a girl, but then saved it. She wanted to see the look on his face when she introduced herself. Whether he would be shocked, or disappointed, or happy...

Janet took a shower and then lay down on the sagging couch. She still hadn't cleaned up the spilled Scotch. She'd get to it later. Her breathing was faster than normal, she realized, and she worked on slowing it down.

She would get to see Ur and get to discuss everything they had talked about over email. Would he still think she was worthy of such deep, intellectual conversations when they met in person? After all, the implications of a real meeting were slightly terrifying: she wouldn't have the ability to think over her responses for hours, finding the best words to get her thoughts across. She would be at the mercy of her immediate recall, her most commonly used phrases. She would probably end up saying *like* every other word. Oh, fuck. She wondered if it would be too crazy to rehearse ahead of time.

It was eleven at night, and she was about to go to bed, when she saw a text message from Izzy. *Can we talk?*

Her heart thudding, Janet stared at the text. No three words had ever seemed so ominous. Forget what they said about boyfriends asking to talk—when it came to siblings, it was way worse. You couldn't preemptively dump or ghost a sibling to avoid an awkward talk. Her mouth tasted like ashes again, even though she hadn't smoked.

Finally Janet replied, *Sure, what's up?*

Her phone was ringing before she could even put it back down.

"Janet," Izzy wailed. "Did you see the news?"

"It's nearly midnight," she said. "I'm not watching the news." In fact, she hadn't checked it all day. It was too damn depressing. "What happened? Are you okay?"

"They say there's a Category five hurricane going to make landfall in a matter of days. They're calling it Hurricane Camilla. It'll strike the southeast coast—that's where *we* are!" As though she'd only just realized this, had only just located their house on a map. "We aren't even five miles inland. Apparently that's the radius at which it isn't quite so dangerous. But we don't quite make it." She paused to take a breath and there was the soft, hiccuping sound of her holding back sobs. "We'd probably have to leave anyway. The wind speeds are like... one hundred sixty, one hundred seventy. They're saying it's the worst one to hit the state since Hurricane Andrew in the nineties. Category five is bad, Janet. Bad."

Yeah. Considering that they didn't even make a category six.

"I told Mom about it and she—she said, 'Do you have anyone you can stay with?'" She swallowed audibly. "But she knows I don't have friends outside the state."

"Did you tell her that you'd need to evacuate?" Janet asked. The words *I don't have friends outside the state* bothered her. Didn't she count as Izzy's friend?

"Of course. That's why she said it."

It took a few seconds for Janet to process this. That their mother hadn't offered for Izzy and her family to stay in the house she shared with her sister—she had not expected this.

"Why didn't she invite you guys to stay with her?" she asked carefully.

"Maybe you should ask her that. I don't know, Janet. Because it would be a bother. Because she doesn't want to have to deal with the interruption that Ted and Ruby and, well, all of us, would represent."

"I don't think so. Maybe you should ask her again. Maybe you misunderstood."

"Misunderstood," Izzy repeated, skeptical. Her earlier tone was coming down now from its near-hysterical pitch, growing calmer.

Even as Janet noticed this, she heard the emotions climbing in her own voice, as if it were necessary for them to balance out. "Yeah, I mean, maybe she got the two of us confused. Maybe you should get back on the phone with her and remind her that it's you who's fleeing the hurricane, not me."

"Janet, *why* is it so important to you that our mother hate you and love me?"

The sharpness in Izzy's voice jolted Janet back from the phone. For a moment she couldn't think of what to say in response. Then she realized how odd it was that she was already preparing her reply, rather than simply absorbing what Izzy was saying. It was the same way she thought of her replies to Ur—she would mentally type out her response to him even while she read his messages. As though her own words were more meaningful than anyone else's.

"I don't know if it is important," Janet hedged. But it was.

"It definitely *seems* like it is. Like you don't believe that she could possibly be the same person to each of us."

Maybe because she can't be, Janet thought. "I don't know— never mind. We can talk about that later." She knew they wouldn't. "Since she appears to not be offering you a place to stay, you can stay with me."

"We... we can come up? We can?" The sharpness in Izzy's voice was gone, and she sounded much younger. And confused. As though she didn't know how to react to her sister being nice to her, rather than combative. Janet flushed with shame.

"Of course. Do you think I'm gonna, what, hang up the phone and say *good luck?* It won't even be a problem where my roommate's concerned—apparently, she's going to be staying in California for at least another four months."

Izzy started to cry. "I'm so worried about Ruby," she said. "She's so young. This'll leave such an impression on her."

As her sister continued to talk, Janet realized, with dread, what this would mean: billions of dollars of damage. Millions of misplaced residents. Ruby and Terry and Henry and Izzy and Ted and Janet all trapped together in the same four-hundred-square-foot apartment. And there wasn't exactly a lot of open space in it; her room was full of a dresser exploding with expired makeup and a mirror with Post-Its stuck to it like flaking scales. Ancient magazines, crusty mugs and glasses—Oh shit, she still hadn't cleaned up the spilled Scotch. Her bedcover was now a foul-smelling lump on the floor.

As she hurried to the kitchen to grab paper towels, she put her phone on speaker and kept talking to Izzy. "When are you coming up?" she asked. She pressed a towel to the floor; it drank up the Scotch in less than a second. She kept putting more and more down, but they got soaked through immediately, like butterfly wings emerging from a chrysalis—wet, soft, malleable. "I'd suggest sooner rather than later."

"Well, I was thinking about that," Izzy said. "I agree, sooner rather than later. I know a lot of people aren't going to leave until it's almost too late. That's Florida for you." She managed a laugh. "I don't want to be part of the airport bottleneck. Or God forbid, the highway bottleneck. I'm checking tickets right now. Is tomorrow okay? Or... or the day after, actually? Friday. That should put us squarely in the middle of the people leaving ASAP, and the people putting it off to the last possible moment." She sighed. "You were right. I'm sorry I didn't listen to you or believe you at first."

Janet came back from the kitchen with another wad of paper towels. Kneeling to press them on top of the first sodden lump, she said, "It's okay. You don't have to grovel. I already said you could come. What time will you leave?" Her bedroom smelled like a distillery. She opened a window with one hand, holding the phone with the other.

"Six a.m."

"*Six?*"

"Believe me, people don't like flying at six a.m.," Izzy said with another laugh. "Thanks again, sis. Mom's going to get the shock of her life. And Auntie too." She yawned, a strange hooting sound that Janet used to make fun of when they were kids. "Sorry. I'm exhausted. I can't believe I didn't hear about this until tonight. I've been all over the place."

"I should let you go," Janet said. "You sound tired. See you Friday, right?"

"See you Friday." There was a release in Izzy's voice, like a sigh. As Izzy hung up, Janet realized that she would have to be awake and at the airport by nine a.m. Since it would be a workday, she'd have to keep up with the grievance letters on her phone, but by now it wasn't difficult to figure out what people were grieving about—medical, psychological, marital—and recommend them specialists with a flick of her fingers. It had become automatic.

Then there were the Unsolvables, of course. Janet had been referring to them by this term in her head, although her supervisors (as mysterious and unseen as her neighbors) would probably not approve. The Unsolvables were those people whose grievances could not be solved by a qualified professional in any area. Their grievances were related to the state of the world at large, or to its effects on their own microcosm, and could not be fixed by anyone in a chair or office or desk. People who were anxious that their children would witness water wars in their lifetimes, that their grandchildren would never know what a forest looked like. People who were overwhelmed by the experience of living through a mass extinction.

Ur was one of these Unsolvables. Janet knew she would be one of them, too, if she were writing grievance letters.

As a special bonus, when Janet looked at many of the grievance letters just the right way—squinting and reading between the lines, as though trying to make out what was going on between the slats of wooden blinds—she was able to glimpse the real grievances behind the purported ones. Sure, HK938283 was complaining about his wife's irritability and how he felt purposeless when it came to his work, but there was the question of what was really troubling him. It could be the state of the world in general. Maybe he felt purposeless overall, and his putting it onto his family and work was just a coping mechanism, a way to shrink everything down and make it appear more solvable.

Even though it was, of course, Unsolvable.

CHAPTER 17

Anna

The remainder of Warren's party was a kaleidoscopic blur. People clustered in groups like herds of spooked animals; some left immediately, practically running off the roof, while others stuck around and drank in the adrenaline. Their voices floated around Anna, worried, disturbed, exhilarated: "What the fuck just happened?" "Did they say *fraud?* I didn't quite catch it." "Looks even more dramatic on video, see?"

Anna stood there for close to a minute after they took Warren away. She couldn't move. Her legs felt like stalks about to crack.

"Hello?" someone said, and she turned.

It was the silver-haired man that Warren had been talking to at the party, the one who had confronted the cops. She couldn't remember his name at the moment. Something Straut, Yohann's father. This close up she could see the gold rings around his pupils like bits of broken glass, the oil gleaming on his nose. "Hello," he said more loudly. "Can you speak? What's going on?"

She shook her head.

"I need to know what's happening," he said, impatient. "What did Warren tell you? I know you're his whore, but I doubt you're just arm candy. He must have told you something about all this mess."

Abruptly she remembered how the pupil was actually a hole, and she could see it now in this man's eyes: two pits. Looking into them, she felt something inside her detach and wheel away into the blackness.

"Hel*lo?*" His eyebrows arched. "Do you speak English?"

She realized he had hold of her arm—how bizarre, she hadn't even felt it. She wrenched herself away and walked quickly across the roof for a few steps; then she began to run.

"Come back!" he yelled, but she was already off the roof and through the door. Clattering down the stairs, bursting through Warren's apartment, past the bookshelves and electronics and couches. The place was deserted. Slowing down, she saw herself reflected in a multitude of surfaces—mirrors and the shiny fridge and the darkened windows—flushed and sweating as she walked unsteadily through the rooms. Dozens of Annas surrounded her, each one different, but all alike in the same terrible way. She couldn't pause. She had to keep moving. The apartment was a tunnel, the belly of a snake that would spit her out again through the entrance.

Then someone crashed through the stairway door behind her and she took off running again, out the front door and into the hallway. No one was here either. It felt too silent, as though people were jammed into the crevices of the walls and hiding behind the columns, all watching her, all holding their breaths. She bundled herself into the elevator and stabbed at the Lobby button.

The lobby: hushed marble, glassy floor, scraped-open ceiling. Here, too, it was utterly deserted other than the guy behind the front desk. Where had everyone gone? They all seemed to have disappeared, flickering out of existence as soon as they'd left the party. It was like a horrible dream, the kind one had while gripped by a 105-degree fever, frantic and thrashing.

Heart hammering in her chest, the sound of her heels clacking on the floor, the doorman behind the desk staring at her as she hurried away. God knew what he must be thinking, seeing one of the tenants dragged away in chains—in handcuffs, rather —and now his girlfriend running after him.

No, not his girlfriend, she reminded herself. As the silver-haired man had said: his whore.

Finally, in her apartment, she could breathe fully again. She realized that this whole time she had been breathing only with the upper part of her lungs, shallow and frenetic, close to hyperventilating. She collapsed on the sofa, staring up at the ceiling, a hand to her chest. Drawing the air in and out.

The empty walls of her apartment closed around her like a pair of lungs. She'd only turned one light on, the lamp at the foot of the couch, and it cast a warm amber circle of light around her. Amber, she thought: the ooze that trapped insects. Freezing them forever in time. Outside the illumination, shadows spilled like liquid up the walls.

A smell hung in the air, heavy and rich, the scent of olive oil and garlic and tomato sauce. Someone in a neighboring apartment must be cooking. She wished more than anything that she was part of that family, that she could be spirited away and end up there, an extra figure at the table, no confusion and nothing wrong.

It was a few minutes before she could piece together what had happened, sort the events in her mind and realize them fully. They loomed out of the darkness, indistinct silhouettes that grew more and more defined until she could no longer deny what they represented.

Warren had been arrested for fraud. Okay. Breathe, she told herself. First: What was fraud? The accumulation of money for personal gain by dishonest methods. Something like that.

She jumped up into a sitting position, her hand going to her throat. With shaking fingers she undid the necklace Warren had given her. The lightness of the metal was now completely unsurprising. In the dim, yellowish light, it looked like cheap jewelry from Asia. Fake hollow metal.

She balled it in a fist and threw it at the wall. It didn't hit as loudly as she would have liked and slid limply to the floor outside of the circle of lamplight, where it lay like a discarded, calcified skin.

Anna texted Warren. She sent him three question marks, lined up in a row: *???* It went unanswered. She wanted to send him something else—*Are you okay? Do you even have access to your phone?*—but it would be pointless. If he could, or would, reply, he would do so in response to her first text.

She took stock of her money again. She had enough to live on for quite a while, even if she kept sending portions of it bit by bit to her parents. But that hadn't been the point. Merely *living* on it hadn't been the point. That was what her retail job was for, and sugaring had been entirely an investment for the future. She had intended to do this for a long time, enough to be safe in the face of whatever disaster would eventually descend on the planet. If everything had gone according to plan, in ten or fifteen years she and her family would have had enough money to ride out whatever crisis was coming.

But then again. Even the word *safety* was fast losing its meaning. She forced herself to look at her plan head-on. Preparing for local food shortages and rising costs was one thing, but what about the extreme heat waves and water wars of the future? In that worst-case scenario, you would probably have to be a billionaire to reap the true safety that would come from money. The kind of safety that could only be achieved by retreating into bunkers specially built for the apocalypse. She'd heard of these places: massive vaults that would house the super-rich in walls of gleaming silver, miles of tunnels, everything cast in perpetual artificial daylight. Metal tombs descending deep into the earth.

The thought made her stomach bottom out. It was possible that this entire undergoing had been doomed from the beginning, that it had been an exercise in self-deception.

She had not thought this clearly about her plan in a long time. She was used to regarding it sideways, out of the corner of her eye, as though it were an unpleasant shape she needed to keep track of but never look directly at. She had tried not to think about it the same way she tried not to think about how Warren's body looked when he was on top of her.

Maybe the money had stood in for something other than future safety. Maybe she had just wanted to feel cherished, the way Warren had made her feel sometimes, during the good times, the bright times. Maybe she hadn't wanted to expend any effort, other than using her body—and was that really an effort for her? It had come almost naturally.

She felt empty, like a stretch of beach after the tide had pulled away, littered with detritus. But her detritus was not shells and driftwood and sea glass. It was jewelry and bags and clothes, the fabric ragged and choked with saltwater, beginning to molder on the sand.

Only a few minutes later, Anna faced another unpleasant surprise. When she went to check the status of her bags on one of the resale websites, she had received not one offer, but instead a notification from the site itself, automated but somehow still dripping with derision: *We have detected fraudulent activity on your account. Please follow link to view message.*

"What the hell?" she said aloud. The officer's voice ran through her head again: *Warren Gohrmansen, you're under arrest for fraud.* Her jaw felt loose and slack, her stomach watery. Dutifully she clicked on the link and read the message.

User Ptitsa112, we have received complaints from multiple shoppers on the quality of your items. In particular, listing #2 was identified as being a counterfeit due to the stitching on the seams and the tags on the inside. Due to the consistency of these markers across all items currently for sale, your account is suspended until further notice.

In addition, a user named Bumbleb33 had left a short, scathing review for her shop. *CAUTION! The items being sold here are blatant knockoffs. For someone who calls herself a "connoisseur of designer pieces" this is surprising and disappointing. Your shop is a disgrace!!!*

Anna slumped back against the couch. The laptop slid off her lap and onto the velvet.

So the bags were fakes. She couldn't get anything for them. She couldn't even get close to the supposed retail price.

Anna started to laugh, very quietly. Even she had thought something was wrong with the bags' stitching and tags—of course actual designer resale experts could spot it. It was all too obvious. If she thought about it, it had been obvious from the first time she'd heard Warren say, on that beautiful heated rooftop, *What do you think of these?*

It felt karmic, in a way. This was what she got for feeling sorry for him. For feeling affectionate enough to allow him to change the terms of their agreement, for being weak and soft. She remembered Yohann Straut at the dinner party, the questions he had asked. His eyes at one moment amused and sparkling, the next devoid of any emotion, like drops of cold black water. At least he had tried to keep his father safe, to steer him away from a sketchy business deal. The same could not be said for Anna, or for her own safety.

The detritus glittered mutely on the beach. Even the gulls didn't want it.

Anna did not know where this left her. As a matter of fact, she did not know who this "her" even was. There were a number of them, stacked like Russian nesting dolls, from oldest to newest, smallest to largest: the farm girl from Siberia. The failed model. And finally, the largest doll, the thinnest and most elaborately painted shell on the outside: the sugar baby. Or as men like James Straut would say—yes, that was his name—the whore.

But who was Anna really? She realized that there was another, tinier doll inside the first one. Barely a speck, its painted features blurry and abstract because of its size. The real Anna was the smallest Russian doll clustered inside its larger clones, rattling inside all of those hard shells. So small as to be unidentifiable, sunken down to near-nothingness in the central black.

Gemma

Gemma skipped all of her classes on Wednesday and Thursday. The thought of going to class and sitting in the dark, echoing lecture halls, with her phone by her side and no one to text, trying to focus on psychology and Mesopotamian history and calculus, was nauseating. There was no way they could expect her to show up after her one idea for a video had been torn apart, and her boyfriend told her he wanted to open up their relationship. There ought to be a mental health day she could take advantage of.

But she didn't sit in the apartment all day, either. The idea of staying there was worse than that of going to class. Even though Derek only came home after seven or eight, the apartment constantly smelled like him: his cologne, his coffee mug by the sink with its dirty brown ring on the inside. It sounded like him: the echo of his voice ringing through the rooms, the music he liked to play late at night. It even looked like him, because he had left his sweatshirt lying on the back of the chair, a pair of jeans on its seat, and his sneakers right next to it, as though he had just vacated this outfit and left it behind in an approximation of his shape.

So she wandered around. The city was full of tiny, heartbreaking details: a lone baby shoe in the gutter, slowly caking with filth; a clumsy, rusting heart scratched into a bus stop pole;

dead leaves losing their color and turning mushy underfoot. Everything falling apart to rot. She watched women walk by and imagined that each of them was the woman Derek wanted to "open up" his side of the relationship for.

A dark, gritty rage swirled inside her stomach. Rage not only at him but at herself as well. She had really thought she was going to be a successful influencer with her lovable partner and aesthetic New York apartment and beautiful little life. She snorted, but timed it badly with a sip of her drink, and some coffee came out of her nose. Wiping it, she thought: what a joke. It wasn't just her classmates, with their critiques and criticisms, who had told her it was a joke; Derek had told her that much as well. Everything that mattered so much to her was disposable to him.

Well. Nobody would want to watch a video about *that*.

Skipping her creative writing class on Thursday was the most difficult. She knew everyone would assume that she wasn't showing up out of humiliation. The smart thing to do would be to go to class and act like nothing was wrong; she wouldn't even have to say anything. She could just sit there for the required amount of time and then leave.

But she couldn't go. She couldn't. The thought was like a wall in her mind.

She sat in a Starbucks on campus, her laptop open to an empty webpage, her mind open to the same kind of emptiness. She watched the time slide away in great chunks. Right about now they were debating whether to start the class even though not everyone (meaning Gemma) was there.

Right about now they were coming to the conclusion that she wouldn't be there.

Right about now they were actually starting class.

All the sounds in the coffee shop gathered strength and funneled directly into her ears: the barista calling out names, the clacking of keyboards, the panic-stricken grinding of the coffee machine.

She typed a few words in an empty document. *Cold air, early autumn, idiot girl.* A triumvirate. She looked around the room, searching for inspiration. A woman stalked by, her hat gleaming with glossy black feathers. She thought of birds, and then butterflies, and then moths. She wrote this down, but *moths* turned into *mothers* in her brain and spilled out onto the document. She regarded her stupidity for a while before highlighting everything and stabbing Delete.

What would she do now? She couldn't continue to live with Derek, not after what had happened. It was funny, because Gemma had never considered herself to have much of a backbone. In fact, she'd always pictured her insides as rather squishy and yielding, unlike the merciless hearts of her classmates who gleefully swapped stories about the guys they'd left on read that weekend. But perhaps even this spongey foam material could stiffen into something harder, like dried coral.

She would have to look for a roommate. Even with her mother's money, she couldn't afford to live all on her own, especially not within any convenient distance of NYU. So she unlocked her phone and downloaded a couple of those corny roommate apps she had seen advertised on the subway.

That was enough for today. Maybe tomorrow she could actually start hunting for roommates.

But drawing this out wasn't a good idea; it meant it would only be longer before she moved out. The whole process of transporting her wardrobe, accessories, books, miscellaneous items across town... it made her want to cry out of sheer exhaustion.

An unexpected side effect of being in Starbucks was that she couldn't cry. This wasn't her room, where she could lay about weeping for hours on end. The public setting of the coffee shop forced her to have control over her emotions.

Although maybe it had been a bad idea to come here. It was growing reminiscent of her creative writing classroom: a circle of faces surrounding her, her own face growing bloated with unshed tears.

Derek wouldn't be home for several hours. That meant she could sit in the apartment for a while, be alone. Cry. All day, if she wanted. At least it wouldn't be in a loo this time.

Just as she was about to get up, a flier landed in her lap.

She glanced up, blinking, as though it had descended from the heavens. But it was a guy who had tossed it her way, a guy in a baseball cap and a camouflage shirt. "You're coming, yeah?" he said. He was British, like her. That was the strangest thing—she hadn't heard one British voice since she'd gotten off the plane. The sound of his accent transported her back home for a moment—not her so-called home in Chelsea, but real home, with gray skies and familiar faces and steaming cups of tea.

Gemma was about to ask, "Coming where?" but he had already moved away, throwing the fliers like frisbees across the room (in fact, someone yelped as one hit him in the neck). The barista, instead of throwing the guy out, was grinning behind her hands. Maybe she was in on it.

Gemma examined her copy, expecting it to be for some play or sports event or something. But it wasn't for any of those. The writing across the top of the flier said ENVIRONMENTAL PROTEST. Below was a drawing of a gull with oil-drenched wings and huge sad eyes. It was an amateur drawing, with too much focus on the details and not enough on the proportions of the bird, making it look both overly worked-on and crude.

She opened the flier to see several bullet points. They listed supposed landmark events she had never heard of: the decimation of 25% of the Amazon Rainforest. The destruction of two-thirds of Australia's Great Barrier Reef. The extinction of the orangutan.

Gemma scanned the list, an empty feeling building in her stomach. Well. When put together like this, those landmarks looked ominous.

Then again, whoever had designed these fliers was probably trying to make the situation look more ominous than it really was. And this protest seemed like it might be a bit dodgy. Gemma had never been to a protest before, only seen them on the telly; her primary impression of them was a crowd of people marching and holding signs, yelling, their faces stretched in rage and indignation. It seemed like an environment one could get trampled in. Influencers didn't go to protests.

Then again, it wasn't like she was an influencer, or would ever be one. She turned the idea over in her head, in her mouth: it didn't taste like bitterness or disappointment or the salty tang of tears. It didn't taste like anything at all. It was underwhelming in a way. Surely Gemma needed more fanfare at this moment, more sturm und drang. Something that would edify the death of a short-lived yet intense dream.

When Gemma glanced back up and looked around the room, no one else was looking at their fliers. Their faces were completely blank, their attention absorbed by their phones, their laptops. Fliers lay scattered around on the floor, abandoned on tables. The guy who had yelped had discarded his on a nearby counter.

It was funny, but Gemma could picture them tearing the fliers apart the same way her classmates had torn apart her intro. Pointing out all the mistakes, the inconsistencies, the typos and misplaced commas and lack of believability. Going over them with a red pen, filling the pages with a spiderweb of corrections and criticisms.

As she stood up to go, she tucked the flier into her bag.

Gemma and Derek hadn't exchanged a single spoken word since he had told her he wanted to open up the relationship. All she had texted him was that she would be looking for a new roommate as soon as possible. He'd replied with *Ok* and *Sure you don't wanna talk?* but she had ignored both of these messages. She'd even muted his texts. Tonight, her plan was to sequester herself in the bedroom in case he tried to talk to her. He was still sleeping on the couch every night, so, mercifully, she had the room to herself.

She spent the rest of the evening slumped on the floor against the bed, the metal frame poking into her back, looking for potential roommates. As she searched, the hours and the shadows both extended. The drawings of flowers framed on the wall grew thinner and frailer with the lengthening of the day. They became uglier and uglier. Eventually they were worse even than the sketch of the bird on the flier, and she had to take them down and set them on the floor and turn them around to face the darkness. Gemma and her mother were the only things on the wall now.

When she heard the front door close, she didn't react or look up. The hollowness in her stomach expanded like a black pool moving through her body, filling up all her limbs. The room turned airless. Derek walked across the kitchen and microwaved his dinner. There was no anxiety in the sounds of his movements, no worries other than an animal instinct, a desire to be fed.

The noises pressed into her consciousness. They intruded as she scrolled through the messages she had gotten. Someone had a studio in the East Village, but it was way out of her price range. Someone on the Upper East Side was offering a potential option, along with someone really far downtown. She glanced up at the photograph on the wall. The two of them were murky in the darkness, features barely recognizable.

She went out into the dining room. "I'm moving out," she told Derek. "I found a place somewhere else in the city. I'm taking most of the kitchen stuff."

He looked at her, mouth slack. "What? Why?"

"Because I cook more than you. And I bought it, anyway."

"No, why are you leaving?"

"Because I don't want to be here anymore."

He was gazing at her as though she were a work problem he was trying to figure out. But there was surprise on his face, too— apparently this was a development he hadn't anticipated. "Let's sit down and discuss this, hey?"

She couldn't imagine why he was so surprised. Surely he hadn't assumed this was some temporary rift between them, something that could be patched up through a dinnertime chat and some compromise.

But then, they had undergone far more conversations in her head than in real life. To Derek, the last time they'd interacted was when she'd said *That's unfair* to his proposal and then left the room. For all he knew she was just a bit upset, and would be coming round shortly. (She wondered what kind of conversations *he* had been having in his head, and with whom.)

"I don't think that's necessary. What is there to discuss? How you want an open relationship, but only on your side? Do you really think I want to discuss that with you?"

His face twisted in something like embarrassment. "I was too reckless—too hasty in bringing that up to you. We don't have to do that if you don't want. It was only a suggestion."

"Well, thanks for letting me know we don't *have* to do that. That's really generous of you." Her voice turned bitter. She'd never spoken to him like this before. Or, indeed, to anyone. She kept thinking about the word *pointless,* how everyone in workshop had seemed to be dancing around that term if not outright saying it. How it had been used to describe the story of her life and therefore her.

"I'm not sure what to say, Gemma. I think you're being unfair. Jumping to conclusions about what I said, so to speak. I didn't mean—I wasn't giving you an ultimatum, or anything. I just got carried away with some thoughts I'd been having, and I figured we were the kind of couple who could discuss these things openly, without any need for negativity or... or anything reactionary. I figured we could share our thoughts. I guess not," he added, very softly.

For an instant she wondered, with the habitual sting of guilt, if she *was* being unfair. If she was jumping to conclusions too quickly, villainizing him. It was just like those circular conversations with her dad about moving to New York, the ones where nobody won and he switched up his mood on her every time they spoke about it so she never knew which version of him she was going to get. Endless scrabbling, flapping useless wings and going nowhere.

She didn't think she was, though. She was pretty sure Derek simply sucked. Just in case, she tried to view the current situation through different eyes. If Mum were here right now, watching them, what would be passing through *her* mind?

The idea was hideous: it sent a dizzying wave of shame

through Gemma's chest. Worse than the workshop, worse even than that scrutiny.

"Why are you just repeating back what I said to you last time?" she asked.

"What?"

"The other night, I said you were being unfair. Now you're repeating it back to me. As though it's unfair of me to react to a situation that *you* put me in."

"Okay," he said. It was somehow less of a response than silence would have been.

"And we're not a couple," she added. "For the record. And I'm moving out next week."

She had so much more she wanted to say, much more, but she restrained herself; she had the idea that spewing vitriol at him would render her the less dignified of the two of them. She wasn't sure why, but she had some idea that he would come up with something about emotions, and logic, and the differences between the two genders.

It was not as hard as she'd always thought it would be to break away from him. She should have known it from the beginning, when she'd first started her last-day visualizations—even then, when she had imagined that Derek would soon be dead and gone and the two of them separated forever, she had not come anywhere close to the grief of her mother's death.

In her room, Gemma packed some preliminary bags, disposing of everything she could live without and arranging the rest into her suitcases. There was surprisingly little of it.

CHAPTER 19

Janet

On Thursday, Janet awoke with a sense of exhaustion. She'd slept nine, almost ten hours, which should be enough, but when she woke her mind was bleary and slow to start. Her chest felt ponderous, dragging her earthward. It was as though sleep were clogging her brain, grinding down the gears, scattering dust through the cogs of it. It took two cups of coffee before she was ready to begin the day.

She checked her work email to see a message from Ur. It was right at the top of her stack, as though it had been arranged that way. He had written,

Hi Owl! Thanks for accepting. I've got to admit I'm rather excited to meet you.

This is extraordinarily last minute, but I'll actually be in the Manhattan area later today, if you wanted to meet then? If that's fine with you. If not, no worries. Here's my number in case you want to figure out the details that way. In any case—looking forward to it.

-Ur.

A ten-digit phone number closed the letter. Janet sat up straighter and considered. Starting tomorrow morning, Izzy and her family would be here, which meant she probably wouldn't be able to get away after that point.

Janet had a moment of doubt as she added his name and number to her phone contacts—Ur seemed so short and inadequate, like a grunt—but she figured she'd ask him his real name when they met. She didn't want to scare him off, especially as he was a university professor and probably had more of a reputation to uphold than she did. And he didn't have her name either.

She sent a text, saying only, *Hey it's Janet. I mean OWL, lol. Oops, now you know my real name!*

Five minutes later, he replied: *Fantastic. Janet, how does 5 pm at the Monahan sound? It's a restaurant/bar on 12th and Seventh avenue. Is that convenient for you? I don't exactly know where in Manhattan you're located, so I'm kind of grasping at straws here.*

She'd never told him where she lived, she realized. He was probably assuming she lived further downtown than she really did, as going all the way to Twelfth Street would be quite a hike for her. But she didn't want to text him telling him to come all the way up to East Harlem, for fuck's sake. And he was coming from Brooklyn. Or the Bronx, she couldn't remember. It had definitely been one or the other.

Finally she replied, *Yeah that sounds great. See you then :)* and tried to bury her disappointment that he hadn't told her his name, too.

By now, Hurricane Camilla was in the New York news. They were predicting wind speeds of 175 mph and catastrophic damage: severe beach erosion, flooding several miles inland, and power loss for as long as three weeks after the event.

It was only when Janet read this last point that it really sunk in. She would have to house her sister and her family for *three weeks.* Maybe more. Her head filled with visions of screaming babies and sticky-faced toddlers. The sharp, ripe scent of shit-sagging diapers. Ted padding to the kitchen every morning in a crumpled pair of slippers. Her sister cluttering the bathroom with scented candles and unnecessary toiletries of every possible breed. Indulging in her spa-like "self-care rituals" while Janet was trying to sleep.

Then: "Jesus," she said aloud. "What the fuck is wrong with me?" Her family was fleeing a life-ruining hurricane, not staying for a vacation. And it wasn't like her sister couldn't spend any time with her mother and aunt. They'd definitely want to see her and the family, and she couldn't imagine Izzy wanting to stay cooped up in her tiny apartment all day. Maybe her mother and aunt would even volunteer for babysitting while Izzy was working remotely. She was still fairly sure Izzy had misunderstood when she'd said she couldn't stay with them, but she knew better than to get in the middle.

She double-checked the transport to the airport the next day and then tried to push it out of her mind. Work beckoned. Unfortunately, work that day was more disturbing than usual, and she wished she could get it to beckon someone else instead. It was like some bizarre software glitch was causing her to get the worst letters of all the grievance counselors. Her first one was from a wife who had found child porn on her husband's computer—featuring their own children. This was some dark shit. Janet actually had to step away from the computer for a few minutes. But if she was affected like this just reading about it, what about the wife? Or those FBI agents or cops who had to actually handle the material in question?

Janet pressed her hands to her eyes; it didn't bear thinking about. The soon-to-be-ex-wife had already contacted the police, so Janet didn't have to go through the process of sending law enforcement to the source of the grievance letter. All she had to do was send the woman a set of psychiatrists and therapists. But it felt less than useless.

The next grievance letter was from a father who was worried about his son's heroin addiction. The next was from a mother whose twin daughters had run away. The next was from a girl who had seen a dead dog by the side of the road and couldn't stop thinking about it. *It shows up in my dreams,* she wrote. *I go to bed knowing that as soon as I close my eyes it'll be at the foot of my bed, staring at me.*

Janet's own thoughts kept going back to Ur, imagining what he would look like when she saw him in a few hours. What she knew so far was that he was a thoughtful, brooding college professor who struggled to teach anthropology to technology-addicted students. This encouraged the mental image of a tall, lean man with dark hair and haunted eyes, perhaps carrying a coffee or hip flask around. Taking brooding swigs out of it between classes as he pondered the meaning, or non-meaning, of life.

Janet bit her lip in excitement. He was such a cliché, but he was *her* cliché, dammit. Or at least, she wanted him to be. What he looked like wasn't even too important; even if he turned out to be fifty pounds overweight or as woolly as an Angora rabbit, she didn't really care. It wasn't like she was planning to marry the guy. Just having someone to talk to, to really connect with on the same level that she had sensed in their messages, would be more than enough.

Throughout the day, the air in her unheated apartment grew colder, until Janet was shivering in her desk chair. Finally she draped a sweater around her shoulders and continued working. It was like the landlord suffered a new bout of mental anguish every time he turned the heat on. If she was lucky it would crank on sometime in mid-December, just around the time her corpse was stiffening with frost.

Janet checked the journey downtown several times to make sure she wouldn't be late. All she had to do was get on this train, and then that one. Easy. Except for the journey to see her mother and aunt, she hadn't been on a train for nearly two weeks.

Before leaving, she went to the bathroom to put makeup on. It was dumb, she knew, but she couldn't help it. It was the first time she'd worn makeup since the date with Liam. What a waste of shitty CVS eyeshadow that had been.

Her skin was pale and wilted, like a plant kept in a dark basement. Leaves crumpling and yellowing and turning to dust. The shadows under her eyes were as dark as bruises. She smeared foundation over her face and applied a touch of blush to her cheeks. The result looked bizarre and unnatural, but this was how she had always applied makeup. It only appeared strange right now because she was used to seeing herself bare-faced. If she washed it off and tried again she would just be wasting time.

She washed it off and tried again.

By the third time she was sweating and there was a wild look in her eyes. *It's not so important! Just go!* she told herself in exasperation. *You think Ur is going to be wearing makeup?* But she made herself dust the blush on again, lightly, so little she could barely see it, and apply powder to the oily spots on her nose and cheeks, and only then could she consider herself ready to leave.

She was, of course, late. She sat on the subway with arms and legs crossed. There was a tense, jittery feeling in her jaw and molars, a pressure coming up from deep within the gums. She ground her teeth and clicked her jaw over and over again. The stares of the other passengers prickled her skin, but when she looked up, no one was paying attention to her.

When she got out on Twelfth Street, it was five minutes to five and she still had to walk four avenues west. Showing up right on time wasn't important these days—every single guy from a dating app she'd met had been at least ten minutes late—but Ur was a college professor, not a Tinder date, which meant he probably valued punctuality. She pictured him tapping his foot, glancing impatiently at the door to the restaurant.

Janet barreled past the other walkers on the street, weaving in and out of groups of people and racing through intersections seconds before the light changed. By the time she got to Twelfth and Seventh, there was a stitch in her side and she'd started sweating again.

She was six minutes late. She texted Ur: *Here! Sorry I'm late :(Are you going to fail me?*

It was easy to almost miss the Monahan. Despite the name, it was a humble-looking place, with silver diner-style tables gleaming in the dimness. There were only two other people inside, both alone and eating their meals with dour concentration. She hesitated at the host stand; she couldn't exactly tell the host that she was looking for someone named "Ur." But the host didn't even ask her if she was waiting for someone, just led her wordlessly to a table in the corner and plopped down a menu, which landed with a *thwack* like a slap.

The two other diners didn't even glance at her. Clearly neither of them were Ur. And clearly he didn't value punctuality as much as she had thought.

Her last text message to him had gone unanswered. Reading it over again, it looked stupid, awkwardly flirtatious. *Are you going to fail me?*

There were a few framed photos on the opposite wall, all of them featuring a round-faced, mustachioed man shaking hands with various men and women. Janet didn't recognize any of them. There was a black-and-white one featuring a woman who might have been Lucille Ball, but then Janet noticed a cell phone in someone's hand. There were far fewer photos than in most of the big-name restaurants that prided themselves in being "celebrity hotspots." Here, they were widely spaced and barely took up a quarter of the area they were displayed on. Janet was a little embarrassed that they were up there at all. It was like making your birthday public on social media, something she vaguely remembered from middle school, and then having only two or three people wish you happy birthday. At that point, you should just hide your damn birthday.

She flipped through the menu—bar food, bland, aggressively American—and put it down, unable to concentrate. Ur still hadn't replied. Maybe he wasn't going to show up at all. She had been hungry earlier, but now her stomach was tight and cold, like a cramped muscle.

Her phone lit up and she glanced at it automatically. *Hello Owl/Janet, I'm so sorry. I will be there shortly. Forgive me!*

Every muscle in her body relaxed. She realized she was looking back and forth, back and forth, from the door to her phone. The anticipation was making her grind her jaw again. She ran through some witty conversation openers in her mind, hoping he wouldn't think she was stupid or silly in real life, in an environment where she didn't have the time to think over her replies and phrase them just right.

Just then, the man at the other table got up. With a trickle of dread she saw that he was heading towards her, and when she met his eyes—reluctantly, an unwilling glance—he was looking straight at her.

Not now, she thought in despair. It would be terrific if Ur came in and saw her engaged in conversation with some random guy. He had a mop of dirty blond hair and soft, muddy features. This close he smelled like mothballs, like a closet that hadn't been cleaned out in ages. Dust and dark and damp, fungal socks. She raised her eyebrows and affected as unwelcoming an expression as she could. It didn't work.

"Owl?" he said.

It took her a few seconds. It truly, actually did.

When she opened her mouth, nothing came out, but he recognized something in her expression. Some realization, dawning.

"Or, if you prefer, Janet?" he continued. "Sorry I'm a little behind. Things got in the way."

He pulled out the chair across from her and sat down. The only other diner in the place, a middle-aged woman with jowls, was watching them with interest.

"I..." She glanced at her phone again, and then at the door, as though she might see Ur—the *real* Ur—walking in any second. "Sorry, who are you?" Maybe this guy wasn't even him, she thought, in a flash of desperate hope. Maybe he had simply guessed her name. And also happened to really like owls.

"I suppose you know me as Ur. I apologize for not telling you my real name, but I'm a bit paranoid over the internet."

Like she cared about that right now. "Why..." She glanced at the table he had vacated. There was a plate there with the craggy remains of a salad on it. A glass of water, half drunk, the sides cloudy and stained. "Why didn't you greet me when I came in? Since you were there all that time?"

"I don't very much like eating in front of people. It makes me self-conscious. I never eat in front of others if I can help it." He was leaning forward now, his arms on the table, his hands clasped. His hair was greasy at the roots, stiff with oil. He looked at her with an expression that was imploring, almost tender. "Do you feel the same way?"

"No. I thought you were going to walk in over there... never mind," she finished weakly. He was looking at her, expectant, like nothing was wrong. Like this was completely normal behavior. Ur the smart, handsome college professor was fast disintegrating in her mind, turning into a formless collection of words and impressions. "Anyway... where were you coming from? Have you been in the area all day?"

"Indeed. I had an interview down here earlier, so I thought it would be prudent to stop in for a bite to eat." The way he spoke was all funny. Over the emails, she had pictured him with a refined way of talking: maybe a British accent, maybe just a clipped, old-fashioned tone. Then, the antiquated phrases had made sense. But in person Ur had a bland, Midwestern voice, and it sounded like he was in a low-budget Shakespeare play, imitating archaic speech patterns without any understanding of them. The effect was jarring, unsettling. "The food is serviceable. I recommend the onion fries." He put a hand on the menu. "Or the pork sandwich."

"So... what kind of an interview did you do?" she asked desperately.

"Ah. I do have to admit, it isn't my proudest moment, but I'm on the lookout for a contractor position. It's been a while since I've had a steady source of employment and I'm willing to tolerate basically anything they throw at me."

"You're looking for a job?" The door to the kitchen swung open and the smell of burnt coffee filled the air, bitter as stomach acid. "I thought... aren't you a professor?"

"I'm sorry?"

"In one of your letters, one of the first ones, you said that you teach anthropology." Her voice sounded like it was coming from somewhere distant. The next table, maybe. "You said it was difficult to get students to pay attention, because they kept, like, wanting to modernize the early humans. Remember? You said that?"

"That's brilliant." His eyes widened, as though she'd just

given him a great idea. "I would love to be a professor. However, that seems a little ambitious."

Fuck it. She gave up trying to be nice to him. She remembered something he'd said in one of his other letters. The thing that contradicted what he had said before. "Yeah, you didn't even go to college, right?"

"I went to Cambridge," he said, puzzled. "In England. If you don't think that counts as college, well..." He chuckled, looking uncomfortable. "You must give me *some* credit, you know, Owl. Do you prefer Owl or Janet? I must admit I think Owl is rather cute." He grinned; his teeth looked mossy, unbrushed. Something clanged in the direction of the kitchen. She missed Liam.

"Should I just call you Ur?" she said.

He shrugged. "You can if you want to. It's honestly been some time since anyone called me by my true name—Ur feels more like a proper moniker than anything else."

"Really? Even your family doesn't call you by your real name?"

"I don't have any family here. They all live overseas. I haven't seen any of them in years and I don't speak to them much."

"I thought you said your family lives in Detroit."

He looked at her blankly. "Why would I say that?"

Janet had a lot of experience with liars. Men who exaggerated their height on dating profiles, who claimed to know the authors she referenced, who canceled last-minute because of "family emergencies." So she was pretty good by now at sniffing out the signs of dishonesty. But she didn't see those signs—a sheepish expression, darting eyes, a desire to end the topic of conversation—in Ur. What she did see disturbed her far more. He wasn't even lying. When she'd referenced Detroit, which she *knew* he had written about in one of his letters, he'd truly had no idea what she was talking about.

She brought a hand to her mouth, and then lowered it. "I'm sorry," she said. "I don't feel very good."

His brow furrowed, as though he suspected her of faking. That was a laugh. "Really?"

She nodded furiously. "Actually, I think I'm going to shit myself."

"Oh dear!" He pushed his chair away from the table with a hideous scraping sound. There were at least five feet in between them now, presumably in case Janet started spraying projectile diarrhea everywhere.

She leaped to her feet and ran out of the restaurant. After its gloom, the October sunshine was brilliant, glittering off the fenders of parked cars and the spokes of bicycles. She jogged a couple of blocks, taking two right turns in a row, before she slowed to a walk. It wasn't close to sunset yet, but the city was filled with an apocalyptic orange light. It was like the inside of a yellow prism, overlapping and deepening to ochre.

When she checked her phone, she saw a new text from Ur: *Dear, I honestly think that was rather rude. Come back and let's talk it out?*

Talk what out? she thought, and blocked his number.

She had been right from the beginning. She would never know what was on the other end of those grievance letters. With Ur she had thought she glimpsed another person, someone like her, someone she could talk to, relate to, trust. But all she had ever seen was a shadow.

CHAPTER 20

Anna

Thursday was a gray, grim day, with the promise of rain that went unfulfilled. At work, Anna angled her phone surreptitiously behind a stack of clothing and searched the news for any information about what had happened with Warren. He wasn't well known, so there were no headlines screaming *FRAUD!* or *INDICTMENT!* Eventually she found what she was looking for: a single, well-placed article in the WSJ.

It presented a background of him—forty-four, single, fabulous apartment in one of Manhattan's wealthiest districts—and then a description of what had happened. He had been involved in an illegal attempt to swindle some new business partners (the Strauts, she mentally filled in) out of money. Apparently, his funds had been running dry for quite a while. Anna realized that the bags and jewelry might just have been a postponement of the inevitable. The question of how long he would have been able to get away with the substitution—that all depended on how much slack she would have cut him. She told herself that she wouldn't have allowed it for any significant amount of time—but then again, she had accepted that it was all right when he'd first suggested it. She had been willing to bend the rules of their arrangement just for the privilege of a sense of security. This could have gone on forever.

The idea was nightmarish. That she would have been so complacent, so unguarded, that she would have allowed this to happen to her. She was weak and innocent after all, no matter how hard she had tried to hide it.

And now she was alone. She had no close friends, only a few acquaintances she had met through modeling. They liked one another's social media posts but their conversations were superficial, light, skipping across the surface like a stone skimmed over water. None of them even knew what she had done to make money. None of them knew her.

Night came. A day separated from Wednesday's events, Anna became more aware that it wasn't entirely Warren's fault what had happened. She couldn't hate him for it. Indeed, she understood him. He had had her, for a time, and hadn't wanted to lose her, even when he ran into financial troubles. She could relate to that. She wanted to hold onto things too. But you couldn't lie to things, and he had lied to her.

Although she wasn't sure which version of Anna he had even lied to, which Anna was the one he'd wanted to keep. The girl who had laughed at his jokes, or the one who'd thought of her ex-boyfriend when Warren was inside her and counted down the days until she was free of the need to be with him?

If she were Warren, she wouldn't want that Anna either.

He still hadn't replied to her last text to him. From what she knew about criminal proceedings, he probably wouldn't have access to a phone until his bail was posted, which might not be for a couple more days. So there was no need for her to keep looking at her phone. But she kept doing this anyway. It was more of a tic than anything else, a nervous habit. She wasn't even sure she *wanted* him to respond. Yes, her primary source of income had dried up, and she was floundering without a safety net, falling at great speed. But she felt a tingle of dread when she thought of him now.

She put her hands to her temples, feeling the skull underneath the skin. She had found that focusing on the immediate future was a good distraction from the perils of the big picture. When the rest of your life was too overwhelming, just figuring out what you were going to do for the weekend was a start.

But Anna usually spent the weekend, or at least part of it, with Warren. Without him, there was a conspicuous gap.

Thinking about it now, she found that although they had spent many days and nights together during their six-month relationship, it seemed like much less time than that. And she had very few concrete memories of their time together. It was like an illustration in a book, barely glanced at and immediately slammed shut: the details were already fading. Warren's face and voice were still clear to her, but the months she'd spent with him were beginning to feel like they had happened to a different part of her, some other girl she was sharing her memories with.

The details of her time with her ex-boyfriend had not faded. His face was no longer something she could call to mind, but the smells and sounds and sense-memories from their six months together persisted. That half-year stretched out and took up a disproportionate amount of time in her mind; even their Florida vacation had felt like so much longer than four days. Her ten months with Warren was a flicker in comparison.

She allowed herself to think of their breakup now, cautiously at first and then less so. There was no reason not to; she didn't need to focus on Warren anymore. She had no one else. She could finally allow herself to spend time with the ghost in her mind.

At a certain point, not long before she turned twenty-one, Anna had realized that she was going nowhere. Her supposed work was running back and forth across Manhattan to modeling castings, trying to impress casting directors who would glance at her for a few seconds—always lazily, always like they had something better to do—and then dismiss her. Her jobs grew fewer and further between, the money they paid her disappeared nearly as fast as she got it, and every day there were more terrible events in the news: pandemics, wildfires, droughts, floods. She would scroll on her phone and absorb one article after the next.

Day after day they built up inside her, filled her like brackish water.

Her boyfriend told her she worried too much. He gave her hugs and kisses that brought her away from her thoughts in the moment, but as soon as she was alone, the images once again filled her mind: broken supply chains, hurricanes devouring towns, cities wreathed in flame. In the face of these future events, everything she did felt increasingly futile. She was existing on borrowed time.

She could not afford to go to college and get a degree without paying off loans for decades afterwards, and even if she could, it would be a waste. The kind of money she needed could not be achieved in this way, not unless she was able to put herself through years and years of medical school, and of course she couldn't. And it would probably be too late by then anyway. She could get a job as a barista or bartender or store clerk, but even if she worked full-time, she would be living paycheck to paycheck.

That was when she learned about sugaring. A girl she met at one of her castings told her that she had stopped trying to book huge campaigns. "I just go to these for fun now," she said, hoisting her leather bag further onto her shoulder. "It's not like I don't have the time." From the way the other girl handled it, Anna knew the bag was expensive, but she had no idea how much it cost or what brand it was. She didn't particularly care; it looked like any other expensive bag. But then she thought of how much it would go for once sold, and what the girl received in addition to bags, and something inside her began to tick. It sounded like time running out.

Anna knew she would never book a huge campaign. She would never again achieve the hip measurement she had been able to at eighteen—a number of inches that was impossible now because her hip bones themselves seemed to have shifted, grown broader. And even if she did, the money she could make sugaring would easily eclipse it. Even the models she saw in Chanel beauty campaigns did not make as much as the girl she'd met at the casting.

Her relationship with her boyfriend became something

almost shameful. At her castings—which were also growing fewer and further between—she looked into the faces of the other models and knew that none of them were living in near squalor with a man their own age, a man who made less than they did.

She knew she needed to let him go. The way she felt with him was so far from the practical frankness of that girl she'd met, who was, even if she didn't know it, preparing herself for the future. Anna needed to do this as well. Being with her boyfriend made her alive and happy, yes, but it also made her feel trapped and helpless whenever she thought of the years to come.

She knew what she needed to do.

The memory crystallized, shattered around her.

Now she was more isolated than ever. She'd chosen the wrong man—and wasn't that pathetic, too, that she'd been so dependent on Warren that him losing his money hurt her so badly as well. She had thought such a relationship would be less pathetic than being emotionally dependent on someone else, being weak in the way being in love made you, but perhaps it was all the same in the end. Being human meant that you were dependent on others in one way or another, and it was up to you to choose what kind of weakness you wanted to have. Anna had not only hurt her ex-boyfriend, who had never taken advantage of her love for him, but had ultimately replaced him with a man who lied to her and exploited their arrangement.

Selfish, she thought in disgust. Selfish and stupid, the worst combination.

She wondered what she could do that was not stupid and not selfish.

For starters, she could attend the environmental protest that the freckly woman had told her about. She stifled a laugh at the idea. As if that could fix her, could make her herself again.

Despite her doubts, she looked it up. She didn't have to do much searching; apparently it was a fairly big protest. It was taking place on Saturday, which she had off from work anyway —she'd requested weekends off when she first started, to make room for sugar dates—and over three hundred thousand people had already pledged to attend. She scanned the description, which was available on several news sites: it would start around noon, at the very bottom tip of Manhattan, and continue uptown. She tried to picture herself there. Surrounded by strangers, by people who didn't care about her, people who couldn't use her for anything, people who didn't even know she was alive. People she had never hurt or let down or depended too much on. People who didn't think of her in any particular way at all.

It sounded like what she needed.

Later that night, she threw away everything in her closet that she didn't like, could not resell, and had worn only for Warren. There weren't a lot of these items, but the process dragged on and on until it seemed that she had been staring into her wardrobe for days. A sensation of panic lurked in the back of her mind, as though at any moment Warren might come marching back into her life and she had to divest herself of any unwanted items before this happened. She found herself throwing away some other things, too, items Warren had not gotten her but which she had purchased for herself and associated with him: the fishnet tights he liked, the blue heels she'd been wearing when she met him, the vermillion lipstick she'd had on the first time she'd given him a blowjob, ringing red afterwards like a bloody bruise.

She ended up staying up so late that Thursday night melted into Friday morning. This brought with it a memory, of her and the ex-boyfriend, and their sleeping schedule. They had not had the most regular circadian rhythms. Sometimes they would stay up through the entire night and watch dawn spread over the sky, a drop of light water spreading through a darker liquid. They'd lie cradled in the crisp eggshell cusp of morning, legs mixed up with sheets, everything the surreal washed-out tones of a Polaroid. Colors gone through the laundry a few too many times.

Anna's lack of sleep and mental exhaustion weakened the

barrier in her brain. Made it porous. The memories returned; they were stained-glass, dripping with saturation, more real than the sheets under her back and the faint early-morning noises coming in through the window. She submerged herself in her past. This water wasn't that of sleep, half an inch deep and impossible to sink into: this was chasmic, bottomless. An ocean.

CHAPTER 21

Janet

Friday came, as Janet had known it would. She rested her head on the car window, but this was a bad idea, as she was already getting a headache.

Ruby hadn't stopped wailing since they had gotten into the Uber. Izzy, next to her, was keeping up a breathless stream of conversation which didn't leave many gaps for Janet, but this was fine with her. She was pretty sure if she opened her mouth she'd join Ruby. Ted was attempting to keep Henry and Terry entertained, which was difficult because Izzy kept talking about more and more disturbing things. They kept looking at their mother with wide eyes and then back at each other, as if to say, *Bro, are you hearing this?*

She realized she was imposing adult qualities onto them. Ur would definitely not approve. So she imposed the qualities even harder, until she was imagining Terry and Henry discussing stocks and business plans over lunches at the King Cole Bar.

Izzy tapped frenetically on her phone as she spoke. "Okay, so here's the latest update, right here—they're saying there's going to be downed power lines, every building up to maybe a couple miles inland is going to be destroyed, and there'll be catastrophic flooding, flooding like never before, waves as high as buildings, it's going to be horrible." She paused for breath. "It's hitting Monday. Did I tell you?"

"Several times," said Janet. "It's on the news here too. I've seen a ton of stories about it."

"Yeah, just making sure. I kept having this horrible dream, you know? On the plane? Where everyone was underwater and I kept trying to eat this sandwich but it was all soggy. I kept wondering how on earth I could breathe, you know, being *underwater*, but then I got distracted by the sandwich and its wetness."

"She slept like a champ," Ted put in. There was the sound of rubber striking the seat. "Terry, stop that, or I'll take away your Planet Destroyer." The noise of quiet, resigned disappointment. "Yeah, so, Izzy slept the entire plane ride. Didn't even wake up for the snack cart."

"How did you manage that?" Janet asked. She knew she could surreptitiously answer a grievance letter or two on her phone right now, but she didn't really care if she got fired. In fact, what had once been anxiety about losing her job had been edging closer and closer to apathy, and had lately metamorphosed into something approaching longing.

"I'm not sure. I think the child behind me kicking my seat kind of soothed me to sleep, like a rocking chair." Izzy smiled. "It doesn't *sound* very soothing, but it was, in a weird way. I actually think having kids has gotten me more in touch with my own inner child." She looked at Ruby, and there was real love in her eyes, tenderness as raw as a wound. Janet had to look away.

When they got to 104th Street, she tried to hurry them inside as quickly as she could. But Izzy didn't miss the trash scattered like confetti all over the sidewalk, and Ted's eyes darkened with disdain as he spotted the overturned garbage can on the corner. They hauled their bags inside in two trips. Janet kept reminding herself that Izzy and Ted's entire life was in these bags, that they had nothing else. At least the elevator was working.

As soon as they stepped inside Janet's apartment, it became smaller. It was like when you visited your childhood classroom or pediatrician's office, years later as an adult, and everything seemed to have shrunk, the ceiling lowering as though by hidden mechanisms.

"Lovely," Izzy said. "The place looks just like it does on our FaceTime calls. I think…" She looked around. "Yes! I recognize that pot, that pot right over there."

Janet followed her gaze to the plain ceramic pot which hadn't housed a plant for several years. There was still some crusted dirt at the bottom.

"Sorry the place isn't bigger." Janet wished she had gotten a few more hours of sleep. It would really help her tolerate Ruby's renewed wailing. The sound felt like something personal, as though Ruby were crying in direct opposition to the empty pot and the peeling wallpaper and the microscopic kitchen. Actually, she probably was. "If I'd known you guys were coming a few years ago, I'd have looked for a larger place to move into." She laughed and Izzy laughed and Ted laughed. Ruby, Terry, and Henry did not laugh.

"It's perfect, Janet," Ted said. "I've got to admit, I wouldn't even have a problem with a basement. After all, in all honesty, you're saving our lives." He ran a hand over his forehead. "It still feels unreal. I can't believe we've just fled our only home."

Izzy elbowed him. "Stop being so serious, Ted. I'll cry. Again."

"I should probably get out at some point and leave you guys to settle in." Even as she spoke, Janet wondered what she would possibly do during this time. Walk around East Harlem for three hours, maybe, see how many catcalls she could rack up.

"Oh, we can go for walks and stuff," Izzy offered. "Take the kids to Central Park? I know you've got a lot on your plate with work during the week."

"Yeah, true." Janet's stomach curdled at the thought of work. "I'm trying not to work too much, though. I think I need some exposure to the outside world as well."

"Well, if you were looking for something to do, I heard about this protest on Saturday. It's about the environment, so I figured you might be interested."

"An environmental protest?"

"Yeah. I thought it might be your kind of thing." At Janet's questioning look, she added, "It's not until tomorrow. But if you want to get out of the house, it's something to do. You'll also feel like part of history, I guess, as apparently it's supposed to be pretty big. I'd go myself, but I have to watch the kids. Because Ted," she added in an undertone (Ted had walked slightly away to show the twins the kitchen, or what there was of it), "has been an absolute life-saver these past couple days. Not a literal life-saver, like *you*, but more metaphorically. He was handling the kids the whole time I was trying to figure out what to take with us—and they were scared, you know, they try to be brave in front of you, especially Terry and Henry, but they're pretty freaked out by this whole thing. I felt like I was in Sophie's Choice when it came to some things, with packing. I know it seems like we've taken a lot, but we left most of our life behind."

"I know," Janet said. "Don't worry about it. I'll do whatever I can to help."

Janet lay awake that night, trying not to roll off the couch. Wrapped in all her blankets, she felt like a burrito balanced precariously on a narrow ledge. In a fit of generosity, she'd given Izzy and Ted her bed, and the kids were all bundled together in her roommate's bed. The rooms still smelled like Febreze, because earlier that evening Ruby had finally stopped crying and had an attack of colic. Apparently this was something of a pattern for her. Janet recalled Ted poking his head out of the bathroom, saying wisely, "What goes in must come out."

The heat was finally turning on in the building, maybe because the landlord had heard Izzy was coming. The hiss of the steam pipes made the apartment sound like it was coming down around her, deflating like a used balloon. She breathed in and out, imagining that the sound was actually that of her inhalations and exhalations.

Staring into the blackness, she pictured herself going to this environmental protest. She'd looked it up and her first thought was that it seemed like something Ur would attend.

Except... that was some BS. Because he wouldn't. He might believe he'd attended, or that he was attending, but he would never actually show up. It would get crossed off the mental list he had in his head and vanish into the white somewhere. The space where his teaching career and college education and Brooklyn/Bronx residency also lived. Along with who knew what else. Ironically, if Janet wanted to avoid him, the protest seemed like the perfect place to be.

CHAPTER 22

Anna

O n Saturday, before leaving for the protest, Anna applied anti-aging cream. It seemed suitably ironic to wear to an event centered around the decomposition of the Earth. No, not decomposition. Destruction. Decimation. Desecration.

Outside, the atmosphere crackled with the premonition of a storm. Slow and cool, the air moved over the buildings, funneling beneath a dense and sheetlike sky. It was dim for noon. Anna took the train downtown and thought of more D-words as she rode. Deforestation. Degradation. Desolation.

At the tip of the city, the buildings were huge and remote and cold. They spoke of money and harsh, metallic smells— coins, which by now were nearly obsolete, and the mineral deposits at the bottom of the ocean. She thought of Warren again and tried not to. He was like a scattering of dust she kept trying to wipe off her mental screen.

The sound of the protestors filled the air. It was already after noon and they had started to walk. There were so many of them, far more than Anna had expected—they filled the streets in a surging mass. The sight made her catch her breath. After the noise, the colors were what grabbed her attention. Their clothing was comprised of a psychedelic rainbow of shades, colors that cast the monochromatic gray and white buildings into a two-dimensional flatness. Many of the protestors carried signs. These signs, too, came in every possible variation: a few bold lines scrawled on cardboard, elaborately drawn or painted images on white backgrounds. Enormous banners unfurling across the width of the street, carried by several people. They included pictures of birds and animals and the Earth in flames; messages calling out corporations and politicians, the people at the top who had the most influence on climate change and, according to the signs, the least compunction to do anything about it.

Many more of the protestors did not carry signs, though, and Anna's momentary doubts about whether she should have brought a sign, or arrived with more of a plan, faded. She jogged to catch up and melted into the crowd. Many of the people here were younger than her, only teenagers. There was a multitude of faces: a wide-eyed girl whose braces flashed in the sun; a man whose glasses kept sliding sweatily down his nose; an older woman with steely, glinting eyes and long braided hair. According to the website, they were going from one tip of Manhattan to the other, all the way to Inwood. How many miles was that—ten? Twenty? Anna had no idea, which was embarrassing. She had lived here for four years; she should know these things by now.

A few people peeled away as they continued to walk, but more joined, and she realized that there would be some that stuck on throughout the entire thing. The man on her right, for one—he had painted his face and arms and every other exposed part of his body with blue and green and brown, supposedly to represent the Earth. Beside him, his companion, who seemed like he might be his boyfriend, kept telling him things in a low voice like "We should go home, Carl" and "Did you *seriously* have to paint yourself, nobody else is painted." Carl ignored these weak attempts at discouragement and kept walking. A woman in front of Anna looked like she might stay for quite a while, too; she was wearing springy, comfortable-looking running shoes, and each time she took a step her tanned calves flexed with boundless energy.

Anna didn't intend to be one of the people who stayed for the whole walk. She would go home soon. She kept telling herself this as they passed her neighborhood and kept walking, through Little Italy and the NYU campus and the Flatiron District. She hadn't gone home yet.

Maybe it wasn't too late, she thought in a burst of hope. Maybe this protest would actually do something, hold back the clock on the destruction that was pounding at the door of civilization, and buy everyone a few more years. A few more exhales. The money she was saving, the investments she needed to keep track of, the plan that she rarely allowed herself to look at head-on: maybe these things were not as important as she had thought. For years now she had prepared herself to brace against a horrible, inevitable future, but it was possible that this future might not be as bad as some people said. Maybe her money would not be necessary after all—or, if not that, maybe the oncoming disaster would not be so bad that her money wouldn't make a difference. Perhaps she, and others as well, could be saved.

More people were joining now, in the afternoon, because it was a weekend. Anna had a suspicion that many of them hadn't even planned to attend; they had just seen the wave marching past their windows and decided to join. There was a muscularity to it, like a long, sinuate, multi-jointed limb forcing its way through the streets.

The Empire State Building was behind them now, rising out of a sea of needles, piercing into the gray sky. Glancing back at it, Anna no longer felt the same awe she usually did when she saw it. Now it just looked like another unnecessary item in the congested city, sharp and ugly and cruel.

Anna wound up walking next to a girl with a pale face, dark bushy hair, and wide eyes. She wasn't carrying a sign either. She looked young and frightened of everything and Anna found herself deliberately keeping in step with her.

At one point the man ahead of the girl stopped abruptly, and she bumped sideways into Anna and yelped. "Sorry," Anna said, not sure why she was apologizing.

The girl skipped a few steps to regain her balance and kept walking. "No, no," she said. She had plump, pillowy cheeks and long black eyelashes, like a doll. An actual doll, not Warren's type of doll. There was an aquiline, aristocratic curve to her nose. She was wearing a leather jacket that looked much too fancy to be attending a crowded protest in; there was already a splotch of fresh-looking paint on the elbow. "It was my fault." She had a British accent, and there was a slowness to her voice, a sadness; it dragged like an anchor in murky water.

"Don't worry about it."

"I don't even know what I'm doing here," the girl confessed. Anna could barely hear her over the crowd. "I just got a flier for this event the other day and decided to come here. Mostly to get away from my bloody apartment. I guess that's a pretty selfish reason for coming."

"Are you kidding?" Anna thought of the woman at the party, how she'd spoken of the people who came here. She wished she could send her a selfie with the crowd in the background. "I don't think so at all."

The girl tugged her jacket tighter around herself. She offered a smile that looked ragged, the texture of paper left out in the rain. "I'm Gemma." There was something clinging and ingratiating about her voice, but it was so much the opposite of the way the people at Warren's parties had talked to Anna. It actually sounded as though Gemma cared what Anna thought of her, rather than speaking to her purely out of boredom or a need for distraction.

"Anna. You didn't bring a sign either?"

Gemma shook her head. "Didn't really know what to put, and besides, I'd feel silly carrying a sign saying something I don't know... ugh, sorry, I'm all mixed up. I don't know anything about this. Apparently I've been doing all the wrong things, being non-sustainable and such. I'm an ignoramus." She sighed. "I probably didn't even pronounce that right."

"It's okay," Anna confided, feeling safe and anonymous in the middle of the crowd. "I don't think anybody's about to quiz you on the pronunciation of the word. Besides," she added, "I don't think the two of us bringing signs would make that much of a difference anyway. It's more important that we're here."

They crossed through Times Square, through the enormous futuristic lights and the constantly playing videos. The bright neon colors pushed back the daylight, thrusting the area into a premature twilight. The faces on the advertisements and videos stretched gargantuan and surreal: gleaming white teeth like icebergs, hair like the blurred trunks of trees. The noise of the crowd seemed to increase as they passed through the area, as though they were competing with the fifty-foot signs.

After Times Square, a squadron of cops appeared, telling them to divert down another street. Anna and Gemma went to the right; the protest now filled two avenues, bloating them to bursting. Nearby, there was the sound of shouting; Gemma shrieked as a woman pushed her, staggered, and almost fell to the pavement. The woman snapped—with quite a bit more vitriol than Anna thought was needed—"Watch where you're going! You crazy or what?"

Gemma took a startled step backwards. On Gemma's other side, another girl rounded on the woman. She was Asian, wearing cargo pants and a holey sweater, and looked like she wanted to fight someone.

"What the hell is wrong with you?" she demanded. She looked for a second like she was about to punch the woman, who was a lot bigger than her. Gemma looked back and forth between them, her expression that of a startled chipmunk.

"If you can't play nice, get out of the crowd!" someone else shouted. The Asian girl shook her head and ducked out of the march, and when Anna saw Gemma following her, she did too, without even thinking about what she was doing.

Outside the crowd, on the sidewalk, Anna took stock of their new companion. She was a dour-faced girl with inky hair and a distracted attitude.

"I joined on a whim," the girl said, shifting her weight back and forth from one foot to the other. "Maybe not too smart, huh?"

"I think that was just a blip." Anna sank down onto the

pavement, crouching on her heels. All the blood in her body seemed to be collecting below her ankles. She wished desperately that she could lie flat on her back and put her legs skyward. She didn't do this much walking at the store; most of her day consisted of standing around. "I liked the rest of it okay. There was plenty of good energy."

"Do you think it will even make a difference?" the girl asked, staring back at the crowd.

"For whom?" Anna asked.

"Um. I don't know." She frowned; she appeared not to have been expecting the question. "Everyone. The world at large. The planet."

"I think the planet is too big to take any notice of us," Gemma said. "It made a difference for me, though."

"It *made* a difference? Don't tell me you don't want to rejoin," Anna said, glancing back at the crowd. But she hesitated as well. Right now the noise coming from it was louder and more chaotic, as though the protestors had changed their mission in the last sixty seconds. Or maybe it was because the three of them were outside the crowd, the way even laughter could sound aggressive when you were in another room, not part of it.

She realized something else—while glancing around at the other people in the crowd, she hadn't seen any of the expressions she'd seen at her countless parties and excursions with Warren. There had been none of the cynicism, the barely concealed boredom, the faint and derisive amusement. There had, however, been a collection of other, often vivid emotions on their faces— uncertainty, hope, anger, joy, sadness, as well as some she had not been able to identify. They reminded her of the old Anna, the one she had been as a teenager, as well as when she was with her ex-boyfriend. An Anna she had almost forgotten. Simple and straightforward, even vulnerable, not hidden behind layers and layers of other selves.

"I'm not sure. I'm kind of tired," the Asian girl said. "I'm hosting my sister and her entire family because of the hurricane in Florida. There are five of them." She looked exhausted just from mentioning it. "I'm Janet."

"Anna." She would go back, she decided. Her feet only hurt a little. She wanted to walk until they were even more sore. It felt good, like hard work.

"I'm Gemma," said the curly-haired girl, as though worried they might have forgotten about her.

"Are you sure you don't want to rejoin?" Anna asked them again. "I'm going to."

Janet shrugged, shifting her weight. "I hope I don't run into that lady again." It was the same tone of voice Anna had used when she was trying to have other people convince her of something.

"You won't." Gemma sounded older all of a sudden, her tone almost scolding. "She's clearly miles away by now. Look at how fast that crowd is moving."

"True," Janet said, grudgingly.

"If you don't want to, it's up to you. No one's going to pressure you." Anna glanced at Gemma, guessing that she might want to rejoin too.

This glance between them appeared to be what jolted Janet into action. "I don't need to be pressured," she said. "I was thinking all day about this protest. Daydreaming about it. Dreaming about it even."

"Are you sure they weren't nightmares?" Gemma suggested.

"No," Janet said. "I'm not." She smiled wryly. "I'll protect you if you protect me. Deal?"

"I don't think we'll need that," Anna said. "But sure."

They rejoined the crowd. They remained together, the three of them, like a phalanx. There were no more pushy protestors, and no real need for their formation, but they stuck side by side anyway. Janet's surly expression had smoothed somewhat, as though the chaotic energy of the crowd were not adding to her own emotions but rather substituting itself for them. As though she were becoming less trapped in her brain, less *herself*.

Or maybe that was Anna projecting.

Around the Upper East Side, the crowd began to thin. Janet

began to limp slightly, perhaps for dramatic effect. Anna took this moment to say, "I think I'm done for today." Today—as though there would be more protests. Well, maybe there would be.

"Me too," Janet said, as they left the crowd and gathered by the curb. She bent her leg, regarded the bottom of her shoe. "I think my soles are worn out. Probably my soul as well. Christ, what a terrible pun; please ignore it."

Gemma snorted with laughter. Anna didn't, though; she was focusing on the earnestness in Janet's voice, the young, hopeful glint behind the shield of self-deprecation. Maybe it was this that made Anna say what she said next, or maybe it was the way Gemma held her hand in front of her mouth as she laughed, like a shy little kid. Or maybe it was both of these things combined.

"I was wondering if either of you might want to meet up for dinner tonight," Anna said. "Or an impromptu glass of wine, or something like that. Not now, but in a few hours, maybe?"

Another thing: the thought of going back to that apartment, alone, where she wasn't who Warren or Dasha or her mother thought she was—it was suffocating. But strangers, like these two women, didn't have a pre-existing idea of her. She was an unoccupied space, an outline she could fill in herself, all over again.

Janet and Gemma looked at each other. "Right, well, that sounds pretty good," Gemma said. "I'd give anything to get out of my place right about now."

"I hope you're not a murderer," Janet added. "Although at this point, maybe it wouldn't be too bad. Even if you *are* a murderer, you can't be worse than some of the people I've met lately." She laughed. "And, provided I make a narrow escape, I'll have a fun story to tell my sister's kids."

They exchanged contact information and then departed their separate ways. Above them the clouds unwound in shades of deep gray and gold, the colors of vanishing bees.

CHAPTER 23

Gemma

That evening, Gemma took the train and walked a few blocks to the restaurant. She hadn't even gone home first to change, instead spending the last couple hours at a coffee shop; she'd be showing up to dinner in the same outfit she had worn to the protest, complete with her leather jacket with a splotch of green paint on the elbow. She found it difficult to care. The atmosphere in the apartment with Derek had begun to feel wispy, insubstantial, as though the air had thinned out. Trying to breathe in there was like trying to suck oxygen through a straw. Derek had spoken to her a couple of times since their conversation on Thursday, but it was in a strange, robotic voice, asking inconsequential things—"Is it cool if I have a friend over to watch this game later?" "Do you want the rest of the pasta?" —to which she'd responded with only a nod or a shake of the head.

She had the sense that he was saving something up, some last-ditch attempt at stopping her from leaving, but hadn't thought it was necessary to act yet, because although her suitcases sat ready in the bedroom, her toothbrush remained by the bathroom sink. (A phrase came to her, like a line she had heard in a dream: the essentials hadn't changed.) Of course she could simply sneak in and leave sometime during the middle of the day. But maybe he hadn't thought of that.

Gemma had found a few potential roommates on the app, but she'd hesitated on confirming any appointments to see apartments. It was silly, because there was no harm at all in looking, and she was away from Derek's place most of the time now anyway—hanging out at coffee shops before and after her classes, reading, looking at blank pages on her laptop and trying to write.

But she hesitated despite herself. She hesitated because Derek was the only person in New York who was also connected to her mother, even if indirectly. Without him, there would be no links left back to her; there would be no one who had known Gemma while her mother was still alive. Moving would be like another death.

After all the crowds and noise earlier, the streets downtown now felt empty, cloaked with an anticipatory hush. Overhead, the sunset made the sky look like it was melting. She switched back and forth between believing the other two women would show up. At times she thought she would be the last one to get there, that she'd been worrying for nothing. At other moments she could picture herself sitting there as dusk crept over the streets, staring out from her table at an emptying restaurant, avoiding the pitying glances of the hostess.

As it turned out, Gemma wasn't even the first one there. She arrived to find the tall girl with the Russian accent, Anna, already sitting at one of the tables. The restaurant had low, intimate lighting. Plants rose in the corners, snaking up the walls and attaching to a trellis overhead, filling the air with a rich green scent.

Anna had on a wide-brimmed hat, dark jeans, and a silky, slippery-looking blue blouse. Her lips shone red; her gold earrings glowed bright in the verdant gloom. She looked like a model, like an image girl sitting at a table purely to give the restaurant the appearance of popularity and class. Gemma felt chunky and awkward as she approached. What would this glamorous person think about her pathetic, futile attempts to become an influencer? Anna was probably one of those girls with 100K followers on social media.

"Hi," Anna said. There was something stiff about her manner, the same attitude Gemma had picked up on in the protest. Then, even when she was walking, Anna had held herself as though she were being observed from every angle. Now, as she gave Gemma a little wave and smile, her movements were similarly restrained and measured. It was like there was a deeply caring, maternal personality in there, but it was sealed up behind a layer of ice.

"Hey," Gemma said. She pulled out a chair and sat down and they smiled at each other across the wooden table.

"So, uh." Anna put a hand to her hat. She gazed into the distance for a few moments, and Gemma had the impression that she'd forgotten she was even there. Then she laughed and said, "This is kind of strange. I almost feel like I've sabotaged everyone's evening. I'm sure you must go on a lot of outings."

"I don't go out that much." Gemma fiddled with her utensils.

"Really? Someone as young as you?" Anna cocked her head. "How old are you, anyway? Eighteen?"

"Nineteen."

"Wow, I wish I were still nineteen. It seems like ages ago." Then she paused, her voice growing soft, contemplative. "And also like five minutes ago."

The two of them shared slightly uncomfortable smiles. Gemma glanced at her phone. It was already eleven minutes after eight. "Do you, um, think the other girl's going to show up? What was her name?"

"Janet," Anna said, just as someone walked into the restaurant and approached their table. It was precisely the girl from earlier. She was dressed in a plaid skirt and a heavy-looking denim jacket. She also had on mismatched socks.

"Sorry," Janet said, pulling out a chair and plopping down. "The last time I freaked out about showing up late to a meeting, I got completely screwed over. Ugh. Sorry if I kept you guys waiting." She smelled like a mixture of Febreeze, pine needles, and campfire smoke.

"It's okay," Anna said, tilting her head again. It looked like the sort of gesture she would have picked up at a society function or debutante ball. "I suppose it's kind of awkward to coordinate when there are three people, right?"

They all looked at their menus for a minute. When the waiter came they ordered: Gemma got a watermelon cocktail and a salad ("He didn't even card you," Anna said in admiration after the waiter left; "Don't take it too harshly; *I* definitely would have carded you"), Anna got white wine and pasta, and Janet just got water. "I'm not hungry," she added when the waiter paused after her drink order. After he drifted away, she told the table, "I already ate a ton of airport food yesterday. I thought I was gonna be sick at one point on the walk."

"Airport food?" Gemma asked. "Why?"

"I was there on Friday, picking up my sister and her family from their flight. I think I told you guys, right? Apocalyptic hurricane? Nobody believing me until it was almost too late?"

"Yeah, but why would you eat it?"

"My sister and her husband *love* it." She performed an Italian chef's kiss. "It's expensive, so they automatically think it's somehow *better*. Same with the books they find at airports. Suddenly a paperback thriller or beach read is irresistible literature. You could take them shopping there and they'd go absolutely wild—sorry. That's mean of me. I shouldn't make fun of them in front of strangers."

"Well, not quite strangers," Anna said, glancing between the two of them. She seemed to have a real interest in sustaining this meeting, more than either Janet or Gemma. It was as though she were about to initiate them into a cult. Then again, Gemma thought she might welcome a cult as long as it kept her away from Derek. "This is kind of awkward, huh?" Anna flashed another smile. Gemma had the sudden impression of her practicing the expression in the mirror.

"I think if you say one more time how awkward this is, this girl's going to get up and leave," Janet said, and nodded in Gemma's direction.

"I'm not," Gemma protested.

"You're literally on the edge of your seat, poised to flee." Janet regarded her more closely. Her dark eyes were so keen, so intense, the opposite of Anna's dreamy gaze. "Your accent is cool. Where are you from? Ireland? Britain?"

"London."

Janet's eyes widened as though Gemma had named an impossibly exotic locale. "Nice. My sister went to London last year."

"Have you ever been?"

"Nope. Too poor." She shrugged.

The waiter came back with their drinks, depositing Janet's plain glass of water almost mockingly in front of her. Gemma realized that the other girl's lack of food and drink might also be reasons to leave the restaurant in a hurry if she needed to.

And she might need to. Anna had been right; the meeting was hideously awkward. This, Gemma reminded herself, was why she didn't have friends or hang out with people around her own age. She wasn't sure about Anna, but she could easily picture Janet skulking around the NYU hallways, gossiping about boys and Tinder dates and who she'd slept with the previous night. In fact, with her wry smile and expertly winged eyeliner, she could easily be one of the girls who'd prompted Derek's decision to open up (his end of) their relationship.

Gemma took a sip of her watermelon drink to distract herself; the heat of the alcohol momentarily wiped all thoughts of him from her brain, and she could breathe again. She had gone to class yesterday, but it had only been a lecture. She wasn't sure if she would be able to face the writing class again on Tuesday, but she also knew that the longer she left it, the more difficult it would be. In this way, it was just like moving out. The thought prompted a vision of an alternate future: one where she hesitated and hesitated and finally never moved out after all, and listened every night to Derek having sex with various girls in the other room.

"So, why did you go to the protest?" Anna asked Janet. Her

words were long, stretched out like strands of cotton candy. "I don't think we got your story."

Janet took a breath. "I feel like it's a shame that there isn't more being done about the environmental damage that's going on. I thought I might as well show up and lend my voice to everyone else's." She paused. "I was surprised that so many people showed up, actually. It seems like... I don't know. Other than one person, no one I met ever seemed to really care."

"But maybe that's just the people who can't do anything," Anna said.

"I know, right, that's the horrible part. It's not even our fault. I mean people like us." She glanced at Gemma and Anna in turn. "Everyone who can really *make* an impact tends not to do so because they're too old and selfish for it to matter, or they think it's too expensive to stop using carbon, or because the process of change is just too scary. I also got sick of my job. Needed a break, needed to get out of the house, which is also my office. Conveniently."

"What's your job?" Gemma asked, feeling like all she ever did was ask more and more idiotic questions.

"Online therapist. But not like you're probably thinking. I don't have regular clients. No, my job is much more *diverse* than that." Janet chuckled, lacing her skinny fingers together. "I receive a bunch of grievance letters, every day, basically telling me what problems the writer is experiencing in their life, and I match them up with specialists I think will help them. Psychiatrists, doctors, marriage counselors... shit, gynecologists... you name it. And they write to me about pretty much everything. It's like being the recipient of the toxic sludge in everyone's mind." Her voice deepened to a burrish drawl with the word *sludge.*

Anna glanced at Gemma, and Gemma could practically read the thought in her head: *So that's why she's like this.*

"That sounds really tough," Gemma said. "I don't know if I could do it."

"I don't think you could. You look too..." Janet gazed at her again. "Too startled and innocent. Like a field mouse. What are you going to do with your life, anyway? You're, what, seventeen? You probably still have a career counselor."

"I'm nineteen," Gemma said, flushing. "And I'm still in school. But I wanted to be an influencer for some time. To, you know, make vlogs and videos. Then I decided that wasn't going to work out, so... well. Back to the drawing board." Once again Gemma realized how silly and childish her dream had been. But she didn't feel judged; rather, these two women were looking at her not only like they sympathized, but also as though they had made several mistakes of equal or greater idiocy in their lives— and what was more, expected to make even more of these mistakes in the future.

"You have time," Anna reassured her.

"*Good*," Janet proclaimed. "Good for you. Those so-called influencer people are some of the most vapid, shallow creatures imaginable. You can do much better than that."

"You think so?"

"Definitely. All they do is sit around and wait to... wait to... be waited on. What do you do?" she asked suddenly of Anna.

Anna swallowed. "I was a model." She hesitated, looking into the depths of her wine for a moment. The candlelight illuminated it, turning the glass radiant, the inside of a filament lightbulb. "My last boyfriend recently got arrested for fraud, so I'm kind of trying to process that."

"Holy shit," Janet said. "Are you okay? I mean, you didn't get arrested too, right?"

"No." Anna's smile was small and, Gemma thought, bitter. "I didn't have anything to do with it."

"Lucky," Janet said. "I'm not sure I could have escaped a situation like that unscathed. With my luck, I probably would have been arrested instead of the guy that actually did it."

"Good thing you weren't at the party then."

Janet frowned, but didn't say anything else. Their food arrived and Janet watched Gemma and Anna eat. "What did you think of the protest?" she asked them.

Gemma waited for Anna to answer, but since Anna had just placed an enormous forkful of pasta in her mouth, she realized that it fell to her to speak. "I felt very out of place," she confessed. "I'm pretty sure everyone else there knew more about the climate stuff than me. I never paid much attention. I mean, I didn't even know what a fossil fuel was until maybe a year ago."

She didn't think this was such an earth-shattering admission, but Janet gaped at her as though she'd said she didn't know her own name. "You're serious?" She motioned to the waiter and ordered a glass of red wine.

"Was that because of me?" Gemma asked.

"Only a little."

Gemma still liked Anna more, but she was starting to warm up to Janet as well. She did swear a bit too much, but at least she was interesting to talk to. And Gemma didn't have to play the same game with either of them that she had with Derek, pretending that Janet or Anna was about to get hit by a truck the next time they stepped outside.

"I think this pasta is really good," Anna said, chewing slowly. "Janet, you're sure you don't want to order some food?"

"Yeah, I'm good. Don't worry, I can hold my liquor."

"That's not what I meant."

"I was thinking of bringing a sign," Janet said, apropos of nothing. The waiter brought over her glass of wine and she took a sip immediately. "To the protest, I mean. I had a lot of ideas. Stuff about the droughts, the wildfires. The extinction of all these species. About the hurricanes in Florida, which I now have near-firsthand, personal experience with. That would get me some, like, bonus points, right? But I eventually decided not to."

"Why not?" Gemma asked. She expected Janet to say something like *Too much effort* or *It wouldn't make a difference*, but instead she said, "I couldn't think of what to say, which issues to focus on. Even a broad term like climate change seems to miss so many other things. People think of climate change as nothing more than rising temperatures. They don't really associate it with all the other effects, like increases in mosquitoes and ticks and all the diseases they bring. Or more pollen and pandemics and floods. Or no more chocolate or coffee or bananas. Stuff a lot of people wouldn't even think of."

"You know a lot about this," Anna said. No change had appeared on her face throughout this speech, not even when Janet mentioned the things about ticks and chocolate and coffee, which had been surprises to Gemma.

"Yeah. You have to do your own research at some point. You don't get this traumatized by checking the news." She laughed. "Well, maybe a little traumatized. It's probably a bad idea, though. To do my own research. It makes me feel so much worse to read about all that stuff. More helpless."

"But you feel better after attending the protest, right?" Anna asked.

"Maybe," she said. "If I don't think about it too much—yeah. I do."

To Gemma, Janet looked like she was trying to see something a certain way, like when you concentrated on one of those trick images—old lady or rabbit, skull or woman looking in a mirror—trying to shift your vision the other way around from what it was accustomed to. Gemma could relate. She could see her attendance at the protest one way, as a pointless distraction from a shitty living situation, or as another: an Action, a break in the recent paralysis that had overcome her.

The sense of paralysis was the worst; it was the feeling of Not Doing Anything that crawled over her whenever she walked from coffee shop to coffee shop, prolonging her stay away from Derek. Or when she went over her lighting or background in preparation for the influencer video that would never come. Or when she looked at the blank page on her Word document and finally closed it without typing anything. Whenever she sat down in front of her laptop these days, an empty document open before her, it felt like there was a flashing neon sign in her brain going: WRITE. NOW YOU MUST WRITE. NOW YOU MUST PRODUCE BEAUTIFUL WORK. The pressure built and built until it collapsed in on itself, like a species grown so massive it could no longer bear its own weight.

She had only felt something different from this overwhelming paralysis on two recent occasions: when she'd confronted Derek, and when she'd attended the protest earlier today.

How to make this feeling last?

She had been thinking about these things all wrong, she realized. It wasn't the change of moving, the finality of closing a door on Derek and her old dreams of being an influencer, that signified death. The paralysis itself was death.

"So don't think about it too much," Anna told Janet. "You know, I didn't make a sign either. In fact, there were a lot of people I know who would have laughed at me if they'd known I even went."

"Damn. What kind of people are you hanging out with?" Janet was drinking quickly. Her lips were already drenched dark purple from the wine.

Anna hesitated. "I wasn't sure at the time. I thought that the circle I was involved with, I thought the things I got from them —that they would protect me. But maybe not. In the far future, either way, I think everything would fall apart. I'd get older, and..." She trailed off, her hand creeping to her neck. Shadows played along her collarbone, along the bones and tendons that framed the hollow of her throat. "They don't matter, the specifics of it. But I kind of realized that that environment wouldn't be good for children, maybe not even for me. I forgot who I was when I was in it. I needed to do that in order to even exist there."

Gemma was dying to ask what sort of environment this was —surely she couldn't just be talking about modeling—but Janet spoke first.

"Yeah. I mean, I'm never going to have children, but I don't think any environment is too great for them right now. No pun intended."

"Why don't you want to have children?" Gemma asked. She wished she could say something that wasn't a question.

"Because they're doomed!" Janet said, a bit too loudly. She took a ragged breath and lowered her voice. "They'll be doomed no matter what. This entire planet is fast becoming a hellscape. You didn't realize that from the protest? They weren't exactly saying now's the time to get merry and be fruitful. Or whatever the saying is."

"Be fruitful and multiply," Gemma corrected automatically.

"That rings a bell," Janet said, raising an eyebrow. "Are you religious?"

"Not very. I was raised Catholic. But I've been lapsed for a while, and now I don't really believe in God at all anymore. Since my mum died." Gemma knew she shouldn't have had so much of that watermelon cocktail. "I sort of just... stopped. The belief turned off like a switch, all at once. It was pretty unnerving, actually. Like a double loss."

"Oh, shit." Janet put her glass down. "When did it happen?"

"April... near the end of the month. It was beautiful weather, really."

It definitely had been. The sky opening up crystalline and gorgeous, the inverse of the dark pit in the ground. Every second taking Gemma farther and farther away from her mother. The gap between their lives growing ever longer, never shorter: distance that could never be crossed, time that could never be gotten back. Her mother's face blurred and muddled in her mind.

Don't cry, don't cry, she thought frantically. There was a heaviness in her chest, like the storm that was supposed to come earlier that day.

Janet, her eyes wide, reached across the table and patted her hand awkwardly. And before Gemma realized what was happening, Anna had gotten up, come around to her chair, and given her a hug.

"I'm sorry," Anna said. For a moment, Gemma was enfolded in a crush of floral perfume and the airy smell of white wine and the scent of fur, or something similar, something animal and soft. Something warm in the middle of a coldness.

"I'm sorry," Janet added, as Anna sat down again.

"Yeah... me too. I have lots of memories of her, though, so it's not all too bad." Gemma attempted a brave smile. "Before she died we went to London and saw Big Ben and Parliament and all those places, made a day of it. We had tons of people take pictures of us. We're probably in the background of hundreds of tourist shots."

Janet frowned. "Big Ben?"

"Yeah. The clock tower."

"For real? I wonder if my sister saw you." She turned to Anna. "Remember I was saying, she went there last year? I'm pretty sure she went in April."

"Wouldn't that be a coincidence." Anna's smile was slightly admonishing, but Janet didn't seem to notice.

"I don't know," Gemma said. "We saw a lot of people there." Then she remembered what Janet had said about her sister's big family. There had been children with the harried-looking woman who'd snapped them in front of Big Ben, bundled up in tiny jackets, their cheeks brilliantly red in the cold. "Wait. She's Asian too, right? How many kids does she have?" The idea seemed funnier and funnier as she spoke. There were probably millions of Asian tourists who came to Big Ben every day. "Don't tell me... two?"

"Three." Janet's shoulders slumped.

"Oh, well. The woman we saw had two. Anyway—"

"Wait!" Janet almost shouted. "Ruby was with a babysitter on that vacation. I remember because of how much of a wreck that babysitter was afterwards—Izzy thought it was hilarious. And since Ruby wasn't there, that means..." She leaned forward and extended a hand into the air, as though she were on the cusp of finally grasping an unsolved mathematical theorem. "That means *you wouldn't have seen her.*"

"We wouldn't have seen her," Gemma agreed.

"Yeah, you wouldn't have," said Anna. Her smile wobbled as she glanced at Janet; she was clearly forcing back a laugh at the other girl's impassioned expression.

Janet relaxed into her seat again. "That's incredible. Wow. I can't even *believe* that."

"Me neither. It's amazing." Gemma had her doubts that they had actually run across Janet's sister and her family, but it wasn't like they would ever know for sure anyway. Not unless she asked Janet to verify with her sister, in any case.

And she didn't want to do this. She wanted that last London day with her mother to stand in glorious significance. It would be the site of a meeting that had turned out to have reverberations far into the future—and, especially if Gemma and Janet ended up staying in contact, the meeting would continue to have meaning in perpetuity. Her mother would not be restricted to the vanishing past, but would instead forever flow into the present, the way a stream feeds into the sea.

CHAPTER 24

Janet

In the end, Janet did order food. The place was quite a bit cheaper than she'd anticipated from the looks of Anna—and Gemma, whose jacket alone looked more expensive than most of Janet's closet. She got some fancy beef and beet bowl, mostly for the alliteration, as well as another glass of wine.

There was a blazing energy working its way through Janet's body, which might have just been the alcohol, but also the fact that she was finally talking to people who actually *got* her on some level. Okay, the Russian girl was a little overly poised and appeared to be in another world half the time, and the British girl seemed a bit scared of everything. But they understood what she was talking about when she spoke. It was enough to make her feel alive again, for once, finally.

It might also have been the fact that it looked like Izzy had met this Gemma girl, several months ago, all the way in London. What an insane coincidence. It was the kind of thing that wasn't actually supposed to happen in real life, and Janet's first thought had been that she could put it in her next letter to Ur. Then she remembered that, of course, there would be no next letter to Ur.

There would be no next letter to anyone, because five minutes ago in the bathroom, she had emailed in her notice of resignation. Hasty, yes, but she'd had the chance to send in her last piece of grievance letter correspondence surrounded by the smell of stale urine and shit, and she hadn't wanted to let the opportunity go to waste.

Janet stifled a burp and reminded herself to slow down on the wine. By the time dinner arrived she was on her third glass. Meanwhile, Anna was elegantly nursing her second glass of white wine, and Gemma kept glancing around the room whenever she took a sip of her drink, as though expecting someone to swoop in and exclaim, "Aha! A minor!" Janet felt a stab of nostalgia. What it had been like to feel rebellious when drinking alcohol. And she was only twenty-two, for god's sake. She wasn't that far from Gemma's age.

"I'm kind of scared of going home," she confessed. "I can only imagine what my sister's been up to in my absence."

"You think she'd ruin the place?" Anna asked in concern. "Burn it down or something? Is she very disorganized?"

"Oh no, she wouldn't burn it down or anything, but she would probably get the idea to redecorate and put up aesthetic fall decor with little pumpkins or, you know, 'cute' goblins or something like that. She can be kind of annoying."

Gemma looked like she was about to say something, and then didn't.

"That doesn't sound annoying," Anna said softly. "That sounds wonderful."

"Yeah, I mean, I don't know. Family can be annoying sometimes."

"I really miss my family."

Gemma didn't say anything.

Fuck. Janet tried not to let her emotions show on her face. She had messed up, offended them—not just one, but both at the same time. That took skill.

She took another swallow of wine. It was dark and rich and tasted like the way she had pictured purple grapes as a child, before she'd ever eaten them (the Ha family was not big on fruit), her imaginings based only on illustrations in books. Aesop's Fables, for example—that picture of the fox rearing up, trying to grab the heavy-looking violet bunch in its teeth. Janet had imagined these grapes as full not of clear sweetish juice but a black-purple sap. When she eventually tried real grapes, they had been disappointingly saccharine and watery in comparison.

"Sorry," she said, but she wasn't sure anyone heard her. She said it very softly. Probably, she realized a few seconds later—as though she were watching herself from a distance, with a few seconds' delay—on purpose.

When she tuned back into the conversation, Anna and Gemma were talking about some guy named Derek. Gemma's face had hardened into something almost intimidating.

"You did absolutely the right thing," Anna said as soon as Gemma had finished her sentence. "What a douche this boyfriend was. Reminds me of... some people I won't name." She had a pinched, mysterious expression. "Anyway, that's in the past. The recent past."

"You don't have anyone special in your life right now?" Gemma asked.

"Not recently, no," Anna said. "There was the boyfriend I mentioned, but I didn't really love him, so into the trash heap of memory he goes."

"The trash heap of memory," Janet mused. "I like that."

"Isn't that a Dali painting?" Gemma asked.

"No," Anna said. "That's *The Persistence of Memory*. I saw it at the MOMA a few months ago. My trash heap boyfriend took me."

"Beautiful, like a circle," Janet remarked.

"Why was he a trash heap?" Gemma asked.

"He wasn't *really*. He wasn't what I needed, though. I mean, he was rich? And that helped?" She was losing her poised tone, beginning to sound lost, like her thoughts weren't laid out clearly before her but instead disappearing into a distant mist. "But I was losing myself when I was with him. The way he saw me was off, different from who I really am. And I began to see myself that way too."

"I don't understand," Janet said, raising her eyebrows, although she thought she did. "Was he your sugar daddy?"

Anna's face tightened.

"No judgment," she added quickly. "I think everyone would

do that if they could. Hell, I'd have five or six of them, and rotate."

"I don't know about that," Gemma said. "Some of us value monogamy."

"I was joking. I wouldn't..." Everything Janet said was coming out wrong. "Sorry. Never mind."

"Yes," Anna said. "He was."

Janet hadn't expected her to admit it so readily. She almost said *No judgment* again, but then she realized how it might come across, as though she were the perceived judgment holder and only she had the ability to save Anna from being judged. Instead, she took a sip of wine and waited for Anna to elaborate.

"He was an okay person," Anna eventually said. "He wasn't a villain or anything. But when he lost his money, well, aside from being dishonest about it, he wasn't doing anything for me, and I didn't need him anymore. It sounds callous, and I feel bad saying it, but... that's how it is."

"Well, of course," Janet said. She didn't think it sounded all that callous. "You think if you lost your beauty, you'd still be doing something for him? Or if you lost your youth? When, rather. A relationship like that is a simple transaction, so no need to feel all guilty about not valuing him as a *person* or anything. I mean, I don't know you guys or your relationship. But it really seems to me that you're attempting to manufacture guilt where there isn't any there naturally."

"I hope he's okay, but I haven't been able to get in contact with him. I didn't exactly try very hard. Although, there was actually someone else." Anna's expression changed, growing a little more lost. "I was very young—still older than you, though, Gemma—and we only dated for six months. We were pretty poor. We went to Florida together, once. That was it for our romance." She wrapped her fingers around the stem of her wine glass, deliberate and contemplative, like she was searching for a hand.

"Florida?" Janet sat up straighter, half-laughing. "Is this my cue?"

"Why would it be?" Gemma said.

"My sister lives there, remember?"

"Where in Florida?" Anna asked absently. Still gazing into her wine.

"Fort Lauderdale."

Anna frowned. Something flashed across her face, something fleeting and spectral. "Really?"

"Well, yeah. Why not? I'm the first one to say it. I wouldn't have gotten the idea anywhere else. Why? Don't tell me that's where you two went?"

"Yes. We stayed with a friend who had a house right by the beach. That place was magnificent. I'll never forget it."

"Well, that's not where my sister lives. She's a lot further inland. We do know one person who lives by the beach, but I think—yeah, she told me he was one of the first to evacuate. He's definitely got enough money to buy another house."

Anna was silent. "Sorry," she said. "It's just kind of weird to imagine that that house will be gone soon. I heard about the hurricane on the news, you know. It's not like I live there or anything, and I'd never have seen it again. It was a really nice place, though. It had blue walls, huge windows, a tiny fountain. It's not something I'd want to think about getting destroyed."

The description triggered something in Janet's memory. She'd visited years ago, when she had flown down to see Izzy, and she still recalled some of the more elaborate (and tacky) furnishings. "White interior? Greek sculptures dotted in random places throughout, like he was trying to live out a Met Museum fantasy? But also trying to counteract some of the modern art in the bathroom?"

Anna nodded. "Yes, that's exactly what it looked like. The bathroom was all done in this beautiful marble, dark and glossy. It echoed like... like the inside of a seashell."

"And the shower blasted from directly overhead with the pressure of a thousand suns?"

Gemma looked back and forth between them, her eyes wide.

"Zack?" Janet offered hesitantly.

Anna shrieked. Gemma jumped. Janet spilled her wine. "That was his name!" Anna said. "You know him?"

"He's a friend of my sister's," Janet said, feeling a little shell-shocked. Anna was staring at her, amazed, hypnotized.

"My goodness," Gemma said.

Janet started laughing. "Izzy! I can't wait to tell her. This is fucking crazy. She'll never believe me."

"No, this is *impossible*," Anna said, looking at Gemma, remembering. "How?" She cleared her throat. "Janet. Is your sister actually several different people?"

"Is your sister actually three sisters in a trench coat?" Gemma suggested.

"I don't think so," Janet said. "I guess she just, like, knows a lot of people."

She was about to say something else to Anna, but Anna looked like she was deep in thought. She was gazing at the wood grains in the table as though they contained pictures only she could see. Or as though she were trying to see something in them.

Looking around, Janet noticed that the restaurant was closing down. Crazy—she hadn't even thought they'd been here that long. But the waiters were wiping down tables and stacking chairs at the back of the room and giving them increasingly pointed looks. Janet knew it was time to ask for the check, but she let a few seconds pass first. Finally she spoke, they brought it, the three of them paid, and the last guests trickled out like embers in the dimming light.

Janet came home with the wine still swirling around her head. The ghost of yesterday's headache was beginning to resurface. She paused in the musty-smelling hallway outside her apartment, not wanting to barge in on unsteady feet. She could hear sounds from behind the door: a child's burble of laughter, Ted's low voice, his words blurred and indistinct, Izzy's higher-pitched tones. It was an alien experience, and she stood there motionless, surrounded by wallpaper the color of dead autumn leaves. Janet had never before heard any noises coming from behind her door, because no one else was ever there. Even when her roommate was home, she never had any friends over, and rarely watched TV or talked on the phone. It felt bizarre, standing there, listening.

Finally she let herself in. Both the living room and the kitchen had been transformed in her absence. The living room was full of toys, stacks of games, and little boxes of raisins and fruit snacks. At least there were no actual snacks on the floor. But the house was *full* in a way it had never been before. Izzy had even decorated the formerly empty windowsills: there was a framed photograph of Izzy and Ted, as well as an older one of Izzy and Janet. Janet didn't recognize it, didn't remember posing for it. But it was her, probably around age thirteen or fourteen: there was the firmly set jaw, the sour, sarcastic smile. The recognition made her feel suffocated—too much of herself, everywhere, even with her sister and her family here—and she looked away.

Izzy and Ted had cooked dinner earlier, as evidenced by the smell of oil and garlic in the air and the dishes soaking in the sink. The countertops were gleaming and freshly washed. Izzy had even set up a few tchotchkes on the kitchen counters: a plump egg timer, salt and pepper shakers that fit together in the forms of kissing elephants. There were a couple of new recipe books on the counters, the contents of which could probably be found online.

Noticing her gaze, Izzy said, "I thought we'd maybe try a game night one of these days." She gestured towards the stacks of Monopoly, Scrabble, Chutes and Ladders. "They're kind of childish, but as you'll find, three-fifths of my family is comprised of children. So, we've had to adapt." She laughed. "They've taken over."

"Wow," Janet said. "I thought I would just sit broodily in the corner with a glass of Scotch and watch you all play. But if you're inviting me, I guess I can't say no."

"Don't be like that." Izzy bent down to attend to Ruby, who was crawling around the room like a short, giggling caterpillar.

Janet reminded herself again that everything Izzy and Ted left behind would certainly be destroyed in the hurricane. Who knew what these items might mean to them, anyway? Maybe the recipe book had been a wedding present. Perhaps Ruby had been conceived in full view of those amorous salt and pepper shakers. Taking on Ur's supercilious, judgmental attitude would do her no good. She would try not to think too hard about what the salt and pepper shakers might have seen, though.

Another thing: the apartment no longer looked strangely small, as it had when they'd first entered. In fact, it seemed to have grown larger. Even with all the added stuff and five more people, it was as though the walls had expanded to fit. And even though the same lights were in place, it was somehow less dim and gloomy. Like there were more surfaces to reflect on. More things for the light to touch.

Then she remembered, in a rush, what she had done at the restaurant. Tapping at her screen in the bathroom, erasing a potential future in mere seconds. Her job hadn't been great fun, but it had *paid*: for food, rent, her student loan debt, all the things that were necessary for her continued existence. That was the important part. That was why people *got* jobs. And she'd thrown hers away because of one bad choice.

She knew she should be experiencing heavy, reverberating pangs of regret right about now. She wasn't, but she should be. Maybe they would kick in tomorrow; maybe she was in some form of shock.

"We left some dinner for you in the fridge," Ted said, breaking her out of these thoughts. "In case you get hungry later. We noticed there wasn't a ton of food around here."

"Thanks." She couldn't believe it, but she was hungry again. She made herself a bowl of the leftovers—tofu stew with brown rice—and ate it standing up in the kitchen. When she came back into the living room, Izzy was playing with Ruby on the couch, sitting cross-legged and holding her daughter's hands, moving them up and down and making a joyful expression every time she did so. On the floor, Ted was showing Terry how to solve a crossword puzzle. Henry was lying on his back beside them, examining the ceiling and trying to find patterns in it.

Janet felt out of place, but Izzy gestured for her to sit down on the couch next to her. "How was your day?" Izzy asked as she sat. "Did you meet those girls for dinner? The ones from the protest?"

"Yeah. They were pretty cool, actually. I didn't even have to fake an attack of diarrhea to get away."

"What?"

"Never mind." She would tell her about Ur later. Maybe. She ought to tell *someone,* after all. It was just too good not to tell. Hell, maybe she'd tell Anna and Gemma. They didn't seem like they'd judge her.

She remembered again: she'd just quit her job. She'd have to find a new one. It was like she had to keep reminding herself to feel bad about it. Because whenever she thought about the fact that she would never again have to read a grievance letter, never again have to infer exactly what kind of specialists a person might need from a two- or three-paragraph missive dashed off in five minutes... she didn't feel anything but relief. Every other emotion about the situation was something she had to consciously manufacture.

"What about the protest itself?" Izzy asked. "Did I miss a lot?"

"I..." Janet watched Izzy smooth Ruby's hair and make a face at her, puckering up her lips like a fish. Ruby squealed with laughter, the sound reminiscent of air squeezing out from a packing bubble. "It depends on how you think of it. I liked being there, but at the same time, it still feels like I haven't made any difference. I'm just one person out of thousands. It's good that so many people were there, though. I didn't expect there to be."

"Did it make a difference for you?"

"Yeah, but—that's not the point. It's not supposed to make a difference for me. It's meant to make a difference for the planet, for the world."

"But you're *part* of this world!" Izzy cried in a British accent. Janet immediately recognized the reference to a scene from *The Two Towers,* where Merry is begging Treebeard to do something about Saruman. It had been so long since they'd watched those movies together, at least six years—how could Izzy still remember?

Janet smiled weakly. "I guess I am."

"What with the hurricane and everything," Izzy continued, "I think now is the perfect time for a protest. It will probably get more traction than if the hurricane hadn't happened. If you think about it, it couldn't have happened at a better time. Optimism? Is that how it works?"

"I wouldn't know. But I think that's the general idea."

Ruby squeaked and Janet glanced over at her, startled.

"Do you want to hold her?"

"I don't know. Does she enjoy being held?" She regarded Ruby with caution.

"Of course! You're her aunt! And you're probably a welcome departure from the people she's been trapped in close quarters with for the last two days. Just let her come on over." Indeed, Ruby was already toddling across the couch in the direction of Janet with the expression of a crazed adventurer. When she fell into Janet's arms, she was soft and warm like dough and smelled, for some reason, of fennel.

"*Ba*," Ruby pronounced, gazing up at her. "Gramma?"

Izzy snorted with laughter and buried her head in her hands. "No!" she said in despair. "Not grandma! *Aunt*! Don't be insulted, Janet, I'm not even entirely sure she knows what it means."

"Aunt," Ruby said. Her mouth was so small, her eyelashes so long. It sounded like *Unt*.

"Yup," Janet said. "That's me. Wacky Aunt Janet."

"Cookie?" Ruby suggested hopefully.

"No more cookies," Izzy said. "Try talking some philosophy, sis, maybe she'll understand in some small corner of her brain."

"Or we could just teach her her colors."

So they spent some time introducing Ruby to the world of primary and secondary colors, which she absorbed with wide-eyed wonder and the occasional sound of disagreement. The whole time, Janet held her. She seemed quite content in her aunt's arms.

"Do you think she'll have a good life?" Izzy asked. There was something new and open in her face, an almost pleading expression.

"I hope so," Janet said, and it felt like the truth. "I think so."

This second sentence felt like a lie. But maybe hope was not as meaningless an emotion as she'd always thought. Maybe it even had the potential to be stronger than pure belief, because hope, after all, was what had brought the protest together in the first place. She was sure that a lot of the other protest-goers had had their doubts about it, too, that even as they marched they were suspecting it wouldn't make a difference. In the crowd, she had felt it: their uncertainty, their lack of conviction. But they hoped. That was why they were there, in the end.

Ruby looked up at her. Janet looked back, and when the toddler's face broke into a wide, gummy smile, eyes squinting with delight, she was unable to prevent herself from smiling back. The expression felt strange on her face, too vulnerable, but Ruby didn't seem to notice. She just smiled at her aunt as though she were seeing only the brightness of the future, as though she were drinking in all the joy that could possibly be found in the years to come.

CHAPTER 25

Anna

Going home that night, Anna felt like she had stepped into the past. It pooled around her body, clinging to her ankles in oily strands. The tiny bird silhouette on her wrist—goose, gull, ghost—flickered in the dim streetlights. It almost looked like it was moving. Trick of the light, she told herself. Trick of the light, of too much alcohol.

She unlocked her door and re-entered her apartment. It looked smaller than it had when she'd left. Quieter, too. The paint duller. The furniture older, in the process of becoming fossilized.

The necklace was still in the corner where she had thrown it all those days ago. It was probably her imagination, but it looked like there was already a thin coating of dust on the metal. She picked it up and dropped it into the garbage.

She had never decorated this place much beyond the furnishings Warren had given her, the vase and the jewelry box and the dressers and the sofa. But there had been no reason for her to restrict herself so tightly to Warren's vision of who she ought to be. No reason other than the fact that she had needed to play the part of Warren's doll as much as possible even when she was away from him, in order to feel like less of her true self. To protect that innermost Anna from what her life had turned into.

Her feet hurt like crazy; she could picture the blood pooling in the lower halves of her legs and her feet, making them ache and pulsate. She lay back on the couch and elevated her legs on the wall, letting the blood rush back to her head and her heart.

Throughout that entire dinner, she had never had to try to convince herself that she belonged there, at that table, that *this was who she was*. She had just existed. How long had it been since she'd done that? Since she'd felt like herself again, the smallest Russian doll inside the other doll-layers, covered with a skin-coating of dust. So small it was not really a doll at all, but more like a seed.

Sunday brought with it an overcast sky and dim, bleary light. A dour mood had settled over Anna too, and when she spoke to her parents that afternoon, it was hard for her to fake any cheer. Even her mother sensed that something was wrong. This was surprising, as Anna had never really thought Ksenia paid much attention to her daughter's moods. Her worrying had always seemed to be an emotion that existed independently, like a tree bending and writhing without the influence of wind. But today she paused in the middle of a story about Anna's brother's new security officer job, and said pointedly, "Anya. What's the matter?"

"Why would anything be the matter?"

"You're quiet. Your energy is low."

Anna blew air out through her nose. A mistake: her mother's gaze only sharpened. A sigh meant trouble underfoot.

"I'm... not great," she confessed.

Ksenia remained quiet, waiting for her to explain. The tactic worked, as it always did. Anna continued, "Something went wrong with someone I was seeing."

"A boy?" The word she chose sounded almost infantile. Anna realized she had no idea how her mother saw her, whether it was as an adult, a young woman, or still a girl. In her maternal mind, perhaps the current image of Anna was forever obscured by that of a towheaded child in corduroy overalls and tiny socks, a ghost-picture that would never fully fade.

"I suppose," Anna said, as though Warren were some in-between figure, not quite a boy and not quite a man. "It wasn't anything to do with me in particular, not directly. He had some money issues and got in trouble for it, legal trouble."

"But it has affected you directly."

"Yes." Anna picked at one of her nails, knowing she couldn't reveal any more than that. "It has." She had a sudden tearing feeling: her mother would *never* know how to reach her, how to comfort her, in this situation. Her pale blue eyes were full of sympathy but not empathy, concern but not understanding. Because it was impossible for her to understand. Anna could never tell her what the arrangement had really been with Warren, how it all boiled down to money and transactions and the exchange of flesh for digits in her bank account. Her mother didn't know about these things. She knew about cows and their kind eyes, and horses and their innumerable neuroses, and tractors and their rust and grumbling. She knew how to coax a fire into life without a match, how to use fresh milk to make yogurt and cream. Things Anna missed, things she would never be able to do now, with her perfectly manicured fingernails.

"So I'm kind of lost," she continued. "I don't know what's going to happen to me, really."

"But the troubles were with him, no? Not you."

"True. But I can't see him, I can't speak to him... the whole essence of the relationship is basically lost," she added in a flash of boldness.

"Well, of course you were with him for his money."

"What?" Anna wondered if perhaps she'd missed something, had said something and then promptly forgotten. "How did you —why did you say that?"

Her mother looked amused. "It's clear to me, because the very first thing you did was to separate yourself from it. You said it wasn't a direct problem with you."

"Oh." Anna felt herself shrinking.

"Then you pointed out that he had money troubles."

"Yes."

"So? Clear to me. When we're ashamed of someone we separate them from ourselves, first of all. And then when you talked about the issue with money, and without anything... else..." she circled a hand in the air, "about him, I got the idea that you aren't worried too much about him right now."

"I am. I am worried. But honestly, I'm more worried about myself." It was freeing, in a way, to give voice to her own selfishness. The freedom that came with speaking the truth. Because it was the truth: her worry for Warren was a vague, abstract emotion, eclipsed by the much stronger and more pointed anxiety for herself and her own future.

"Good," Ksenia said pointedly. "That's *exactly* what you should be doing."

"Oh?"

"*Oh*," she repeated, with a trace of exasperation. "Yes, *oh*. Do you think anyone other than me and your father think of your safety, health, and happiness more than our own? We're the only people who will. Besides us, you only have yourself. You're still young, Anya. Do you know how many people you will meet in your life? Unless you are very, *very* lucky, none of them will ever put you first. You have to look out for yourself. You can't afford to not worry about your future, especially these days."

"I thought I was lucky with him," she said softly. It was the sort of thing a lovesick teenager would say—or heartbroken, rather. Why had she thought *lovesick?* It wasn't a word mix-up, a consequence of trying to think in English.

No, the word *lovesick* had flashed through her mind because as her mother said, *Unless you are very, very lucky,* she'd thought of someone else. Someone she had known once, a few years ago. Who had made her realize, for the first and only time in her life, that she was capable of caring about someone else much more than about herself.

Her mother thought she was referring to Warren. With skepticism, she said, "Was it luck, or a favorable circumstance that you brought about?" She raised an eyebrow. "And now he no longer seems to be favorable, given what you liked about him in the first place. Something else to remember, Anya: luck doesn't occur in the form of a person. It occurs in the patterns, the things that happen to you. People are just part of the pattern. They are incidental."

"So..." Anna hesitated, wondering how to phrase her next question. They didn't usually have this type of conversation. "What are you saying? I'm a person. Do you think I'm incidental?"

"In a way, yes." Her mother laughed. The lines on her face creased, faint and fragile like rivers seen from space. "You are very special, of course. But to me, you're my daughter above all else. You're *daughter* more than you are *Anya*. If had given birth to any other girl instead of you, I'm sure I would love her just as much."

Anna had the feeling that if they had been having this discussion at some earlier point in her life, even just a few weeks ago, she would find these words disquieting. They spoke to a vanishing of herself, a wiping-away. But now, they were comforting. With the wiping-away came relief, and a kind of freedom.

CHAPTER 26

Gemma

I t was the first time since Tuesday that Gemma was truly gutted over Derek. Not because she suddenly missed *him*, missed staring wistfully at him over the dimly lit kitchen table as he lost himself in his sports videos, but because she so badly wanted to tell him what she had learned. Earlier today, she had met someone whose sister might have taken the last picture she had with her mother. Those sorts of things didn't happen all the time. It was a tenuous connection to her mother, her mother still alive in someone else, someone other than Derek.

But she had no one to tell.

When Gemma got home on Saturday, Derek was hunched over his phone and ignored her when she came in. But this wasn't a bad thing, she reminded herself. She narrowed down her options, and found her number-one potential roommate, Theresa, in the Upper East Side apartment offer. She kept thinking *potential,* as there was no guarantee she would take the apartment. It was smaller than her place with Derek, for one thing. (Although she was finding it extremely hard to care about these things. Small might very well mean cozy.) Apparently Theresa went to bed at around the same time Gemma did, so not too late, and slept a solid nine hours every night. She also tended to work a lot and spent a lot of evenings out at the gym or with friends. She didn't even smoke weed, a quality Gemma had been hard-pressed to find on the app—it seemed that not only did most of the people there smoke constantly, they insisted that you smoke *with* them. So by the time she found Theresa, it felt like she'd happened upon a one-in-a-billion occurrence.

Late on Sunday morning, she took the train uptown to visit the apartment. She'd left her suitcases, full of everything she would want to take with her, by the door of the bedroom. How strange that when she came back, it would be for them, not for Derek. How strange that the very reason she'd had for taking that apartment in the first place was now her reason for leaving it.

Theresa's building was on 77th Street. It was ancient, pre-war, smelling of resin and sawdust and something else Gemma couldn't name, something that reminded her of blistering radiators and ballet classes on a splintery wood floor. The elevator was one of those ones where you had to pull a handled door open to enter. She rode up in silence, running over questions in her head. She'd written down a list of them but had forgotten to bring the list.

The fifth-floor hallway was dim; at one end there was a window, through which murky light shone, fighting its way through the foggy buildup of grime on the pane. It was only noon, and early autumn, but it felt like a midwinter afternoon with the faint gray light and lack of sun. With a feeling of mounting dread, Gemma walked to Teresa's door—double-checking her phone, yes, it was this one—and knocked.

"He*llo!*"

Gemma's first impressions of Theresa: lavender perfume, an Afro, unexpected height. She swayed like a sunflower in the doorway. "I love your accent!" she said, as soon as she heard Gemma's answering *Hello.* "Where are you from? London?"

"Yup. Got it in one."

"Well, come in, come in, don't stand there. Don't want you to linger in that hallway any longer than necessary." Theresa made a face, and as she stepped aside so Gemma could enter, she understood why. The room was full of light. It streamed in through the windows at the end of the living room, touching everything—the dark red sofa, the gold-trimmed coffee table, the cluttered ornaments on the desk. She hadn't seen it so bright in a room in months. The kitchen was little more than a nook, and the living area wasn't exactly large, but the light seemed to open everything up. Well. This was a surprise.

"You weren't kidding. I love the light in here."

"Uh-huh," Theresa said proudly. "The windows are south-facing. It's surprising how many people don't pay attention to the orientation of the windows in apartments they're looking at. East- and west-facing windows only directly get morning and late afternoon light, and north-facing windows get no direct sunlight at all. South-facing is the best. It was one of my biggest reasons for choosing the place. I'm like a plant, I need sunlight."

Gemma looked around, finding potential spots for actual plants. Here, they might actually be able to grow. "You gave more thought to it than I did," she remarked.

"First time looking for an apartment? It's so complicated, isn't it?"

"Yeah," Gemma said, after a pause. "I didn't even have to look for my last apartment, I just moved in with my boyfriend... at the time."

"Ah!" Theresa said pointedly. "We've had enough with him, yes? It's much less stress living with a girl, I can tell you. Of course, I'm biased, you know, looking to get a roommate, so you probably shouldn't listen to me. But... listen a little." She winked. She showed Gemma the bathroom, which was marble, thankfully mildew-free, and smaller and narrower than the bathroom at Derek's but with much more stuff in it. Gemma actually found herself appreciating the shampoo bottles, hair products, and scrubs on the counters. They gave the bathroom a vaguely spa-like feel, instead of making it look like nothing more than a place to do your business, shower, and brush your teeth. The utter lack of any products in Derek's bathroom—other than toothpaste, a toothbrush, and combination shower gel/shampoo—had made Gemma feel silly when she'd unloaded her toiletries upon moving in. She even remembered him giving her a glance when she added a new body scrub at one point, as though thinking, *Oh great, another piece of shit I have to put up with in my bathroom.*

"And now let me show you the bedrooms. Don't be shy, and don't mind the horse posters, I can take them down if you want. I just liked them there to provide a bit of atmosphere when I walked past the room." She said it offhandedly, as though to convince Gemma it was no big deal.

"The horse posters?" Gemma prepared herself for a room that looked like a ten-year-old had decorated it. But as they walked into the empty bedroom, she saw that there were three large posters on the otherwise unadorned white walls. Only three. One was of a Friesian tossing its head, arching the glossy black musculature in its neck, veins visible against skin the texture of satin. Another was of a white horse emerging from the mist, its muzzle the dark gray of rainclouds, its eyes doll-lashed and inquisitive. The third, which hung above the bed, was of a mare and her foal.

"I should've taken them down," Theresa admitted, knotting her hands together. "I just, I don't know, I really like them. I think I hoped I'd find another horse obsessive." She gave a stilted laugh. "It's no big deal to take them down, though. Say the word and I will. I have a few in my own room, of course, but I got used to where these were, and...."

Gemma couldn't look away from the third poster. The foal was standing beside its mother. The mare, an Appaloosa, was turning her head to place her nose against her baby's cheek. The foal's eyes were bright and eager, and it had taken one spindly leg off the ground, as though it would break away at any instant and return to playing. But the mare's head looked solemn. She seemed to be pressing her nose to her foal's with a quiet sadness, as though to say, *Stay a little longer.*

"My mum used to take me riding," she said. She hadn't expected to say it. She felt her throat tightening, the space in her chest growing smaller and smaller. For a horrible instant she thought Theresa would say, *Oh, how lovely! Tell me about her!* and then Gemma would cry. But Theresa saw something in her face, or heard something in her voice. After a few moments she said, meekly but with empathy, "I'm sorry."

"They're beautiful posters though." She paused. She got ahold of herself. "I really like it, Theresa. I think I want the room. No, I do want the room."

It was nice, for once, to know what she wanted. And she thought that if her mother could see her right now, she would be nothing so much as proud.

"I want you to move in too," Theresa said. "You seem nice and normal, which can be a big ask these days."

"Could I move in this evening?"

"You're... kidding?" Theresa squinted at Gemma. It took a few more tries before she could be convinced that Gemma really did have all her stuff packed in a couple of suitcases, and she really did want to move in as soon as possible.

"It's the boyfriend, isn't it," Theresa said at one point, and when Gemma nodded, she nodded too, as though they shared a solemn secret. "I get that. I had to break up with my ex-boyfriend when I discovered he was helping run a dog-fighting ring. It was awful. But at least they all got sentenced for it—with my help."

"Oh Jesus."

"Yeah, so don't go thinking it's you who's the unlucky one, or something. New York men are like that. In fact, you could even say... but I won't go there." She laughed. "Don't mind me."

Gemma signed the lease and sent Theresa her deposit. Her new roommate said a couple more times that she'd never seen someone as eager to move as her, but she said it with admiration, as though Gemma's attitude were a welcome departure from the slow, resigned decision-making of everyone else. "You seem to be one of those people who, when they make up their mind, really makes it."

"I definitely am," Gemma replied, thinking of how to make

a subtle exit that evening. "Or at least I'm trying to be." Maybe Derek would try a last-ditch attempt to stop her from moving out. Maybe he would fall to his knees and plead with her. Maybe he would cry. Maybe he would rage and storm around. She hadn't seen these sides of him before, but who knew what might emerge.

After Gemma's tour of the apartment, she went straight to a bookstore in the area that she'd been wanting to visit for a while. With her eyes pulled in several directions at once, turning from one row of books to the next, she flipped through the newest hardcovers at the front of the store. By the time she came home, it was mid-afternoon and the apartment was empty. Derek was often home on Sundays, scrolling on his phone on the couch or watching something on his laptop.

Trying not to think of where he might be, she meticulously divested the bedroom of any last traces of her life—a stray pair of socks, her hairbrush, a candy wrapper beneath the bed—aware that she was biding her time. After she had removed every last possible remnant of herself from the apartment, she looked through the kitchen and bathroom for anything she might have forgotten. Just in case he showed up to throw himself at her feet and beg her not to leave.

As the time ticked by she felt stupider and stupider. The darkening apartment told her that she had no more business here, and every minute she remained would be a return to the paralysis, the sickening slog. Maybe if she waited too long she would forget how to leave.

The suitcases were easy to carry. She took an Uber uptown, and on the way, she found herself thinking of her mother, picturing her face and her smile and her voice. Her voice was the hardest to call to mind: she had to remember the phrases her mother had said often, the ones that were so familiar to her that she could "picture" her voice perfectly. Things like *That's all for today, everyone* (when someone had made a bad joke or an awkward comment) and *Oh fiddlesticks* (when she stuck herself with the sewing pin) and *There she goes again* (when Gemma was doing something noteworthy, or silly, or often anything at all). And of course *Oh well* whenever anyone made a mistake or something bad happened. Stupid things, pointless things really, but full of meaning for the two of them.

She kept thinking of her mother all the way until the car pulled up on 77th Street. It was the longest Gemma had thought about her without crying.

CHAPTER 27

Janet

On Sunday afternoon, Janet woke and realized that she was less heavy. Less leaden, less like a murky body-soup dragging itself towards the center of the earth, and more like a being comprised of coils of energy. She sat up and felt none of the same soporific morning sensations she had grown so used to feeling over the last few months.

Well, maybe a little. Her dreams pulled at her, inviting her to fall back into them. Her limbs were foggy with sleep. But it was late morning already. The apartment was empty and held a startled, hushed feeling, as though everyone had just left. Bowls stood in a distracted line next to the sink; when Janet went over to look at them, she saw that they were still wet.

She glanced at her phone. It was almost noon. Izzy had texted her, asking her if she was awake yet and that they'd gone to Central Park, and would be coming back by two p.m. *We wanted to take you but I wasn't sure if you'd be ok with being woken up, lol!* Janet read the message a few times, wondering what it would have been like if she had woken up in time. If Izzy really would have invited her out with them.

She decided to find out, and texted back, asking if she could join them at the park. When her sister replied a few minutes later, saying she'd love her to come, Janet took the train downtown. A long-haired, bearded young man was the only person speaking on the entire subway car. "It's gonna be riddled with toxins," he was drawling. His companion seemed like he might not be fully awake. "It won't be fresh fruit. It'll be *unfresh* fruit." Something unintelligible from his companion. The young man gave a long sniff. "You can riddle your body with toxins if you *want.*"

Janet had never heard anyone use "riddle" as an active verb before. She tried to tune him out; for some reason, he reminded her of Ur. Perhaps if Ur were on this subway car—she looked around surreptitiously, just to make sure he wasn't—he would take on this man's mannerisms the next time he had the opportunity. Maybe that was how he got inspired. Watching other people and deciding which parts of them to imitate.

Janet got to the park at noon. The day was brisk and almost wintery, the pavement scratchy under her boots. A car screeched by, the radio blaring commercials. Janet glanced at it in disbelief, wondering how people could listen to that all day: loud obnoxious voices, advertisements screaming at them. She'd go crazy.

Then again, who was to say she hadn't already? Because, shit. Ur had not seemed to know he was delusional. This was something to think about as she entered the park.

Izzy and her family were at a corner of the park that was half-shaded, half-dappled with light. Ted and Terry were kicking a soccer ball around on a nearby field, running in and out of slices of sunlight. Izzy, on a nearby bench, cradled Ruby in her arms. Henry was crouched in the grass beside her, examining something. The air was thick with the scent of damp, crumbling leaves and gently rotting wood.

When Izzy saw Janet, she waved her over. "Hey!" She was wearing big, unseasonal sunglasses. "I'm glad you showed up. It gets pretty suffocating being in that apartment all the time."

"Yeah, we don't know *how* you do it," Henry said with an affected posh accent, standing up and pushing his stomach out.

Janet squinted down at him and tried—not very well—to imitate his accent. "Thank you, Henry. I don't know either."

Henry shook his head sadly at her failure and then called, "Mom, can I show Ruby the bugs? I'm finding new species."

"Just stay where I can see you," Izzy said. Then, as he began to lead Ruby over beyond the bench, she added firmly, "No, no —literally right there." She pointed to the foot of the bench.

"There's no bugs there," Henry said in disgust.

"Yes, there is. I see one right there."

"That's a *button*."

Finally they reached a compromise, allowing Henry to introduce Ruby to the wonders of nature while still remaining in close proximity to Izzy and Janet. Izzy glanced over at them every few moments, so naturally and smoothly it looked like breathing. Watching them gave Janet a strange, painful sensation in her chest. She remembered what Anna and Gemma had said last night, about how they missed their families. Gemma even more so than the other girl. When she thought about it, in this way Janet was luckier than both of them. Her family, or at least a big part of it, was all around her.

"It's strange to have you guys here," Janet finally said. Seeing Izzy's forehead crease over her sunglasses, she added, "Not in a bad way. Not at all. It's just different. Like new spaces have opened up inside the day. More hours, more time to do things with."

"So time *doesn't* fly when we're here," Izzy tried, with an awkward laugh.

"No, you don't understand. I usually wake up feeling like shit. Either I don't recognize my room for a few moments, or I feel *lost* in it. Or I feel super tired even though I slept nine hours. I don't want to go back to sleep, because my body is stiff and I'm thirsty and I need to pee and I need to do work, but I don't want to do anything either. And I'm always looking ahead to the next thing. I can never enjoy where I'm at in the moment, even if it's something I was looking forward to the whole day. I'm always skipping ahead to the next thing, the next thing to look forward to, except I never quite get there. And I never get any joy from the anticipation. I'm like a... a glitching film. Or a broken record that keeps trying to jump ahead to the next song." She stopped herself before she could come up with any more stupid metaphors. "I don't feel like that right now, though, or this morning. I think it's easier to feel like that when I'm alone."

"You don't have to be alone," Izzy said.

"The funny thing is, I actually thought I met someone. He was..." She cringed at the memory. "He was writing me grievance letters, and I started responding to him."

"But you aren't supposed to do that, right?"

"Don't—yeah. I know I'm not supposed to. But I couldn't stop myself from writing back. It was just a little bit at first, but eventually the two of us were trading these long letters. And at a certain point, he invited me to meet up with him in real life. At a café."

Izzy's eyes widened. It was probably the juiciest story she'd heard all week. "So what happened?"

"He wasn't that person at all. I got to the place where we were going to meet, and... it was eerie, Izzy. He was like some guy playing a part. He kept saying stuff that contradicted what he'd said earlier—like, he said he was looking for a job, but he'd told me previously that he was an employed professor. And then I noticed that he'd never heard of a place where his family had supposedly been living. Crazy shit. He made it all up. It was like he believed it, too. Like he truly believed all the stuff he was feeding me. Like he had mental problems, true delusions. And that's what scared me—how intensely he believed."

"Did you think he would hurt you?" Izzy leaned forward in concern. "Did he try?"

"No, that's not why. We were in public, and I left pretty quickly. But it scared me because I started to wonder how he ended up like that. What went wrong in his life that he was talking to someone over the internet, pretending—and really believing—that he was a university professor, that he lived somewhere he didn't. Like, how did he get there? And he really seemed to understand me, Izzy, like our thoughts ran on the same track. So what's stopping me from ending up the same way one day?"

"You aren't delusional, Janet." But Izzy looked solemn, as

though Janet had touched on something very close to the truth. The knot of fear in Janet's stomach tightened.

"I imagine he got there through some pretty intense isolation."

"You aren't isolated."

"Not anymore. Before you guys came, though? I was. It turns out you can only go on so many shitty Tinder dates before you realize that you aren't really talking to these guys at all. You're talking to yourself and watching them talk to themselves, as though you're separated by a pane of glass. It's like mutual masturbation. But verbal."

"If that's how the dating scene is now, I'm glad I'm not in it." Izzy made a face. "It sounds awful. I don't blame you for disliking it."

"I think I'm going to get in touch with work again about Ur." When she said his name now, it sounded like a non-word, a faceless monosyllable. "Oh, I quit my job," she added. "I guess I didn't tell you."

"No, you didn't tell me." Izzy was sounding more and more worried. Janet felt a bit chagrined—as though she hadn't known that it was not normal to cross professional boundaries with a client and begin talking to them, superimposing onto them your ideal image of someone who Really Understood You. And then quit your job in a wine-riddled display of impulsivity, dooming yourself to scrolling through the pages of online job listings.

"Oh. Yeah. Anyway, I quit. The other day. Yesterday, actually. And..." She looked out across the field, where Ted and Terry were still kicking the soccer ball back and forth. "And I think I should get in touch with them and alert them to his presence. He's probably bugging my replacement right about now, drowning them in letter after letter of cynicism."

"Was that the kind of stuff you talked about?"

"Pretty much. And then we'd congratulate each other on our understanding of it." She stifled a laugh. It felt like it would come out too bright, too hysterical. "It felt really awesome to have someone get me, you know? I felt like for once I was the one writing the grievance letters, except to someone who would actually respond."

"Almost like therapy," Izzy said, contemplative. Her sunglasses flashed in the light as she looked out over the grass; then she turned her head and they reflected Janet's face back to herself at a warped, stretched angle. "Except in therapy generally there is some progress made towards some kind of treatment, or outcome. Not just an echo chamber."

"Yeah," Janet said. "I... Yeah. I can't argue with that."

Izzy was silent for a minute, gazing over at Henry and Ruby. Henry was sitting back on his heels, looking exasperated. "She keeps trying to eat them!" he called over to Izzy.

"Don't let her. Protect them from her hunger!" Izzy leaned back and crossed her legs. "You know," she said in a softer voice, "after I gave birth to Ruby, I had these intense mood problems. I say mood problems but it was really like a cloud was in my brain, a dark cloud. Every time I tried to think about something happy, the cloud would be there. It was one of the reasons we went to London, to try to get away from my black cloud. But the black cloud followed me."

Janet had never heard Izzy confess anything like this before, ever admit to not having the perfect life.

Although maybe she would have, if Janet hadn't always made it so clear she was convinced that Izzy *did* have the perfect life.

"I couldn't find pleasure in anything. I would wake up and want to go right back to sleep. I would keep thinking, Why aren't you happy? You should be. You've got everything you ever wanted."

"Don't you think it's different, though?" Janet said, without meaning to. "I don't have everything I ever wanted. Definitely not. Even at that point, you had a husband and kids. So if you weren't happy, how could I possibly be?"

"But have you ever *thought* you might soon have everything you want? Like—" She held her hand up, began ticking things off on her fingers. "Just a few days ago, didn't you have a lot of the base levels of Maslow's Hierarchy of Needs? One: a job that isn't great, but a job. Two: food, shelter, clothing, the works. And you were building up some of the upper layers of that hierarchy, too. Because you also thought you might have, *three*: someone who understands you, a man, you were pretty sure, an educated, intelligent man."

Yeah, an educated man who didn't go to college, Janet thought. She didn't know how she could have missed that part. He'd written it right out in one of his letters, and she'd skimmed over it, willfully blind. "And?" she said. "This was still just potential stuff. At least the last part."

"But a lot of the positive emotional impact from good things happening actually occurs in the *anticipation* of those things happening. Not the things themselves."

This was true. Janet remembered reading it somewhere, ages ago, and it had stuck with her. Still, she hadn't expected Izzy to start talking about this, or about Maslow's Hierarchy of Needs, for that matter. And her surprise surprised her.

"Unless, of course, you're stuck in a funk like the one you described. Where you keep looking forward but even the looking-ahead doesn't bring you joy. It's more like, *Oh shit, I have this to get through too? And this? And this?* Before, you know, the end."

Janet just nodded.

"So, back to my point," Izzy continued, "with everything else being equal, you should have been at your *happiest* in the last few weeks. But you weren't, were you?" She gave Janet a piercing look, which felt like a rush of cold air. There was no way Izzy could possibly know this. But it was true. Janet hadn't been at her happiest for a long, long time. In fact, in the days leading up to her meeting with Ur, she had been more prickly and irritable than ever, like a remnant of humanity buckling down and gearing itself up for survival in a barren world. Like evolution in reverse.

"Don't you think a lot of my mood might come from the fact of what's happening to the world?" Janet tried. "Climate change, et cetera?" She didn't want to list it all out. It was too much.

"Janet, you're not the only one who's aware of what's happening. I've been reading up on more of this environmental stuff lately, too—yes, more than you probably think I have. And it's scary. But I'm not ready to lie down and die just yet, and I bet that's true for a lot of people. You assume that everyone is ignorant and indifferent, simply because they aren't staggering around the streets wailing and rending their clothes. But that isn't necessarily true. For one thing. How many people were at that protest the other day? Did that look like the face of apathy to you?"

Janet couldn't think of a reply.

"When you told me how you were feeling earlier," Izzy said in a softer voice, "the heaviness, the not wanting to get up, it reminded me of how I felt after Ruby's birth. Even the physical sensations, everything. Have you considered that you're depressed?"

I'm an Unsolvable, Janet thought, with a flicker of humor. "Probably. I'm sure lots of people are. But do you really think that taking drugs to rearrange my brain chemistry is going to fix it? The thought's a little—" She cut off abruptly; who knew if Izzy was on antidepressants herself.

"I'm not even referring to that. Just talking to someone might help. It helped me after Ruby. I talked to a therapist— don't tell Mom—and I also talked to other mothers who were going through the same thing." She pulled her legs up onto the bench, wrapped her arms around her knees. With that gesture, several years fell off like scales, and Janet was looking at the teenage Izzy, with her tattered band tees and soft smudged eyeliner. A girl she'd looked up to, despite herself, instinctively. "That probably helped the most. My kids are wonderful, but they can't relate to me the way another adult can."

"I guess Mom didn't feel that way." The sentence escaped Janet's mouth before it had even consciously processed in her brain.

She waited for Izzy to ask her what she was talking about, but her sister nodded, her gaze still on Ruby and Henry. "I think you're right. And I wonder how it would've been if she had had someone to talk to. Another adult besides Dad. Who was off in his own world most of the time anyway."

"What about Auntie?"

"Nope." She hesitated for a moment, precarious, like someone who had just walked out onto a wire and was considering whether or not to keep going. "You know they weren't talking when Mom was pregnant with me? And when I was little? And when Mom was pregnant with you?"

"That whole *time*?"

"Yep. Auntie discovered she couldn't get pregnant. It was a horrible time. She doesn't care anymore, obviously, but back then? Forget about it. Auntie *hated* her."

Janet stared at her sister in astonishment. It was like reading fanfiction about her own family. Or peering into an alternate universe. Janet had known their aunt was infertile, but she'd never thought it was a problem. Neither she nor her late husband had ever expressed a desire for children—the husband had even seemed annoyed by the younger Janet and Izzy, looking at them sideways when they wandered into the dining room while the adults were having a conversation.

"It was part of the Ha curse, she said," Izzy continued. "She wasn't even a Ha, of course, but she believed she got the curse by association. She told me some of this after a Christmas party, once, when I was about twelve years old. She was *very* drunk." She laughed, but with a straight face. The effect was eerie. "I asked Mom and Dad about it later, and even though they told me almost nothing, I was able to piece some stuff together. Apparently, even around the time *you* were born, they still weren't speaking. Dad was working all the time, and Mom had no one else. She was losing her mind, I think, taking care of both of us and trying to hang onto her sanity."

Janet tried to imagine what her mother might have been thinking, feeling. It was depressingly easy to picture her twenty or so years ago, in their house of broken lightbulbs and cracked laminate countertops. Bent over, back aching as she cleaned up a dark kitchen, the kids in the other room, the air aromatic with spice and the scents of a country she had never even visited. She had probably felt very far from everything that was supposed to be familiar. Maybe when she'd woken up in the morning her own room had felt strange to her. As well as her body, her life. Maybe she woke up thinking, *How the hell did I get here? And why can't I go back?*

"Do you think she never wanted to be a mother?" Janet asked.

"Yeah. I do sometimes think that. She was more of a suggestion than an actual mother, wasn't she? Supervising our grades, arranging birthday parties for us, signing parental consent forms. But it was only the bare minimum, wasn't it? Like when she took us to that gross, cheap restaurant for your tenth birthday and we all got food poisoning. Or how she didn't even glance at our volunteer work in high school before she signed her name. It was like she was playing a role. Performing the way everyone thought she ought to act."

Janet thought of Ur, and a shiver slid through her. "You used the past tense, but she's still a mother."

"Technically, yes, of course. As well as a grandmother." She glanced again at Ruby and Henry. "But I'm not sure she thinks of herself as one anymore. Because she doesn't have to be a mother now. She can just be herself."

"But," Janet said slowly, "wouldn't it be horrible to try to go back to being your old self again, a non-mother, and find out there's nothing to go back to?"

"You're scaring me a little, Janet." Izzy gave a nervous laugh.

"Sorry. We probably shouldn't talk about this depressing stuff."

"No, it's not like that. I like talking to you." Izzy laughed again. "Look at me getting all mushy and sentimental. You know, for the longest time, I thought Mom preferred *you*?"

"Hell no. She preferred *you.*"

"That's what she wanted you to think. I'm sure when it was just the two of you, she said great things about me. But in front of me, when you weren't there, she would always praise you. And I always felt like she took your side in arguments."

"What on earth could she have said about me that was good?" Janet recalled one incident involving a D+ in Latin, her mother practically cackling as she told Janet about Izzy's superior grades. Thirteen-year-old Janet had begun to cry silently, tears trickling into her mouth like raindrops on a windowpane, holding her face down so her mother couldn't see. At the time she'd congratulated herself on her stealth, because her mother had kept ranting for several more minutes before running out of steam. Now she thought that her mother had probably seen the tears and continued anyway.

"She said you were smarter."

"No way. I got worse grades than you."

"So? Didn't mean I was smarter. Only meant I studied harder." She shrugged. "See how it works? Either way you lose. Either you're the overachieving dummy or the slacking genius."

"Oh, come on. I doubt she called me a genius."

"Okay, she didn't call you a genius. But she did say you were naturally smarter." Izzy gave a small smile, but with her eyes behind the sunglasses, Janet couldn't see the entirety of her expression. She had the feeling that Izzy's eyes said something very different from her smile.

But like so many other things, she would never know for sure. All she could do was reach over and put her hand over Izzy's. It gave her the same feeling she'd gotten when she'd put her hand on Gemma's at dinner. Something to hold onto.

At this moment, shouts from Terry and Ted reached them. One of them had managed to kick the soccer ball into a tree, twenty or thirty feet off the ground. It rested gently in the branches like an oversized egg, cradled amongst the leaves. Terry was gleeful, Ted trying to act contrite but within seconds echoing his son's smile, both their faces open and unguarded in a perfect unreadiness.

"We were having a contest!" Ted called. "I couldn't just let him *win!*"

Izzy took her sunglasses off. "Have you lost your mind?" she called in Korean. But Janet caught the flash of an answering smile.

In that moment, Janet realized that she had finally stopped looking ahead to anything else. The present moment was enough, and in it, she was momentarily immortal.

CHAPTER 28

Anna

On Sunday afternoon, Anna took a shower and soaped the back of her neck, her ankles, the thin planes of her wrists. She tried to imagine that Warren would never touch these places of her again. She wasn't sure how she felt about this—it was a bittersweet fade, the feeling of putting something away, something that had benefited her greatly but also caused her entire picture of herself to contract and sharpen to an unknowable singularity.

Now she wasn't Warren's anything anymore. Now she was simply Anna, no more and no less. Without the need to define herself, her edges could swell and expand like a sea, lapping past the borders of her existence. It was just as her mother had said: she was everything and no one. Everything to her mother, of course, and to herself—which was not selfishness but a necessity, because in the fullness of time, she was no one.

But right now, while she was still here, she didn't want to be no one to the people around her. The thought persisted, entering her mind more and more, the shadow of a bird winging in past the edges of her vision: the ex-boyfriend was out there. He was reachable. And, ironically, he was always in the background of her thoughts, even more than her family was. Because she couldn't see him or talk to him. Not even on a screen. She had gotten rid of all the photos of him, all the text messages, everything. But he persisted, a memory of a memory of a memory. Shifting across her vision like the smoky remnants of a dream.

She had deleted his number from her contacts long ago, right after the breakup, filled with shame and guilt and horror at herself. In order to do what she knew she needed to, she had had to erase him from her phone as if he'd never been there.

But there was a note buried deep in her phone, way down at the bottom. It had his number, not that she had forgotten it anyway. Funny how she remembered a single ten-digit number, how it had stuck around so easily—it and its owner's name, although she had tried so hard to banish both of them from her brain.

Her fingers were heavy with anxiety as she typed his number into the keypad. The phone rang once, twice, three times. She kept thinking: *Let him pick up. Let him not pick up. Let him pick up. Let him not pick up.* As though she were plucking petals off a flower.

When he picked up he said not *Hello?* but *Anna?*

Her heart clenched like a fist.

"Hi," she said. "It's good to hear your voice. I just thought I'd call and see how you are."

"Hey. I've been good. It's good to hear you too." He hesitated. "What have you been up to? It's been a while."

His voice pushed her back into the past. She wobbled off balance, falling, tripping down the spiraling staircase of the last few years. And something else, too: despite all the dramatic scenes she'd read in books, Anna had never really believed that your heart could beat all *that* hard during intense situations. She'd thought it must be an exaggeration. Even when Warren was arrested, she had not noticed her heartbeat quickening. But now she could feel her heart banging against her rib cage, sending tremors through her body.

"Nothing too bad," she said. "Nothing too amazing. I was just wondering... are you still in Brooklyn?"

She remembered the wild chases around his kitchen table, the way he had pulled her tight next to his chest so she could feel the muscles there. They felt so close, those days: right up against her skin.

What had ever been the point, she thought, of anything else? If the world truly was ending, she was fucked no matter what. But she still had a few good years left before that happened. There was no reason to waste them with someone like Warren, living a life that took her so far outside of herself, stiffening into a lifeless doll.

"I am. Are you still in Manhattan? You were living uptown the last time I remember."

"Yes. But I'm living downtown now. It's a cute place." She looked around. The phone felt hot where it was pressed to her ear, as though it were a living being. "Maybe not right now, though."

"I've got to ask, Anna," he said after a moment. "Last time we spoke you made it clear you never wanted to see me again. So I've got to ask why you're calling. I've also got to ask what possessed me to even answer the phone. I mean, I thought I had some pride." His tone was serious but there was a hint of something else in it, something light and almost playful.

"Ah, it's me that doesn't have pride," she said. "Look, I only wanted to know one thing, and then I'll leave you alone forever, if that's what you want. And I wouldn't blame you. I wanted to ask, would you like to see me sometime? In person?"

Say yes, she willed him. And he did. It was a hesitant yes, and it didn't promise anything—just a meeting. Maybe nothing more. But she would see his face again, would see the last two years on it, how it had aged and matured along with her own. Would see how he had changed, perhaps. The person he had become.

CHAPTER 29

Gemma

On Sunday evening, Gemma came home to her new apartment for the first time. It was strange to say hello to Theresa instead of Derek, to sit on her bed in the small bedroom and look at the horse posters instead of the "influencer" decor she'd had in the other place. But although they were only pictures, the horses felt more real and consequential to her than those things had. Maybe it was because they were tied so strongly to things that had actually happened, reaching across the low and rolling foothills of memory, instead of popping in and out of a nebulous future she had only vaguely imagined.

Derek had not texted her since yesterday. She wondered if he was back home yet, if he'd noticed her absence, or if he was still... wherever he'd been when she left. But she didn't wonder about it too long. The thought had stopped bothering her after she'd stepped into the Uber, as though Derek were one of those low-frequency noises that caused immense psychological distress in the surrounding area but which, as soon as you escaped it, made your earlier unease seem like an apparition or a dream.

This apartment was quieter than the other; the street outside was less busy, the people moving around more slowly. She'd left behind the youthful rush of Chelsea—the sticky-sweet, blandly interchangeable ice cream and dessert shops, the sailor crushing the nurse in his arms like a trapped bird. The last time she'd seen that mural, days before leaving, she had noticed for the first time how harsh and forceful the kiss looked.

Now she was folded inside the antique dignity of the Upper East Side. As she always did on Sundays, Gemma thought ahead to the next week, to all the things she would have to do. Her creative writing class, if she didn't skip it, was in two days. She pictured the circle of faces, inquisitive and distracted and bored. It wouldn't be her turn to be workshopped again for a while, so she didn't need to contribute anything. And when it was her turn for workshop in a few weeks, she could wait until the very last moment and substitute some old piece of writing for her story—a short story she'd written in ninth grade, even. They'd never know the difference.

But she didn't want to do that. It would be like the paralysis all over again.

She undressed and took a shower and then lay in bed. The room was grayish in the half-dark, the horse posters fast losing their saturation, taking on the muted shades of old photographs. She recalled something she had read once: that at some point in the future, everyone who was alive would only ever have been photographed in color, not black-and-white. Black-and-white photographs would eventually become a relic of their ancestors, as remote as daguerrotypes.

A neighbor across the street turned off their lights, then another. The dots of yellow outside blinked out one by one. Overhead the night grew thicker and darker, threads of cloud turning the sky tattered. Rust crept through the constellations.

Gemma lay awake and tried to remember every detail she could of the last days she'd spent with her mother. Not the day of that April trip but later, when her mother had declined further, when she was too weak to even walk around. The stark white hospital smell, the walls as empty and impassive as the nurses' faces. Everything a reminder that her mother would be gone soon, that Gemma would shortly become motherless, half an orphan. These thoughts had hovered, ever-present, over the last few months, eventually growing rounded and softened as she turned them over in her mind, like stones beaten smooth by the ocean.

Gemma opened her phone, squinted at the rectangle of whiteness in the dim light. She found herself going to the Notes app. Maybe if she wrote some of this down it would leave her brain, stop popping up again and again like demons she had to beat back.

A few words turned into lines and then she'd written so many paragraphs that it was easier to just slide off the bed, flip open her laptop, and start typing. The things she wrote were nothing at all like what an influencer would discuss. Too sorrowful, for one, too vulnerable. Not spicy or glamorous or original. No gloss, no sparkle, nothing but the terrible ordinariness of death. But there was something freeing about it too, about getting it out of her at last.

She pictured the faces of her writing class peers, imagined them reading it, and felt a jolt of excitement. No one could possibly say there was anything missing or lacking, let alone pointless, about this piece—because there wouldn't be.

And another, stranger thing: the faces of some of these peers were shifting in her mind, turning into those of Janet and Anna. Their conversation in the restaurant had been so rich, somehow: so much said and so many changes happening in such a short time. At first Anna's intimidating, overly curated exterior had discomfited Gemma, thrown her off balance and made her wonder why she'd even accepted the other girl's invitation in the first place. But then Anna had revealed more of her life, her real life—slowly at first, cautiously, layers husking away one by one. And there had been her empathy, too, the unexpected warmth of her hug.

And Janet's nervous energy, which had seemed so awkward at first, almost aggressive. She'd been prickly, sardonic, just this side of unstable. But then had come her fervent, victorious realization that her sister might actually have met Gemma and her mother. Her raw vulnerability, her need to believe in this connection.

To Gemma, the encounter with those two girls had felt like a beginning in the midst of all of these endings that she was reading about and living through.

A siren wailed outside, catlike. Someone's front door closed with a thud. But Gemma barely heard these things. She kept on writing about all her yesterdays, and all her tomorrows rushed in through the pages, gliding on swift, rustling wings.

Acknowledgments

Thank you to Christoph and Leza and everyone at CLASH for believing in my book and for their invaluable insight, wisdom, and support.

Thank you to my loyal beta reader, my mom.

Thank you to my friends, both in and out of the Long Covid community, for their encouragement and kindness.

Thank you to Lily (my dog) for watching me in adoration as I typed.

And finally, thank you to Gary: for always being in my corner, and for always being you.

About the Author

Amy DeBellis is the author of the novel *All Our Tomorrows*. Her writing has been published in journals including *X-R-A-Y, Pithead Chapel, HAD, Fractured, Ghost Parachute, Monkeybicycle, Atticus Review, Vol. 1 Brooklyn*, and elsewhere.

Originally from New York City, she earned a BA in English from NYU. She has Long Covid and ME/CFS and is passionate about raising awareness for chronic illnesses. She is represented by Aurora Fernandez at Trident Media Group.

Follow her journey at amydebellis.com

GENDER/FUCKING

Florence Ashley

HOW TO GET ALONG WITHOUT ME

Kate Axelrod

THE MISEDUCATION OF A 90s BABY

Khaholi Bailey

EARTH ANGEL

Madeline Cash

GIRL LIKE A BOMB

Autumn Christian

AMERICAN THIGHS

Elizabeth Ellen

PROXIMITY

Sam Heaps

SAD SEXY CATHOLIC

Lauren Milici

GAG REFLEX

Elle Nash

I, CARAVAGGIO

Eugenio Volpe

9 781960 988317